Starfish

AKEMI DAWN BOWMAN

BLACK & WHITE PUBLISHING

This edition published 2018 by Ink Road
INK ROAD is an imprint and trade mark
of Black & White Publishing Ltd.

Black & White Publishing Ltd
Nautical House, 104 Commercial Street
Edinburgh, EH6 6NF

First published in the USA 2017
by Simon Pulse, an imprint of Simon & Schuster Children's Publishing Division

1 3 5 7 9 10 8 6 4 2   18 19 20 21

ISBN: 978 1 78530 161 2
Copyright © Akemi Dawn Bowman 2017

The right of Akemi Dawn Bowman to be identified as the
author of this work has been asserted by her in accordance with the
Copyright, Designs and Patents Act 1988

All rights reserved.
No part of this publication may be reproduced,
stored in a retrieval system, or transmitted in any form,
or by any means, electronic, mechanical, photocopying,
recording or otherwise, without permission
in writing from the publisher.

This novel is a work of fiction.
The names, characters and incidents portrayed
in it are of the author's imagination.
Any resemblence to actual persons, living or dead,
events or localities is entirely coincidental.

Cover design and illustration by Sarah Creech copyright © 2017 by Simon & Schuster, Inc.

A CIP catalogue record for this book is available from the British Library.

Aberdeenshire Council Libraries	
4013686	
Askews & Holts	16-Sep-2019
JF	£7.99
YPS	

To Ross—the first one was always going to be for you

CHAPTER ONE

M om doesn't show up.

I shouldn't be surprised—she never shows up—but I can't get rid of the empty, twisted feeling in my stomach. Emery always says that being alone isn't the same thing as being lonely, but sometimes it feels like they're *exactly* the same thing.

My mermaid teapot is sitting on the shelf in front of me. I flick my finger against the purple ribbon dangling from its spout. When I made it in ceramics class two months ago, it looked vibrant and smooth. Now all I can think about is how the blue glaze looks more gray than cerulean, how the torso is so unrealistically long, and how bad of an idea it was to make a mermaid teapot at all.

It doesn't matter that the ribbon says "Honorable Mention." All I see is "Not good enough to get into Prism." All Mom would see is "Not good enough."

Maybe I should be happy she isn't here.

I pull the ribbon from the spout and shove it into my bag,

burying it beneath a graveyard of almost-used-up pencils, a sketchbook, and a pack of cinnamon chewing gum.

When I hear laughter, I look up to see Susan Chang—the only other half-Asian girl in our school—clutching a blue and gold ribbon like she's afraid she might lose it. Her mother's hand is wrapped around her shoulder, and her father is pointing at her acrylic painting—an image of a house on a lake, with several geese dipping their toes into the water. It's a sensible piece. It has mass appeal.

Not like my stupid mermaid teapot.

If I could feel anything other than sorry for myself right now, I'd feel happy for her. I've always felt a weird connection to Susan, even though we aren't friends and even though the only things we have in common are our part Asian-ness and a love of art. I guess I always thought we *could* be friends, if either of us had bothered to try.

It's not that I'm desperate for friends or anything. I mean, I do *have* friends. I have Emery Webber, who rescued me from having to eat lunch by myself on the first day of freshman year. And there's Gemma and Cassidy, who are technically Emery's friends, but we all sit at the same lunch table so I think they count.

I had a best friend once too. The kind you see in movies or read about in books. We lived in a different world than everyone else—a world that always made sense, even when everything around us didn't.

We were like two halves of a snowflake—we matched.

But he moved away, and I've been half of a snowflake ever since.

The truth is I'm not really good at talking to new people. I'm not really good at talking to people, *period*.

And anyway, it isn't a friend that I need. Not right now, when I prefer painting to trying to fit in. I need a mom who doesn't look at me like I'm a worn-out piece of furniture that doesn't match the rest of her house. I need a fresh start. I need a real life.

I need *Prism*.

But a purple ribbon isn't going to get me admission to Prism Art School in New York. And it's certainly not going to make my mother proud.

My chest feels heavy, and I try to think of what I'm going to say to her when I get home.

Mom is sitting on the couch painting her nails bright red with a gossip magazine propped against her knees. She isn't looking at me, and she definitely isn't looking at the teapot in my hands.

"How was school?" Mom asks from a thousand miles away.

"Fine," I say. I tighten my bag over my shoulder. Maybe she forgot about my art show, even if I did remind her this morning. And yesterday. And every day before that for three weeks. But maybe she was busy and it slipped her mind. Maybe something came up.

She brushes another layer of candy-apple red over her toenail.

I feel my stomach knot over and over and over again.

My older brother, Taro, steps into the kitchen. He's wearing a gray and red shirt with a University of Nebraska logo printed on the front and oversized glasses, even though the lenses aren't prescription. There's half of a peanut butter and jelly sandwich wedged in his left hand.

"Mom, there's nothing to eat in this house." His voice is gruff because he doesn't know any other way to speak.

Mom wipes a blond curl away with the back of her hand, her eyes narrowed with amusement. "There's a grocery store around the corner. You know how to drive."

Taro makes a noise like a disgruntled cow, and then he looks at me. "Where have *you* been?"

Mom turns away. I feel like it's on purpose.

"My art show," I say, loud enough for Mom to hear. I could lie. I could tell her I won first place—I could make my award sound a lot better than it is. Maybe she'd pay attention. Maybe she'd listen. "I won something."

Taro looks at Mom, then at me, then back at Mom. He looks as awkward as I feel. "That's cool," he mumbles, chewing his sandwich and moving toward the refrigerator.

I think of my ribbon, buried at the bottom of my bag. She'd never see it. She'd never even *ask* to see it. Why not just tell her it's blue and gold?

I sigh. I can't lie to her, even if I desperately want her to care. It wouldn't work anyway. Mom doesn't look at me the way Susan Chang's parents look at her—she looks at me like I don't belong. Sometimes I wonder if it's because I look nothing like her. I have dark hair and a wide jaw and stumpy legs; Mom has loose blond curls, a narrow chin, and legs like a supermodel. We're just *differ-ent*, like we exist on different spectrums. If I lived on an iceberg,

Mom would live inside a volcano. That kind of thing.

But most of the time she looks at me like she doesn't *want* me to belong.

Maybe it's because of what happened with Dad. I think I'll always feel guilty about that part, even if Mom *should've* listened to me.

Why, after seventeen years, do I still crave her approval so much? I have no idea. It's stupid, but I can't help it. Whoever programmed my personality made me overly accommodating. Whoever programmed Mom made her—well, I haven't figured that part out yet.

And then, because Taro can't help himself, he says from over his shoulder, "Mom, did you see Kiko's teapot?" Sometimes I don't know if he thinks confrontation is hilarious, or if he thinks he's helping in his own pushy way.

He's not helping. Mom hates being called out.

She looks up and flashes her peroxide-infused teeth. "Well, what did you win?" She didn't forget about my art show, but she's also not going to acknowledge that she didn't want to go. She's going to pretend like it isn't a big deal, even though to me it's a *huge* deal.

Heat radiates across my face. "Just a ribbon," I say.

A crack appears in her glass smile. "What, like a participation ribbon? You know that's not a real award, right?" She doesn't ask to see it; she laughs like it's a harmless joke—like I'm supposed to be *in* on the joke. Except Mom doesn't laugh like a normal person. She laughs like she's secretly mocking the entire world. That's her "tell." It's how I know she means everything she's saying.

I tighten my mouth. Maybe I should've listened to Mr. Miller and entered one of my paintings in the art show. Maybe then I'd have won first place instead of Susan Chang.

I swallow the lump in my throat. I could *never* enter a painting into a school competition for everyone to see. They're too precious to me. I consider them actual, physical pieces of my soul.

Taro closes the refrigerator door and groans. "Seriously, is anyone going to make anything for dinner? I'm starving."

"You're graduating from college next year; why don't *you* cook a meal for a change?" she points out, twisting the cap back onto her bottle of nail polish. "It would be nice if someone would cook for *me* once in a while."

WHAT I WANT TO SAY:
"I've literally been cooking dinner at least twice a week every week for the last year. How can that possibly go unnoticed?"

WHAT I ACTUALLY SAY:
"I just made spaghetti a few days ago."

She laughs. "I hardly call boiling some noodles in a pot 'cooking.'" She makes a face at Taro as if to ask if he agrees with her.

Uninterested in Mom, me, and the teapot he's all but forgotten about, Taro stuffs the rest of his sandwich into his mouth, swallows the lump of bread, and says, "Forget it. I'm not hungry."

"You guys are so lazy." Mom rolls her eyes. Mine feel like someone has thrown salt in them.

It doesn't matter that I've had straight A's since the seventh grade, a nearly full-time job at the bookstore, or the fact that I've been actively building an art portfolio to help me get into Prism. I'm never doing enough to keep Mom happy. She never notices how hard I try, how much I care, or that maybe I just need to be noticed every now and then. And not just when it's convenient for her.

"I'm going upstairs. I've got work in an hour." I mutter the last part under my breath.

"Do you want a piece of cake before you go? I bought a pound cake from the grocery store. Isn't that your favorite?" Mom's voice drips with something sickly sweet.

I flinch, pausing before I reach the first step. Something tugs inside my chest, like there's a hook pierced into my heart and Mom's words are reeling me back to her. "I'm not hungry. But thanks."

"Okay. Well, I'll save a slice for you and you can have it when you get home." She smiles so naturally, as if she's like this all the time.

She's not, but sometimes she makes it so hard to remember.

I paint a girl with white hair, blending into a forest of white trees, with stars exploding in the sky above them like shattering glass. If you don't know where to look for her, you might not see her at all.

CHAPTER TWO

The yearbook cover is half velvet and half textured. It feels soft and scratchy beneath my fingertips. The inside is filled with glossy pictures of after-school classes, smiling faces, and sports events. Pictures of all the people I've known since kindergarten, who look so obviously different from me that sometimes I feel like I'm a pencil in a box of crayons.

Because I'm the thing that doesn't belong.

I find the only picture of me—my senior picture—and wish it weren't there at all.

But even if I had the ability to erase it, I wouldn't, because Mom would kill me. She loves school yearbooks in a way that I don't understand. Her favorite thing to do when I bring them home is to look at every student in the entire school and decide who is the prettiest girl and the best-looking guy. Then she likes to look at who the school voted "Best-Looking" on the award pages and see if she's right.

Sometimes it feels like she belongs in high school more than I do.

Mr. Miller lets our ceramics class pass around yearbooks to sign because it's Friday and there's only one more week until graduation. I feel too weird asking anyone to sign mine, so I flip through the pages by myself and play my mother's game. Not because I enjoy it, but because if I can imagine who she will pick, I can stop imagining that she'll ever think to pick me.

But I don't need to play the game, really. I already know Lauren Finch and Henry Hawkins are the best-looking people in our class. I don't think anybody in the entire school would disagree.

In the fifth grade I thought I was in love with Henry. Later I realized I was just emotionally rebounding because Jamie Merrick had moved to California. Jamie and I were best friends, and although we never even held hands, I think we had a mutual unspoken agreement that one day we'd get married.

Except long-distance relationships are doomed to fail, especially when you're in elementary school.

Beyond being occasionally paired up for class projects, Henry and I had very little interaction. But I liked him anyway because he was cute and because I missed Jamie.

On Valentine's Day in elementary school, everyone was supposed to pass out cards to every other student in their class, to make sure nobody was left out. I gave Henry Hawkins a different card than I gave all the other kids—it was bigger than the others, and it had a drawing of a character from his favorite cartoon.

Inside it I wrote, *To Henry Hawkins, From Kiko Himura.*

By the end of the day, everyone was talking about my stupid drawing and how Henry was going to have to get a restraining order before I started showing up outside his window in the middle of the night.

It was embarrassing. I wanted to melt into the floor just to stop people from looking at me.

I guess Henry was embarrassed too, because he made his friend Anthony pull me aside to tell me that Henry wasn't into girls who looked like me.

I remember not understanding it. *Girls who looked like me.* Did he mean girls with dark hair? Girls who wore jeans instead of skirts? Girls who didn't have their ears pierced? Or did he mean something else?

For years I watched him hold hands with girls who didn't look anything like me. And some of them had dark hair. Some of them wore jeans. Plenty of them didn't have their ears pierced.

But they all had one thing in common: None of them were Asian.

Now when I have a crush on someone, I don't wonder if they like the same music as me, or if they watch the same kind of movies, or if we'll get along the way Jamie and I did. I wonder if they like Asian girls.

I stare at Henry's and Lauren's pictures. They're both posing like they're on a modeling reality TV show, and above their heads is the caption: BEST-LOOKING.

Lauren Finch is pretty. Not just because she has good skin and the right clothes. She has the right *everything*. She's universally appealing. Her nose is tiny, her eyebrows are close to her eyes, and everything about her is bright and brilliant, like someone turned up the highlights on her real-life filter.

She doesn't have to wonder if guys will like her because of her race. Nobody will tell her she's "pretty, for a white girl." She's just pretty, period.

I don't stand a chance.

Because I will never be bright and brilliant like Lauren. I have pale skin and dark hair, and my eyes are too small. She's colors and candy; I'm pencils and smudges.

I close the yearbook, tired of wishing I were someone else and tired of feeling like everyone expects me to be someone else.

"I know you aren't putting that away without asking me to sign it." Emery plops onto the metal stool next to me. Her shoulder bag drops to the floor like it weighs fifty pounds.

"I thought you'd ditched class after lunch or something," I say with a grin.

"And ruin four years of perfect attendance? Never." Emery scrunches her nose and pats the table. "Come on, hand it over."

I slide the yearbook toward her and laugh. "You might struggle to find any free space."

Emery tucks a curl of auburn hair behind her ear. "Kiko." She frowns. "You haven't asked anyone else to sign this?"

I roll my eyes like it's only a stupid yearbook and why would I care?

It doesn't fool Emery, who sighs like I'm a little puppy who just won't learn. "You can act like you don't care now, but in ten years, when you look back through this, you're going to wish you had made more of an effort."

Sometimes I can't tell whether Emery knows she's the only person I talk to, or if she just talks to so many people that she never really notices. "Okay." I shrug dismissively. "I'll ask Mr. Miller to sign it after you."

Emery snorts and scratches her pen hurriedly against the inside cover. A small tattoo of an arrow sits below her wrist. When she's finished, she slides the yearbook back toward me.

"Thanks," I say.

She taps her taxicab-yellow fingernails against the wooden table. "Are you going to Lauren's party tonight?"

My body freezes. "Lauren Finch?"

"Yeah, here," Emery says, pulling out an orange card from her bag and placing it on top of my yearbook. "They've been passing them around to the seniors on the down-low."

I look back down, reading the rest of the text.

Pre-Graduation Party at Lauren Finch's House
TONIGHT at 7pm
362 Arlington Road

I've never been invited to a party before. Not one without chaperones and sleeping bags, anyway. I don't know why, but it feels intimidating.

"I know what you're thinking." Emery interrupts my thoughts. "You hate parties and people and loud music. But literally everyone is going. You can't honestly miss the last real high school party of our lives."

"I don't hate those things," I correct. I mean, I don't think I do. I've never had the opportunity to find out.

And then I think of Mom. I think of her going through my yearbook, inadvertently reminding me how I'll never be as pretty as the other girls at school, how pretty she was when she was my age, how I'll never be as pretty as *her*, and I suddenly want to be anywhere other than my own house.

I read the card again. It's tonight. I don't have to work.

I shake my head, deflated. "I can't. My mom doesn't even let me wear makeup—in what alternate universe would she ever be okay with me going to a party?"

"Stop letting your mom control your entire life," Emery says in her pretend-robot voice, which always makes me laugh.

"You might be brave enough for parties and tattoos and doing whatever you want, but I'm not," I point out.

Emery lights up and claps her hands together. "That reminds me, I'm getting a new one done next weekend. Do you want to come with me? You can meet Francis. She's amazing. Honestly, if I didn't already have this set plan for medical school, I would totally be a tattoo artist. Her shop is incredible."

She lifts her bag up, sticking out her tongue like it really does weigh fifty pounds, and rummages inside for her sketchbook.

Unlike mine, which is completely black on the outside, Emery's is covered in stickers, concert tickets, and tape. When she splits the book open, I watch her flip through sketches of cartoonish women, all dressed like futuristic gangsters and armed with some kind of weapon or another. She stops at a black-and-white image of a girl with pigtails and a giant bubble between her lips. She's holding two pistols—one has LOVE written on the barrel, and the other reads HATE.

"That's amazing," I say, a little breathless. Emery's love of art is probably the reason we've managed to stay friends for the last four years. That and our shared experience of having parents who don't let us invite friends over. "Where are you getting it?"

"On my side. I think it's going to be really painful. Will you be my emotional support?" She pushes out her bottom lip.

"Yeah, I'll go with you."

Her voice goes up an octave. "You could get one too, you know."

"You want to see my mother actually murder me, don't you?"

Emery laughs. "Okay, but at least come to the party tonight?"

And because I feel like saying no will ruin her good mood, I say, "I'll think about it."

Tracing my finger against the edge of the orange card, I tighten my mouth. I don't have it in me to be rebellious. I should—in the course material for Overbearing Mothers 101, I'm probably the perfect example of a person most likely to rebel. But I hate confrontation. And disappointing people. And drawing attention to myself.

Besides, what would I do at a party?

People terrify me. I'd probably spend the whole night wishing I had the superpower to make myself invisible. I don't know how to be any other way. Having fun with lots of other people isn't an easy thing for me to do, especially when it's with people I don't feel comfortable around.

That's why I need Prism.

I want to get away. I want to start over, so I can figure out who I really am and where I fit into the world.

Someday I'd like to feel comfortable enough around people to actually say the things I want to say. I'd like to look around and not feel like I'm the outsider. I'd like a life that just feels calm.

And I *need* to get away, so I can stop feeling guilty about what happened between my parents. So I don't have to feel like the dark smudge in somebody else's life.

I stuff the card between the pages of my yearbook and replace it with my sketchbook.

I draw a girl with arms that reach up to the clouds, but all the clouds avoid her because she's made of night and not day.

CHAPTER THREE

Shoji is sitting on the edge of a low wall when I pick him up from tae kwon do. He's still wearing all his gear, but he has a thin book in his hands. I have to honk to get his attention, even though I'm only a few yards away from him.

He perks his head up and pushes his black hair from his eyes. Unlike Taro's almost-military cut, Shoji keeps his hair long and straight, like he belongs in an Asian boy band.

When we were kids, we would fight about who looked the most Asian. We weren't fitting in at school because we were consistently one of the token minority kids. It was something the teachers seemed to appreciate when casting pilgrims and Native Americans in the school Thanksgiving plays, but it came in a lot less handy when we were trying to make friends. We thought we were just like all the other white kids, but how a person feels on the inside apparently has nothing to do with how they look on the outside.

And I guess if we couldn't feel white in school, we wanted to at home. So the three of us fought for the title of "Most Caucasian-looking of the Himura Children."

Mom always found our game amusing. Sometimes she'd even play along and point out which of our features looked more Asian and which were—as she'd often call it—more "normal-looking."

Dad didn't want to play. I think our contests hurt him more than he ever wanted to admit, but Dad doesn't complain. He's a peacekeeper—he endures. Maybe that's part of the reason I have such a hard time speaking up. I feel like I'm not *supposed* to.

Shoji always had the blackest hair, the smallest eyes, and the roundest nose. He hated it when he was little.

But something changed since then. Now he embraces it.

Even if I asked him, I don't think he'd ever explain why. We aren't like other siblings—we're strangers living under the same roof. And talking about anything too personal feels like we're opening doors we shouldn't.

But sometimes—when the angle is right and Shoji doesn't notice I'm looking at him—I can see our dad and none of our mom at all.

And maybe that's all the explanation I'll ever need.

"Hey," I say when he climbs into the car.

He pulls the door shut and splits his book open with his thumb. "Hey."

It's quiet, but it's always quiet with Shoji. Or maybe it's me—I can never tell. Neither of us are good conversationalists. Sometimes I worry when we grow up we'll never talk to each other again, and it will be because we didn't practice enough as kids.

Some people don't have to practice at speaking—it just comes naturally to them. My brothers and I aren't like that. For us, speaking is hard.

I look down at his book. It's a manga.

When we were little, Dad bought us some Japanese anime DVDs for Christmas. I loved them because they were like moving artwork—Taro and Shoji just liked them because they were cool.

But Mom hated them. She said all the voices gave her a headache. Dad never bought any more of them after that.

After a while, Taro and I found other things to be interested in, but Shoji missed the stories. He said he could see himself in Japanese cartoons in a way he couldn't with American ones, so he started collecting Japanese comics.

Manga doesn't give Mom a headache. At least not one she could admit to.

I glance down at the open page. The writing is all in Japanese.

"Can you read that?" I ask him.

Shoji doesn't move. "Most of it. I'm still practicing."

I'm not embarrassed to admit I think Shoji is a lot cooler than I am, even if he is younger than me. He's always so calm—bordering on mysterious, even. He doesn't wear his heart on his sleeve; he keeps it in a locked box with all of his dreams and expressions because he doesn't want to share them with the rest of the world.

I don't have that kind of control. My feelings tend to burst out of me like I'm a water balloon. Mom always says it's because I'm overly sensitive, but I can't help it. I don't have a box to hide my emotions the way Shoji does.

And besides, everything breaks eventually if it's put under enough strain. Even titanium. That's not sensitivity—that's science.

"Is that the one about demons?" I try again.

"Yeah." He turns the page from left to right.

We don't talk again until I pull into the driveway of our house.

Shoji wedges his index finger against the pages like a bookmark and presses the book against his chest. He grabs the handle of the car with his free hand just as I turn off the engine.

"Uncle Max is coming over tonight."

The first thing I think of is my stuffed rabbit. The second is the feeling that something heavy and painful in the pit of my stomach is making me want to vomit.

"Oh." My hands fall into my lap. "What time?"

Shoji shrugs. I'm not sure if he knows why I don't like being around Uncle Max, but he's not stupid. Neither is Taro, even though he acts like it sometimes. When Uncle Max and I are in the same room together, the tension is suffocating.

Mom says it's all in my head, but I don't think so. He wouldn't have moved out in the first place if things hadn't gotten so weird. My parents might even still be together.

Their divorce is my fault, after all.

Shoji gets out of the car, but I don't follow him right away. I pull the key out of the ignition and squeeze the Batman key ring into my palm. I don't even like Batman, but Jamie Merrick gave it to me when I was six years old, and sometimes holding it makes me feel safe.

Except it's not working today.

My heart starts to race. My head throbs. I feel like I can't breathe. If Shoji knew Uncle Max was coming over, it means Mom did too. Why wouldn't she tell me herself?

I get out of the car because I feel like it's eighty thousand degrees and I need the fresh air to stop my head from spinning.

When I walk inside the house, I can hear Mom trying to get Shoji to talk to her. She has even less luck than I do, and as soon as I step into the living room, Shoji turns for the stairs with his book still in his hand.

"Mom?" I start. I try to calm my voice. Maybe she'll be reasonable if I stay calm.

She looks at me with the kind of excitement a child has on their birthday. "Did you get your yearbook?"

"Yeah, I did. But—"

"—I want to see it!" she says with huge, round eyes.

I pull my yearbook out of my bag and hand it to her. She makes a noise like someone seeing a magic trick for the first time. There's so much awe and innocence and joy—*over a yearbook*. I wish just once she had that kind of reaction over my art. No wonder we have a hard time understanding each other.

"Mom," I start again. "Is Uncle Max coming over tonight?"

"Let's try to be positive today, okay?" Mom says, her eyes pinned to the pages of winter formal. "What a gorgeous yearbook. *Beautiful*."

I don't know what positivity has to do with Uncle Max, or what a beautiful yearbook has to do with *anything*. Staying calm is becoming less and less of a possibility.

I try again. "I'm not comfortable—"

"What is this?" Mom interrupts. She pulls out something from the yearbook and holds it up. It's the orange invitation to Lauren Finch's party.

"It's just a graduation thing. I already know I can't go," I say dismissively. I want to talk about Uncle Max—why won't she let me?

Mom looks over the card. She takes her time, mulling it over like she's considering something important. "Why can't you go?" Her voice sounds distant. Timid even.

My face scrunches. "It's a party," I say, like this should answer everything. Mom has always been strict about letting any of us go anywhere. It took more than a year before she'd let me go to the movies with Emery. She never has a good reason—I think she just likes to be in control.

Mom shrugs. "A party could be fun. You are about to graduate. It might be a good opportunity to say good-bye to all your friends."

I press my lips together. Mom clearly doesn't know me very well.

But she is giving me permission to go to a party—maybe I don't know her very well either.

And then something clicks together. I raise my eyebrows. "Are you doing this because you don't want to talk about Uncle Max?"

Mom laughs and turns another page of the yearbook. "You think there's an ulterior motive for everything nice I do."

That's because there is, I want to say. But I don't, because I'm not an idiot. I'm about to get out of having to face Uncle Max tonight. I would literally spend the entire weekend with a house full of strangers if it meant not having to see him again.

"Okay. Well, thanks," I say.

Mom looks back at the colorful pages in her lap. "Just *gorgeous*."

I leave her alone on the couch.

When I'm upstairs getting ready for a party I never in a million years thought I'd be going to, I hear someone knock at the bathroom door. It's Mom.

"Do you need help with your hair?" she asks.

I scrunch my face. "Mom, you haven't touched my hair since, like, the third grade."

She shrugs. "Can't I help now? I'm good at hair."

I let her in because I'm starved of motherly interest, and it feels nice that she wants to help.

She pulls and brushes and tugs at my hair, and when she's finished, it's pulled back in a bun so tightly my eyes look even smaller and I can barely see any hair at all.

"I look bald," I say blankly.

Mom clicks her tongue disapprovingly. "It looks good. It shows off your face."

"That's the problem," I reply under my breath.

"This is how the celebrities wear their hair on the red carpet," she adds.

"They wouldn't wear their hair like this if they weren't wearing any makeup. Can I at least borrow some mascara or something?"

"Absolutely not." Mom sniffs. "It's way more impressive to be beautiful without makeup."

I stiffen. She's never called me beautiful before. Ever. I wonder when she—

"Girls were always jealous of me when I was in high school because I never wore makeup and I was the prettiest girl in the school."

I sigh. She's not talking about me—she's talking about herself. *Of course* she is.

"I don't look like you, Mom. This hairdo doesn't look good on me. It makes my face look too round."

I don't know how Mom doesn't see it, especially since she's been talking about my big round circle face for as long as I can remember. The round face I got from Dad and not her. The face she's constantly reminding me doesn't look anything like hers.

Hair like this might be flattering on celebrities and Mom, but not on me.

"I'll get some hair spray—don't touch it." She swats my hand away.

I start to tell her people stopped using this much hair spray in the nineties, but she doesn't listen. She smothers me in a cloud of chemicals that makes me cough, and the next time I touch my hair it's so stiff it feels like plastic.

I draw a girl without a face, drawing somebody else's face onto her own reflection.

CHAPTER FOUR

Lauren's house is beautiful. It's three stories and made up of perfect red brick, and it's surrounded by grass and hedges. A constant regurgitation of the top-twenty pop songs bursts from the open door, and a giant, inflatable unicorn is resting its plastic horn against the living room window.

Three girls about my age spill out of the front door, bright red cups in hand. A husky guy wearing a maroon college sweatshirt follows after them and tries to persuade them back inside. The girls giggle dizzily. I'm pretty sure they'll go with him—I've been watching them do this weird dance of should-I-stay-or-shouldn't-I for the past hour.

Because I am still in my car.

I'm creepily parked across the street behind a shiny white pickup truck, staring at Lauren's house like I'm about to walk into a job interview.

Emery keeps texting to ask if I'm here yet, which is making me feel even more paranoid. I feel like someone is depending on me. It's so much pressure.

My heart thuds. When I swallow, I feel my throat close up. I'm so jittery and squeamish and cold that I feel like I'm going to die. Literally, the best thing that could happen right now is that my body could just evaporate into the air and I would never have to face so many people.

I'm worried people are going to stare at me and I won't know what to do or say.

The three girls disappear back into the house, and they are replaced by Adam Walker, a tall blond with questionable balance. I recognize him because he's on the lacrosse team and looks like he stepped out of an Abercrombie & Fitch catalog. And also because we've averaged about two classes together every year since the sixth grade.

He stumbles across the driveway with a goofy half smirk frozen onto his face, and before long he's joined by more people. Eddie Greene, Caitlyn Barrow, and Marc Sherwood, to be exact. They aren't on the lacrosse team—they're just popular.

They all laugh and nudge each other. They're so comfortable in these situations. Not like me.

My phone rings. It's Emery.

"Hey," I say meekly.

"Why are you still in your car?"

"There's a lot of people, and—"

"—I'm coming to get you." She hangs up.

I sink into the driver's seat and tell myself this is a good thing. Being around Emery will make all of this so much easier. I can fake being normal, as long as Emery doesn't leave me alone.

She taps her fingers on the window and pulls the door open. She doesn't hide her confusion when she sees my hair.

"My mom did it," I say lamely.

She gives an abrupt laugh. "Oh my God. Do you think she genuinely thought she was being helpful, or do you think she's afraid if you look nice, people will think you're prettier than her?" I don't say anything because I honestly don't know the answer. She shakes her head and motions me closer to her.

Without waiting for permission, Emery pulls the band out of my hair and scratches her fingers through all the hair spray, shaking my hair like she's trying to bring it back to life. Eventually she knots it back up, looser this time, so that the bun sits on top of my head instead of somewhere near my neck.

"Fixed," she says, giving me an encouraging smile.

Emery leads me across the street. I try to remind myself it's okay. This is what people my age do—going to parties is completely normal.

Adam seems to be walking closer to us as we near the door, his eyes falling on me curiously. "Hey, don't I know you?"

I feel myself flinch, and I inhale his cologne. It smells like spice and pepper.

"Government, right?" Marc says, pointing a finger at me.

Caitlyn shoves him with a hand decorated with too many bracelets. "Like you've ever actually managed to show up to government."

Adam snaps his fingers. "Ah, I remember you now. Kelly! You used to let me copy your math homework on the bus." He reaches for me like he's trying to give me a hug.

"That's not her name," Emery growls, tugging at my arm like she's helping me escape. She leans in to my ear. "He is literally *always* the drunkest person at every party. Just ignore him."

Before I know it, we're walking into Lauren's house, and a mash-up of different sounds floods my ears. A girl wearing a fedora hat is singing "Skinny Love" and strumming her guitar in the dining room. Next to her is an intense game of beer pong. And to the right of them is a group of people playing a video game in the living room.

Cassidy and Gemma spot us right away.

"You made it!" Cassidy exclaims, brushing a strand of hair from her shiny forehead. She's swaying a little, and I don't think it's because of the music.

I can feel Gemma staring at my Spider-Man shirt like she's trying to understand why I'm wearing it. Eventually her eyes find mine. "I like your hair today," she says.

I laugh and glance at Emery, but Gemma's attention has already moved on to someone else. Pretty soon she and Cassidy are talking rapidly to some other girls about people I don't know.

Someone must have lost the Xbox gunfight because there's a series of angry groans near the television. The girl with the guitar starts singing another song. I feel painfully out of place.

Emery says something next to me, but I can't hear it over all the noise.

"Do you want a drink?" she repeats, louder this time.

I shake my head. "I'm fine."

"I'll be right back," she says, and as soon as she disappears into the next room, I feel like someone has yanked my social crutch out from under my arm. I'm floundering. All I can think about is Emery coming back so I can have someone to hide behind.

I look back at Cassidy and Gemma, but they're still deep in conversation. I feel weird just standing there listening. Do other people do that? Move from circle to circle, socializing with everyone like they all know each other? It seems invasive. I don't know the rules.

I want to leave. I don't belong here. But I can't go home—Uncle Max is probably still there, eating dinner at our family table, talking to everyone like he's the favorite relative they've all been missing. It's making me feel so distracted. Thinking of him being so close to my family makes me feel like he's too close to *me*.

I wish Mom would make him stay away for good.

I feel myself still looking around anxiously for Emery. I need my friend right now.

I realize it's probably been only a matter of seconds since she left, but it honestly feels like hours. I don't think I can stay here all night. Not with everything closing in on me because there are literally people everywhere who I don't know and they are having such a good time and, *oh my God*, what am I doing here?

I spin around toward the door, but before I reach the handle, a voice stops me.

"Kiko?"

It's a smooth voice. A sweet voice. Like a glass bell or melted caramel. And it knows my name.

My stomach feels light and foreign. I know this voice. I know bells and caramel. I remember the way he says my name.

I've never forgotten.

CHAPTER FIVE

I turn around. Even though he's shot up by at least a foot and his skin looks baked by the sun, I know it's Jamie Merrick. With scruffy dark hair that hangs above two aquamarine eyes, a sturdy runner's build, and a partially unbuttoned shirt that's drawing attention to the area between his neck and chest, he's completely different from the way I remember him and exactly the same all at once.

"Hi," I say.

"Hi," he says.

It feels like two comets have just collided headfirst into each other, and the aftershock of two hundred earthquakes rolls through my chest.

I'm not listening to the guitar cover songs or the video game explosions or the plastic bounce of Ping-Pong balls leaping from the table. I'm staring up at him like I haven't seen him in years.

Actually, I *haven't* seen him in years. Just in my daydreams, and in the handful of blurry photographs from Taro's eleventh birthday party. I stole all the ones of Jamie from a box in Mom's closet because I didn't think she'd miss them, and also because I'm the one who was always in love with Jamie. I deserved them.

"You got taller," he says with a harmless smile.

"You too," I reply, but it comes out in more of a harsh whisper.

Jamie looks at his drink. After a pause, he asks, "How's Taro? Is he here with you?"

My heart plummets. *Of course* he would ask about my brother. I've never been just Kiko—I'm Taro's sister, or Emery's friend, or Angelina's daughter, or the weird girl from government class.

"He's not here," I say. "But he's fine." At least I think he is. Taro and I don't usually talk unless we're arguing about something, but I don't tell Jamie that. If he remembers me at all, he'd remember my relationship with my brothers.

Jamie raises his brow. "I hope he's being nicer to you these days. I still remember that time you punched him right in the face. Over a song, wasn't it?"

I feel my face flush with an overwhelming amount of heat. He remembers. "I punched him because he wouldn't stop turning off my stereo," I correct nervously.

"You broke his glasses."

"Yeah. I did."

We both laugh at the same time. His laugh is soft and gentle, while mine is awkward and loud.

I quickly clear my throat, and my cheeks darken.

"I thought you moved to California," I say. "I mean, I know you did. But I didn't know you were back in town. I mean, obviously, because we haven't talked in years." *God, Kiko, stop talking.*

He shifts his feet and taps his finger against his cup. "I'm back visiting family. My semester ended last week, so I'm already on my summer vacation."

"Oh, right. That's cool."

It goes quiet.

I have a million questions in my head I want to ask him. *What have you been doing for the last eight years? What are you majoring in at college? What's California like? Have you thought about me at all?* But I don't ask any of them. I just stare up at him like I wish he would do all the talking.

But he doesn't seem interested—he seems like he's in a hurry.

He holds up his cup. "I'm going to get something to drink. Do you want anything?"

I stare at the shiny red plastic. "No thanks. I don't drink alcohol."

There's a glimmer in his eyes, and when he leans closer to me I can smell his aftershave. He smells like ocean and sandalwood, even though we're miles away from any coastline. It makes my limbs feel like licorice. "I don't either. I'm on Sprite, but don't tell anyone. Otherwise they'll spend the rest of the night trying to get me to do shots." His laugh is deep and has sort of a hiccup at the end, but in the cutest way imaginable. I bet even guys secretly find him charming. He's like Captain America and Batman had a baby—he's polite, and cool, and mysterious all at once.

He holds up his cup again like he's giving me one last chance to make any requests. I shake my head, but as soon as he turns for the kitchen I realize now he doesn't have a reason to come back.

You should have taken a stupid drink, Kiko. God.

Jamie doesn't come back.

But Emery does, and she's holding two red plastic cups. She forces one into my hand. "It's soda. Even if you don't drink it, it'll make you feel more comfortable holding it. Trust me."

Strangely enough, it doesn't take me long to realize she's right. The red cup is like magic—I feel like I blend in more. I feel like I look like everyone else. I feel normal.

But then I see Jamie again. He's in the dining room, walking toward the sliding glass doors, with two girls in ankle boots and cutoff shorts. He looks right at me, maybe because he wasn't expecting me to be looking back, and as soon as our eyes click together, he hesitates. He looks at me with something I don't understand—something that makes me feel small.

When he disappears into the backyard with the two girls, it occurs to me his priorities at a house party might not revolve around reconnecting with his strange childhood friend.

And just like that, I feel out of place all over again.

I don't tell Emery about Jamie. I was going to, when less people were around. But the way he looked at me makes me want to keep it a secret. He looked at me like I shouldn't be here, and now I feel like he's right.

Emery tries to help, bringing me into random conversations now and then, but she mostly lets me blend in beside her as best as I can.

I don't know how to act at a party, or where I'm supposed to plant myself to stay out of the way of constant traffic. When

Emery says she has to go to the bathroom, I find a space in the living room, pretend to melt into the wall, and wish I had the legs and self-esteem to pull off ankle boots and cutoff shorts.

"Kelly!" Adam Walker's hands are spread wide like he's about to give me a bear hug. He doesn't follow through with it, maybe because I glue myself to the wall, or maybe because he's *really* drunk and forgot what he was doing.

He leans next to me, his breath sour and smoky all at once. "You having a good time?" he slurs.

I want to tell him my name isn't Kelly, but to be honest I don't really care. I feel like my energy is rapidly depleting. I'm thinking about Uncle Max, and being socially awkward, and how Jamie looked at me like he was making a conscious decision to avoid me. It's draining thinking about so many things all at once, and even more draining to be around so many people. I don't know how other people do it—don't they ever feel like they need to recharge? Doesn't talking to people for so long wear them out?

Adam is still waiting for an answer. I decide he's drunk enough that I don't have to lie in order to preserve anyone's feelings. "Not really." I shrug.

He tilts his head back and groans. "I know, right?" He drags out each word like his speech has become slow motion. "There aren't even any girls here."

I look around. There are literally girls everywhere. Pretty ones, too, and they all look like their wardrobes came straight out of an episode of *The Vampire Diaries*.

When I look back at Adam, he's staring across the room.

Caitlyn is leaning against the wall, her face buried in Marc's neck, and his fingers are hooked through the belt loops on her shorts. Something tells me Adam was expecting the night to go a different way.

Blinking back to life, he looks around at the floor and then at his hands. "Oh, man. Where did I put my drink?" He looks at me like I should know, and then he's smiling. I feel like he thinks we're sharing a secret, except I have no idea what that secret is supposed to be. "So you're friends with Emery, huh?"

I nod.

"How come I never see you at any other parties?" He grins in a way that I guess is supposed to be charming, but his eyes are so glassy and tired that I can't see what any of the other girls at school seem to.

"I don't really like being around so many people. I find it kind of overwhelming," I say truthfully. It's surprisingly therapeutic talking to someone so drunk.

Adam pushes his mouth forward like he's sneering and nods. "I get that. It gets boring after a while, the same old thing. It's just, like, every day is the same and it never changes."

I'm not sure he got me at all, but his loopy train of thought makes me smile.

He notices. "You're different. I like that."

Different. The word makes me feel jittery and nervous, like there's suddenly a spotlight glaring down on me, announcing to the entire room that I'm not like everyone else. It doesn't matter how many red cups I hold—I'll always be *different*.

"Thanks," I say, my arms tightening into my rib cage. Do people always get so overfamiliar when they drink?

I look around again for Emery. What's taking her so long?

"Are you waiting for someone?" he asks.

"Just Emery."

"I'm pretty sure she's out back." He throws his thumb over his shoulder, even though the backyard is in the opposite direction. "Do you smoke?"

"No. I don't drink either," I say, cringing. I don't know why I just admitted out loud how completely unfit I am for a house party. I guess I don't know what else to say. Because I'm not the cool, carefree, fun person who plays beer pong and dances to all the songs on the radio. I don't know the right words to say to sound cool, because "being cool" does not fall within my skill set.

I shift my weight to my other leg, my eyes still scanning the room for Emery. She's trying to enjoy the party—I should just go. I don't want to ruin her night by making her feel like she has to keep checking up on me.

Adam nods too slowly, like it's too difficult to comprehend everything I'm saying. "I want to show you something." He grabs my hand and pulls me away from the wall. "You'll like it. I promise."

We turn down the hall and into one of the rooms. I try to pull my wrist away. "I don't think we're supposed to go in here."

But he pulls back insistently. "It's cool. It's cool."

It doesn't feel cool—it feels intrusive and like I'm going to get yelled at by the owner at any minute for being in their bedroom and *oh my God why are we in a bedroom?*

All my joints go stiff, like they've been fused together with liquid iron. Every part of me wants to object to this—especially when he closes the door—but I am paralyzed with the fear of making Adam uncomfortable. Confrontation of any kind is my nightmare.

He flicks the switch on the wall, and a rainbow-colored chandelier made of uneven pieces of sea glass lights up the room. An unlit candle near the door makes the room smell like lilac. It itches my nose and reminds me of my grandma's house. Maybe I should tell Adam about my grandma—how she lives with three cats and how she once tried to feed me a can of crushed sardines and fed the cats macaroni and cheese. I think maybe it will distract him enough to make him let go of my arm. Maybe it will even make him forget why he brought me in here in the first place.

Adam wanders to the side of the bed, pulling me along behind him like a mindless puppet, and shuffles his hand around the end table.

"This room smells like my grandma's house," I start, but Adam turns to me and waves a remote control in my face.

"Do you like *Family Guy*?" he asks, turning the mounted television on, releasing my hand, and throwing himself onto the patchwork bed. He pats at the space next to him. His eyes are half closed, like he's about to fall asleep.

My eyes dart from the edge of the bed, to the flashing images on the TV, to the door separating us from a herd of loud strangers. And Jamie Merrick.

But Jamie is with his friends, and his friends are the strangers that are giving me an anxiety attack.

I sit on the bed, a foot away from Adam, with my feet dangling over the edge.

Only ten minutes pass before Adam starts to snore. I contemplate leaving, but with Adam asleep, I almost feel alone. Alone is good. Alone feels safe.

Something else is on TV that isn't familiar or particularly funny, so I look for the remote. It's still in his hand, draped across part of the mattress like a body part on a mannequin.

Adam's chest rises and falls, and there's a deep rumble starting in the back of his nose.

I reach across him; I'm sure I can grab the controller without waking him. Just as my fingers clutch around the plastic, his eyes open and his hand closes around my wrist.

Startled, I pull back, but his body lifts toward mine like we're magnetized somehow.

His eyes are heavy and bloodshot. The night has weakened the product in his hair, so the blond waves have gone wild and soft. When he opens his mouth, he smells sour.

"Has anyone ever told you that you look kind of like Princess Jasmine?" He grins—the grin that is supposed to be charming but isn't. "I don't know why I never noticed before. You're really pretty, you know that?"

His words trigger something.

I am eight years old.

The oxygen empties from the room. My eyes won't focus on

anything for very long. They jump from faded paint on the wall to frayed edges on the quilt cover to a David Letterman bobble-head on top of a stack of magazines, on top of an old record player.

Adam runs his fingers along my arm. My mouth is twitching. *There are stars on the ceiling.*

My eyes search more of the room. *Keep looking around. Keep thinking.*

The blinds are bent in the left corner. There's a half-empty container of orange Tic Tacs on the nightstand. An unopened package of peppermint candy next to it. A receipt behind the trash can.

He's closer to me now. His breath makes my eyes water.

I want to reach for my stuffed rabbit, but I'm frozen.

I'm frozen now, too. I can't move. I can only think.

Think. Think. Wrappers. Blinds. Triggers. Bed.

Oh. The bed.

The stars shake, the rabbit shakes, the bed shakes.

I'm remembering what I don't want to.

I need to keep thinking about anything but the bed.

Adam puts his lips against mine. I feel sick. *It* feels sick. He tastes like ash and rotten fruit. He's trying to shove his fat, slobbery tongue into my mouth, but I pin my lips shut because I don't want to do this at all.

But why can't I move?

Everything is shaking but me.

My breathing quickens, and Adam mistakes it for enjoyment. He grinds his teeth against me like we're supposed to mold together, but it feels like two pieces of metal that are shaped all wrong for each other. His fingers close against my head like he's squeezing my skull. Is kissing supposed to feel this aggressive?

I don't know, because I've never been kissed before.

I'm too scared. Everything is shaking and I don't know what I'm supposed to do.

I'm too scared to move. I'm scared of the embarrassment. I'm scared of what acknowledging any of this says about me. I feel completely out of control, and my body feels like it's made out of lead. I don't know how to change this.

I've felt like this before.

I melt into myself, my limbs stiff and my mouth closed, and when Adam is finished trying to smother me with his alcohol breath, I watch him lean away from me.

"Man, I'm so hungry right now." He half chuckles and stares off into space, probably imagining a sandwich. He lets himself fall back to the bed, our magnetic pull severed.

I lunge for the door.

CHAPTER SIX

Walking through the hallway feels like I'm walking through a mirrored tunnel in a fun house. The walls don't stay up the way they're supposed to. I'm dizzy, and it makes me feel weak.

I squeeze the bottom of my shirt in my hands and try to ignore the pounding in my chest.

I need to get to the front door. I need to get to my car. I need to go home.

"You're still here," Jamie says when I emerge in the living room. It's not hard to spot him because he's like a unicorn among donkeys. Nobody else is anywhere near as beautiful. Even the girl sitting on the couch next to him—with her perfect side braid and about five layers of lip gloss—gets lost to the blur that surrounds him. "I thought you went home already."

My mouth feels like it's stuffed with cotton balls. It's too hard to concentrate, so I just shake my head.

His smile fades a little because he's studying me. Everything about me shifts—my eyes, my feet, my hands—everything about me screams something isn't right.

"I thought you didn't drink," he says, and his smile returns a little bit.

"I'm not—" I mumble. "I don't—" I try to swallow the cotton away. "I'm going home. I don't feel great."

"Did you drive here?"

I nod too many times. I need to get out of this house.

He's watching me the way someone would watch an injured cat—not wanting to leave it alone but scared to get too close too quickly. "Are you okay?" His eyes darken with concern.

I feel my jaw shake. I nod once.

He stands up and his lip-glossed companion keeps her eyes glued to the two of us. "I can give you a ride home if you're not feeling well. My car is right outside."

"No," I blurt out, and he looks startled. "I mean, thanks, but I can't leave my car here. My mom would kill me."

The skin in between his eyes scrunches deeply. "Okay. Well, at least let me walk you out. You look like you're about to pass out."

The girl with the braid and lip gloss stands up. "I'm going to get another drink. See you out back?"

Jamie nods. "I'll just be a minute."

I start to object—I even think of trying to find Emery. But I don't want to stay here any longer. I want to go home. My stomach is rotating in so many directions I think I'm going to be sick.

"See you later, Kelly."

I glance over my shoulder—Adam is standing outside the

hallway with sleepy eyes and an unlit cigarette in his hand.

Oh my God, I can't believe I let a smoker kiss me. I want to claw off my own face.

I ignore Jamie even though I'm sure he's staring at me. When we're standing in front of my car, I dig through my bag clumsily until I find the keys. When I pull them out, the metal glint of the Batman key chain dangles from my fist. It catches my eye. It catches Jamie's, too.

I feel myself shrinking into the ground.

"It's weird seeing you again," Jamie says all of a sudden. The corner of his mouth dimples when he smirks. "You look the same, but . . . different."

I'm shaking, and I can't tell if it's the aftershocks of the horrible kiss with Adam, or if it's because Jamie Merrick is standing in front of me with the streetlight pouring across his face like a moonlit mask. His eyes are such a piercing blue. They stand out even more because he has thick, heavy eyebrows. On anyone else, his eyebrows would look like a Muppet character. But on him, they don't look weird—his face just makes sense, quirks and all. Maybe because he's always made so much sense to me.

"Yeah, I guess that's what time does to you," I say lamely.

Jamie looks like he wants to say so much more. It wasn't always awkward between us. We used to be effortless together.

Maybe time has something to do with that, too.

I straighten myself up.

I want to ask him why he stopped talking to me. I want to ask him why we didn't stay friends forever, when we promised each other we would.

I want to ask him what happened after he moved away that turned us into strangers.

But I don't have the time or the courage.

"Well, I hope you feel better. It was nice to see you again." He presses his lips together and looks down at his feet. When he brings his face back up, he looks at me the way I feel—like something inside of him aches. "Good-bye, Kiko."

Good-bye. Not good night. Why does it feel so final?

"Good-bye, Jamie." I turn for the car door, and when I look back over my shoulder, he's already making his way back to the house and his pretty friend inside.

I don't know what any of it means, but it doesn't matter. I feel weightless.

I paint a girl with wings instead of arms, flying along the border where darkness becomes light, unsure of where she's supposed to be.

CHAPTER SEVEN

Emery calls to ask why I disappeared last night. At first I think she's mad about it, but then I realize she's just groggy and hungover. I try to tell her about Adam and Jamie, but both stories are on such drastically different ends of the emotional spectrum that I can't seem to get the words out without downplaying one or the other.

Kissing Adam was horrible.

Seeing Jamie again made the world feel whole.

So I don't tell Emery about any of it. I push my thoughts into a small corner of my brain to deal with later, and I ask about her night instead.

I spend the weekend working on my portfolio. I fill four pages of sketches until I settle on a painting of a woman with a shaved head dancing in a swirl of fire. It takes a long time because there are about a hundred layers of fire all around her. It keeps me busy until Monday morning, so I don't have to think about kissing Adam. It also keeps me from thinking about Jamie's probably-girlfriend.

But it doesn't keep me from thinking about Jamie. He is literally all I think about, even when I'm painting, and usually painting is how I shut out the rest of the world. It's my sanctuary from the thoughts that cloud my head.

But with each burst of color on the canvas, I see dark eyelashes and blue eyes, dimples and a gentle smile, and light radiating from his olive skin, like he's secretly a star that fell down to earth by accident.

By Monday morning, I forget about everything *but* Jamie.

Until I see Adam at school.

He's standing near his locker, hiding a pack of cigarettes in between a folder covered in black Sharpie drawings and an English textbook. My nerves are making me feel sick—I don't know if he'll even remember me or what happened, but I also don't know how he'll act if he does.

Part of me wants to just get our inevitable encounter over with, but as it turns out the universe isn't interested in what I want, because Adam doesn't notice me by the lockers at all.

Later on, in government, I feel like there are tiny bugs crawling all over my body. It's so hard to sit still. I pick my nails under the desk because it's only a matter of time before I see him now. I'm nervous to speak to him for the first time since *that* night.

He walks in with his friend, and when he sees me, his smile disappears like someone's erased it from his face.

He spends the rest of class looking embarrassed and avoiding any direct eye contact with me, intentional or otherwise.

He is embarrassed of *me*.

Of course.

I feel angry. Really, really angry.

I spend the next two classes on the verge of tears. My hands are shaking so much that I can't hold a pencil still enough to sketch.

That part makes me even angrier.

And then I see him for a third time, right outside of the gymnasium. He sees me too, but this time he doesn't seem in a hurry to get away, even though there's only five minutes until the bell rings.

Five minutes doesn't seem like enough time to say what we need to.

"Hey," he says when he reaches me. He's wearing a red-and-gold-striped shirt. It reminds me of Harry Potter. I'm still mad about his reaction in government, but if he apologizes, I might be able to forgive him if he likes Harry Potter.

"Hey," I reply quietly. I look down at my feet. I'm wearing black Converse sneakers and a Legend of Zelda T-shirt. Maybe he'll like video games, too. Maybe I didn't waste my first kiss on a smoker—maybe we have a lot in common that I don't know yet.

Right now I feel hopeful.

"Look, about Friday night," he says with a laugh. It seems harmless, so I smile back. Maybe this is a joke we're going to share for a long time. Maybe we can recover from Friday and be friends, or—

"I would really appreciate it if you didn't tell anyone what happened," he says, almost urgently.

I feel nothing. Everything I thought I felt vanishes, and all my brain leaves me is a stupid look on my face.

"What?"

Adam runs a hand through his blond waves and grimaces. "It's nothing personal. It's just—you know, my parents—and I had too much to drink—"

I interrupt him. "What do your parents have to do with anything?"

His eyes flit across mine, begging me to let him off the hook. He doesn't want to say it out loud. "You're not the kind of girl I usually go out with."

"What does that mean?" I'm shaking.

"I don't usually date Asian girls, that's all," he says finally.

I blink and my eyes go blurry.

"I don't have anything against girls like you," he insists, "but my parents, they wouldn't understand. This is kind of a small town, you know?"

WHAT I WANT TO SAY:
"So you want me to lie about my first kiss because your parents are racist?"

WHAT I ACTUALLY SAY:
"*You* were the one who kissed *me*."

My throat tightens. My face burns. It's not that I wanted our kiss to mean anything—I'm just not sure I'm comfortable with it being erased. *I'm* not comfortable being erased.

Adam shrugs, his jaw clenched. "I was drunk. It didn't mean anything."

I don't know exactly why I'm so mad. I mean, I know why, but I don't know which reason makes me the angriest. I don't know if I'm furious that I wasted my first kiss on a smoking racist, or if I'm enraged that he won't apologize, or if I'm mad that it meant so little to him.

Because it didn't mean a thing to me. It was the worst first kiss in the history of first kisses. But I guess I was going to be okay with that as long as he cared a little bit.

"So." He waits, looking at me with a crazed smirk. "Are we cool?"

I wait a long time before I answer. Not to punish him, but because I can barely breathe. Finally, when my heart slows and I can feel oxygen fill my nose, I show him my teeth.

"We're cool."

He smiles wider. "Thanks, Kelly."

When he walks away, I swallow the lump in my throat that contains the last bit of emotion I had toward Friday night and Adam, and I push it all away.

I draw a boy kissing a girl and the girl shattering into a billion pieces.

CHAPTER EIGHT

All right, spill," Emery says, leaning toward me like she's waiting for me to tell her something important.

I tap my pencil against the blank page of my sketchbook. Mr. Miller is grading papers at his desk. There's not enough time left in the year to get anything in the kiln, so those of us who bothered to show up to ceramics at all have been left to our own devices.

"What do you mean?" I ask quietly, my voice full of shame because I hate what happened on Friday and I hate what Adam said to me today.

"You were being weird at lunch—weirder than usual," Emery points out, smiling. "So, what's up?"

I don't want to tell her about Adam, and not because he told me not to. I don't want to tell her because saying it out loud—forming the actual words of what happened—is humiliating.

Besides, if I tell her about Adam, I'll have to explain why I didn't stop him—why I froze up and couldn't move.

I can't tell her that. I can't tell anybody that.

So I tell her about Jamie instead, because it's a good deflector. Besides, I feel like I've waited long enough—if I leave my thoughts in a corner any longer, I might start to forget them. And forgetting about Jamie is the last thing I want to do.

Emery squeals giddily. "Why didn't you tell me he was there? I would've totally been your wingman. I can't believe he offered to drive you home. How long is he in town for? I hope you got his number or something."

"It wasn't like that. I think that other girl might have been his girlfriend."

"He can't have a girlfriend. Doesn't he know you've been in love with him for more than a decade?"

My face breaks into a smile, and I bury my head into my folded arms. The wooden table still smells like clay. "You're going to make me more nervous than I already am." I lift my head back up so my voice isn't so muffled. "It's been years. He doesn't see me like that. Not anymore."

Emery frowns. "Honestly, you don't understand how this works. People don't insist on driving random people around for no reason."

I pin my eyes to the blank page. "I would. I mean, if someone needed a ride home, you know? What are you supposed to say?"

"You say, 'No. Go call a taxi like a normal person because I don't know you.' Some variation of that." She shrugs.

"Saying those words would cause me actual, physical pain."

"You need to work on that."

"I know." I sigh.

Emery nods. "I bet he'll try to get in touch with you. You'll see."

I twist my face. "I don't know. I think you're reading too much into it. He was just being nice."

"Why do you find it so hard to believe that guys might find you attractive?" she asks seriously. "You *are*, Kiko. You're exotic-looking. People love that."

The word makes me wince. *Exotic.* Like Princess Jasmine. It's how Adam sees me. It's probably how *everyone* sees me. Like I don't belong.

"I don't want someone to like me because I'm 'exotic,'" I say. "It makes it sound like I'm an acquired taste, or something someone tries once in a while."

"It doesn't mean anything bad. It just means you're different," she says.

"Exactly," I say.

She narrows her hazel eyes. "Are you trying to tell me you'd rather be mashed potatoes than crème brûlée?"

"I'm saying I don't want to be the thing that people like once in a while, or because they think it's unique or exotic." I don't want to be kissed by someone who is ashamed about it later because I don't have blue eyes and blond hair and I might disappoint their parents.

I hesitate, pinching my fingers against my leg nervously. I know it's Emery—the last person in the *world* who would probably be mad at me—but I still worry I might've upset her. Confidence is a foreign concept to me, and saying how I feel, out loud, is horribly unnatural. It sounds like I'm yelling my feelings.

I don't want her to think I'm yelling at her, and even if it is completely illogical, I don't want her to be angry with me.

Emery lifts her brow, eyes softening. "I didn't know you felt like that. I mean, I'm sorry." She pauses. "You're not different to me, you know. You're just my friend. My beautiful, timeless, mashed-potato-if-you-want-to-be friend."

I relax, and a grin settles onto my face. "Thanks, Emery. You complete me." And it's true, because I've tethered myself to Emery somehow. I feel protected by her, like I can pretend to be mashed potatoes or crème brûlée or whatever I want to be if I see myself through her eyes.

But the rest of the world doesn't look through her eyes, or mine. They see me the way Adam does. The way Mom does.

I'm not like them.

She holds up her fingers in the shape of a heart. "Now I want to hear more about Jamie. Were his eyes as blue as you remembered?" Her voice oozes with theatrics.

"*So blue,*" I reply before breaking into a laugh.

I let Emery distract me with her questions and jokes and ideas for new tattoos. It helps get Adam out of my head, and for just a moment, I almost forget how desperately I need Prism and how badly I want to feel like I'm part of a world that wants me back.

I draw five humans and one skeleton, and it doesn't matter that the skeleton has all the right bones and joints—he will never be the same as the others because he doesn't have the right skin.

CHAPTER NINE

Taro stands in my doorway. He's halfway through a strawberry pastry. The smell of toasted sugar makes my mouth water.

"Mom's going to strangle you for eating upstairs," I remark without looking at him. I'm pretending to read over the notes for my English exam, but really I'm trying not to think about my wasted first kiss with stupid Adam.

"Where were you on Friday?" Taro asks. He sounds like he already knows the answer.

It pulls my attention away from John Steinbeck. "Why do you care?"

Taro laughs and chews at the same time. "I know where you were. What were you doing at a party? You don't even have any friends."

"Yes, I do," I snap.

He shakes his head slowly. "You don't. You have creepy clay things."

I roll my eyes and turn back to my book.

"Did you see Jamie?"

My cheeks burn. "Who told you that?"

"I *have* friends—friends who tell me when they see my sister leaving a party with some dude." Taro shrugs like I should've expected this. "So are you still in love with him?" He's laughing like he's ten years old and trying to get my attention.

"Why are you bothering me? You literally never talk to me. What does it matter who I hang out with?"

Taro swallows his last bite of pastry. "I'm talking to you now."

I try to figure out what his intentions are. I don't think he cares about Jamie—they used to be friends when they were kids, until he realized me and Jamie had way more in common. And by the crumbs he's licking off his fingers, I don't think he's here to share his food with me.

I think, in his unbelievably off-putting way, he's trying to "hang out."

My brother has never known how to get anyone's attention without being abrasive and blunt and loud. When we were kids, it was the only way he could get Mom to notice him—by *demanding* her attention. It's something I will never be good at.

But maybe his abrasiveness is also his armor. He's loud and thick-skinned. He offends before he can be offended. He laughs before his feelings get hurt.

He stops Mom before she can get to him by getting to everybody else first.

Taro looks around my room, taking in the abundance of art

prints I've collected over the years and the shelves of "creepy clay things" against the wall. "You're weird. Everyone thinks so."

I cringe. The part of me that doesn't believe him thinks he's trying to get under my skin. But the part that does believe him is too scared to hear exactly who "everyone" is.

"You're socially awkward," I bite back.

He laughs again, and I'm grateful it doesn't sound like Mom's. "We're all socially awkward. Mom made sure of that."

I twist my mouth. I don't understand how he can say something so sad and still look so happy. I know some people laugh to hide how they're really feeling, but I don't think Taro is hiding anything. I think he found a way to never let the sadness in. He's strong that way. And part of me wishes he told me his secret a long time ago, but the other part of me understands why he couldn't.

Because my brothers and I can't *all* be strong. Somebody has to be on Mom's target board—I think Taro would rather it was me than him.

When he leaves my room, I'm no longer thinking about Adam or trying to remember what my teacher told us about *Of Mice and Men*—I'm thinking about how my brothers and I have been pitted against one another since birth. We're products of two parents who aren't around—one physically, one emotionally. There's not enough attention for all three of us—there's not enough love to go around. We nurtured ourselves, by ourselves, and protected our hearts even from one another.

We were never going to be close. We were never going to really love one another.

We never stood a chance.

I paint three faceless people—one becomes the sky, one becomes the ocean, and one becomes the sun. They live apart for eternity because they don't belong together.

CHAPTER TEN

Leah is the bald one. Emily is the one with giant lips.

People always say babies are beautiful, but I think they look like alien-turnip hybrids. In fact, they kind of resemble my clay sculptures.

Dad smiles at me with lots of teeth, and it makes his eyes disappear into his face. "Aren't they tiny? I remember when you were this small. Just like a baby rabbit."

I like the way Dad speaks. He likes to compare people to animals, and he always observes the world like it's so new and exciting.

"They are really small," I agree. The twins yawn at the same time. "Oh my God, did you see that? They're in sync already." They might not be beautiful, but they're fascinating.

My little sisters. It feels *so weird*.

"Want to hold one of them?" Dad asks, already scooping one of them out of the white crib.

Bald Leah, I tell myself.

I hold out my arms. Dad adjusts them with his free arm and places one of my new sisters in my hold. It feels strange, like I'm not doing it right. I'm worried I'm going to drop her or break her or make her uncomfortable.

"How were you holding her with only one arm?" I say in a rushed, quiet voice.

Emily makes a little noise from the crib. She sounds like a baby pterodactyl.

Dad scoops her up too, and the two of us are swaying with little tiny people in our arms. He's holding Emily, but he's still smiling at me. He hasn't forgotten me already. Not like how Mom would if something cute was in the house.

I still feel guilty about playing a part in ruining our family, but maybe Dad actually is happier now. In some twisted way, if he hadn't found out about Uncle Max, he wouldn't have these two little babies.

Maybe they are the silver lining. Maybe this means I can let go of some of the guilt.

"How's Serena?" I ask before Dad reads into my expression.

"She's good," he says. "She's with her mom, trying to get a little break." He chuckles. "They aren't always this quiet."

I look down at Leah's squashed little face. Okay, I can *kind* of see why people think they're cute.

"We'd love to have you around more, you know," Dad says seriously. "Serena really wants you guys to bond with the twins. We both do."

I nod, but I don't say anything. I've never truly bonded with

Serena as a stepmother. Not because she isn't nice, because she is—she always hand-makes birthday cards, and she even sent me an e-mail when she heard I was applying to Prism to tell me good luck. But it was never going to be easy to bond with the woman who replaced our family with a new one.

I might have ruined Mom and Dad, but she was the one who took him away.

Dad is quiet for a little while. We sway and listen to the twins breathe.

"Serena cares about you. She really does." Dad's eyes are glassy. He always gets emotional when he talks about his wife with me. Probably because he feels guilty about what happened, but also because I know he wishes we could be a family.

Mom would disown me if she thought I even remotely took anyone's side but hers.

"How are you doing, though? Is your mom okay?" he asks.

I look up and see his concern. Because he knows. He *knows*, and he still left the three of us with her. I know I should probably hate him for leaving, but when I look at Dad, I don't see someone I'm capable of hating.

Because Dad is like a rabbit too. He's gentle and kind and he disappears too quickly, but it's only because he's scared. He doesn't want to hurt anyone, but he doesn't want to get hurt either.

I don't know if that's selfish or not, but I don't hate him for it. Because *I know*, too.

Mom preys on the weak. He got out alive, which is what I'm trying to do.

I turn my eyes to my sister to keep them from watering. "I'm fine. Mom's Mom, I guess."

He nods, and I think he's trying to think of more words to say, more words to explain himself.

So I try to change the subject, because I don't want to waste the little time I get with Dad being upset. "Do they look like me when I was little?"

Dad smiles. "I think so. Except you had so much fluffy, dark hair, like a little wolf cub."

I laugh, watching the twins scrunch their faces in unison. "I wonder if they'll look less Asian than us." I look up at Dad. "Remember when Taro, Shoji, and I used to fight about that?"

"I know it was tough for you guys. I wish my family had still been around. You guys missed out on getting to know that side," he admits, and there's a quiet sadness in his voice. His parents died before he ever met Mom. For a brief moment in time, Mom was all he had. Sometimes I wonder if she preferred it that way, when it was just the two of them and there were no children or relatives to share his attention with. I might not like spotlights, but Mom definitely does.

Dad's the only person I know from the Japanese side of the family—the side I feel like I'm supposed to be connected to, even though I don't know anything about it. Everyone expects me to be Asian, not white, because of the way I look. But I'm only half Japanese—I'm the same amount of Asian as I am white. Why doesn't anyone ever call me half white? It's confusing. I wonder if it will always be confusing.

Maybe Dad's family could've helped with that, if they were still alive. Maybe Dad could've helped with that too. But maybe there just wasn't enough time.

Dad shrugs. "But at least the twins will have the three of you to learn from."

I force a smile. I guess he doesn't realize I don't have anything to teach them.

The door opens from downstairs, and we listen for the slow, shuffling footsteps on the stairs. Serena appears in the hallway. She's wearing yoga pants and a loose shirt, and her auburn hair is twisted up in a high bun. She has lively green eyes and freckles she never tries to hide with makeup. Mom calls her "very average-looking," but I've always thought she was kind of pretty, especially for someone who doesn't paint her face with layers of cosmetics.

Mom didn't like me saying that. She *always* wears makeup.

"Hi, Kiko," Serena chirps. Her smile is bright. "Looks like the girls are still asleep."

Dad leans toward her and kisses her cheek. "We've got it all under control. Did you have a good time? You didn't have to rush home so fast."

She scrunches her nose. "It felt too weird to be away. Thought they might be missing me." She looks at me. "And I wanted to catch you before you left. Any news on art school?"

God, she's so nice. I don't understand how she'd get together with a married man with three kids. It doesn't make sense. "Not yet," I tell her. "I'm still waiting to hear back."

"I'm sure you'll get in. I don't know anyone as talented as you," she gushes.

Yeah, *so nice*. It makes no sense at all.

"Thanks," I say sheepishly.

"How about we take these two little bunnies downstairs, and you can tell us all about what you're working on while we stuff our faces with cake?" Dad offers. "I'm starving, like a bear after winter."

I try not to laugh too loud into Leah's little ears.

Serena brings out a plate of carrot cake and banana bread. I eat one slice of each and wash it down with a can of cream soda. When it's time to go home, I kiss my sisters for the first time and decide that they are the most beautiful little babies in the world. Dad reminds me to come over more often, and Serena reiterates that she wants to see me more.

I tell them I'll try, even though I know Mom won't like it.

I like their house. I like their family. I like how they make me feel like I'm a part of it.

I leave feeling happier than I have in a long time.

I draw a flower with eight petals, and each petal is a dancing woman.

CHAPTER ELEVEN

The last time I saw Uncle Max was when he had shaved all his hair off and looked like an ex-convict. Now that his hair has grown back, he looks like an ordinary, middle-aged father. Except Uncle Max doesn't have kids, and thank God for that.

He finishes his can of beer like he's short on time. Mom passes him another one because she says he's on "vacation." He already told us he got fired from his job, but I guess Mom thinks vacation sounds better.

She's punishing me for going to see Dad and the twins. She has to be. Why else would she invite him to dinner when he was *just here*?

"So what are you studying at college?" Uncle Max asks, smiling at Taro like they're old pals. Uncle Max doesn't look like Mom, except they have the same pointy nose.

"Journalism," Taro says, stuffing his face with steak.

"Oh, that sounds cool," Uncle Max says, flashing his teeth.

"I always hoped we'd have a dentist in the family," Mom

muses. "I read somewhere there's going to be a shortage of them soon—you could open your own practice nearby. Live near home. Wouldn't that be cool?" I'll never understand Mom's obsession with trying to get us to stay close to her. Maybe she's afraid of being alone. Or maybe she likes the *idea* of being a family more than she likes *actually* being a family.

"I don't want to be a dentist," Taro says with disgust. "I don't even like being in school."

He pushes his food around with his fork. Taro's not a dreamer like I am. He doesn't have a great love the way I love art or Shoji loves reading. He's getting a degree in journalism at the University of Nebraska not because it's his passion, but because it was the only in-state college that offered him a scholarship.

Taro has always been smart, but he lacks motivation. He's the person who aces all his tests but doesn't turn in any homework. Maybe it has something to do with his armor—maybe the only way to protect his heart is to not care about *anything*.

"What are you going to do after you graduate?" Uncle Max asks.

"Probably get a job as a bartender and tell everyone how happy I am that I don't have to clean people's teeth for a living." Taro snorts.

Mom ignores him. I could never get away with talking to her like that. She'd tell me how rude and ungrateful and jealous I was all at once. Maybe it's because Taro has thicker skin than me. Maybe it's too much effort for her to try to break through it. Maybe I'm an easier target.

"Well, I think Shoji is going to be my doctor. Aren't you, Shoji?" Mom asks.

Shoji doesn't look up from the manga he's hiding under the table. I don't blame him—his books are my paintings. They're an escape.

And hiding the thing he loves most under a table works for him because he's never cared about getting anyone's approval. He doesn't need to share his comics; he doesn't need anyone to be interested in him. He has more raw confidence than I ever will.

I never learned how to hide my art from Mom. I've always wanted her to be a part of what makes me happy, and I don't know how to turn that off.

Shoji does. Maybe that's why he picked manga—because he knew the last thing Mom would ever want to do is look at Japanese comic books. His hobby was always his and his alone, and maybe it's safer that way. Maybe *knowing* someone will never be interested is better than hoping one day they will be.

Uncle Max turns to me innocently. "What about you, Kiko? What are your plans?"

I shift in my chair, avoiding his eyes. I don't want to talk to him about art. I don't want to talk to him about anything.

"She wants to do something with her art," Mom says without blinking. There's a brief pause. "She went to go see the babies, you know."

I have the sudden urge to stretch my spine, as if every part of my body feels cramped and constricted. I feel protective of my new sisters. I don't want Mom to talk about them. Especially not to Uncle Max.

"I've seen a picture of them. They're cute." She raises her brow. "Except one of them does have your dad's nose. Your grandma's nose, I should say. Just like you." Mom glances at me. It's definitely not a compliment.

She's talking about my wide, round Asian nose. The one she doesn't have. The one that isn't as pretty as hers.

Uncle Max laughs—like, *really* laughs—as if having my dad's nose is the most hilarious thing he's heard all day. "Don't worry." He winks. "They have surgery for that." Suddenly Mom is laughing too.

Shoji shifts, turning his page roughly. He doesn't make eye contact with me, but for some reason I get the feeling he's worn out. Maybe from tae kwon do, or maybe from Mom. He never talks to me long enough to find out.

"You better eat some more steak before your brothers finish it all," Mom warns me.

I blink at her. "I'm a vegetarian. I haven't eaten meat in two years."

"Why do you have to make everything so difficult?" Mom sighs like she's tired. Like *I* make her tired. "I made this beautiful dinner, and you're trying to ruin it with your negativity."

Taro coughs loudly and stabs his fork in another piece of pink steak.

I breathe through my nose. Through my big, fat Asian nose that is good for dinner-table jokes.

"Did I tell you my girlfriend went to art school?" Uncle Max asks after another gulp of beer.

Mom jolts her head back like this is the most exciting informa-tion she's ever heard for the fifth time. "We almost sent Kiko to an art school when she was little, but it was so expensive."

My head snaps to her in surprise. "What?"

She hums like what she just said isn't a big deal at all.

But it's a huge deal to me because it's the first I've heard of it.

"When were you going to send me to art school?" I ask.

Taro snickers into his plate. Uncle Max drinks more beer. Shoji pretends none of us exist.

Mom sniffs. "It was after your second-grade teacher sent her daughter to that place near the lake. Do you remember? Your dad and I did the research and everything. We talked about it."

"Why didn't you ever tell me that? How long did you consider it for?" I'm not trying to be annoying—I'm actually weirdly excited. Because art is my life. Everyone knows this. Mom *especially* knows this. But she has a way of pretending she doesn't. I never thought she cared enough to consider *sending me to art school.* I just want to know the details. Because this might be the nicest thing I've ever found out my mother secretly almost did for me.

"I don't know, Kiko. We googled it, okay? It was too expen-sive." The corner of her mouth twitches in anticipation of what's going to happen next.

And then, very quickly, I see the truth flash across her eyes because I know my mother very well.

WHAT I WANT TO SAY:

"So you didn't almost send me to art school. You asked Dad to look up on the Internet how much it costs, probably to find out how a second-grade teacher could afford to send her own kid. And now you're bringing it up because you think it will make you look like a good parent who tried to do nice things but only couldn't because of the money."

WHAT I ACTUALLY SAY:
"Oh. Okay."

"Becky is really talented. She even plays the piano," Uncle Max continues.

"I was always a very good pianist when I was younger. Remember all those recitals I had?" Mom asks.

They go back and forth like it's a competition.

I glue my eyes to my plate and think about my pending application with Prism until something Uncle Max says makes me feel ill.

"You guys will get to meet her soon, now that I'll be staying here for a few months while I get back on my feet."

I don't say a word.

I look at Taro—he's chewing and chewing and chewing and pretending he doesn't know what's going on.

I look at Shoji—his eyes flick up from his hidden book for a sliver of a moment. It's short-lived sympathy.

And then I look at Mom.

She avoids my stare, probably because she knows I'm imagining they are lasers and whatever I look at will be forced to spontaneously combust.

"Is that a problem, Kiko?" Uncle Max's voice is like steel. He's talking to me like I'm the brat who isn't getting my way. When I look around, Taro and Shoji are looking at me the same way.

Why? they're thinking. *Why do you always have to make everything worse?*

But it's not me. Why doesn't anyone else ever see it? I'm not asking for the world—I just want to be heard, by the one person who is supposed to listen.

"Mom," I start.

She slams her hands on the table, and my entire body jumps back in alarm. Maybe I did manage to make her spontaneously combust after all.

Tears fill her eyes, and it takes only a second before her whole mouth is contorted and she's ugly-crying like she's just had her heart broken.

I don't blink.

Mom presses her face into her hands, and Uncle Max rubs her back like she's an exhausted, overworked mother dealing with a bratty, deadbeat teenager.

"I do so much for these kids. They don't appreciate anything," she sobs into her palms.

"Don't get upset, Angie," Uncle Max says. He flashes his eyes toward me. "Your mom works so hard, and she never asks for anything in return. You guys need to start being nicer to her."

But this has nothing to do with Mom, and she knows it. She's making this about her so she doesn't have to listen to me.

She can't be the villain if she's the victim.

I look at my brothers. I wish they'd help me.

Taro shakes his head. Shoji is looking around for his escape. *Why?* they're thinking. *Why can't you blend in like us? Stay in the background. Don't question anything. Just be invisible. Just be quiet.*

But I don't want to be invisible to Mom. I want to be able to tell her how I feel.

I want her to care.

But she doesn't. Because she blames me for Dad. Because she wishes I was different.

Because *I'm not good enough for her.*

It's not fair.

I don't finish eating. I rush to my room before I start crying in front of everyone at the table.

Why would she do this? She knows he's a total creep. She knows what he did to me. How could she let him back into this house knowing what he's really like?

It's been more than an hour since dinner, and I still can't calm down.

Mom doesn't knock—she opens the door and walks in, and by the look on her face, she was hoping to catch me crying or feeling sorry for myself. I think she not-so-secretly finds it hilarious when other people are upset.

"Do you want to talk?" she asks, half smirking.

"This isn't funny." I stare at her, not crying or feeling sorry for myself. I'm just mad.

"I know that," Mom says. She closes the door and walks over to my bed, sitting down beside me like we're former friends who don't know how to act around each other. "I don't think it's funny. I smile when things are awkward."

I shake my head and don't respond. Everything I want to say to her is drenched with rage. She would use it against me for the rest of my life if I let it slip out.

"Look, I don't know what happened between you and Max, but if we're all going to be living together you need to—" she starts.

"You *do* know," I interrupt angrily. "You know exactly what happened."

"No," she corrects. "I know your side of the story."

My shoulders shake violently. "Are you saying you don't believe me?"

She lets out a sigh. "I'm not saying that. I'm not saying anything, really. I just think you were very young when this 'event' happened"—she scratches the air with her fingers—"and maybe it's not fair to put so much blame on Max."

"Who else gets the blame? Me?" I ask with a knot in my throat.

"Kiko, would you please stop making this so difficult. I mean, it's not like he did anything *that* horrible to you."

WHAT I WANT TO SAY:

"It's disgusting that you'd actually make excuses about what your brother did to your own daughter. It's disgusting that you're questioning whether I'm even telling the truth. It's disgusting. *You're disgusting.*"

WHAT I ACTUALLY SAY:

"Get out of my room, Mom. *Get out!*"

I throw myself up from the bed and hot tears pour from my eyes. I tear open my bedroom door and ball my hands up so tight that my fingernails cut into my skin.

She hesitates at first, and for a second I think she's going to yell at me for shouting at her, but eventually she shakes her head dismissively and leaves.

I slam the door behind her, and the bedroom walls vibrate. I listen to her footsteps move toward the stairs, and when she speaks I know she must have run into my brothers.

"She is *so* sensitive," she says loudly. "You can't say anything to her without her flipping out."

I paint a woman who steals hearts, but none of them fit the hole inside her empty, black chest.

CHAPTER TWELVE

It's been two days since I found out Uncle Max is moving in. Mom and I have been avoiding each other, which usually lasts a few days. When we don't talk, it feels like we're no longer a part of each other's life. It feels like we're complete strangers. It feels more like the truth.

But today she's downstairs screaming at someone on the phone. Someone didn't let her use their stapler after she bought everyone doughnuts last week—seriously, I'm not making that up—and her shrieking voice is making my chest tight.

It reminds me that I'm stuck with her—she's unavoidable, even when I'm ignoring her, because Mom is an actual black hole. She swallows up everything around her so that everything light suddenly becomes dark.

For someone who talks about positivity so much, Mom is the most negative person I know.

I feel like my shoulders weigh more than the rest of my body, and if I don't get out of the house and into the open air I'm going to suffocate.

I text Emery to see if she wants to meet up for coffee, and she texts back pretty quickly that she'll be there in fifteen minutes. She doesn't have to say it, but I know she hates being at home as much as I do.

When I see her in the parking lot, she's still in the middle of tying up her frizzy hair with a scarf. "Too lazy to straighten it today," she says. She's wearing a purple dress with knee-high boots and an oversize crescent necklace. Most of her tattoos run up and down her forearms, with the exception of the turtle on her shoulder blade.

I asked her once what her tattoos meant, and she told me art doesn't have to mean anything—it can just be pretty.

We have different ideas about art, but I think it's cool. There's something inspiring about how casual Emery can be about things I take so seriously that I could die over them.

"I like your hair frizzy," I point out.

Emery pretend punches my shoulder. "Aw, thanks!"

When we get inside, Emery hovers over the pastry counter while I order the same drink I always do, because a vanilla chai latte makes the *world* feel better.

"What's your name?" the curly-haired barista asks.

"Kiko," I reply.

She hesitates, her black marker hovering over the giant cup with uncertainty. She was expecting something simpler to process.

"Sorry. It's Japanese," I apologize. I always apologize to people when my name confuses them. I have no idea why; I just feel like I'm supposed to. "It's K-I-K-O."

The girl scratches my name in. When her coworker calls me for my drink, the cup reads "Kiki."

I sit in the corner with Kiki's drink, and Emery sits across from me with an orange and cranberry muffin and a giant latte.

"Want some?" she offers, holding the muffin toward me.

I shake my head and sip my tea. "Did you book your flight yet?"

She tightens the corners of her mouth. "Yeah. I leave on Monday."

I feel like someone has punched me in the chest. "Seriously?"

She nods. "That's why I want you to come with me to get the tattoo. This is, like, my going-away weekend."

"You mean 'good-bye' weekend," I correct. "You're lucky. I wish I was leaving for Prism early."

Emery's eyes widen. "You got in? Why didn't you tell me?"

I wave a hand in the air quickly, like I'm trying to erase what I've said. "No, no, no. I didn't. I haven't gotten a letter yet. I just meant I wish I didn't have to stay here for the summer by myself." I don't know how I'm going to get through it without Emery, but at least getting an acceptance letter from Prism will keep me sane until I can move out.

"I worry about you sometimes, Kiko."

"What do you mean?"

She shrugs. "You don't really do things on your own. I'm

worried you're going to spend the next few months hiding out in your room not talking to anyone. Plus, you know, your mom." She trails her finger along the edge of the table. Her nails are painted green today, with black stars on her thumbs. "She has a way of making you feel so insecure; I worry it's her way of trying to keep you close. It's not healthy."

Neither is living across the hall from Uncle Max, but I don't tell her that part. Telling her would require me to say the words out loud, and I haven't done that since the day I told Mom and ruined my family forever.

"That's why I need Prism," I say at last.

She's quiet for a moment, studying her half-eaten muffin like she's waiting for it to jump up and dance across the table. "But what happens when Prism isn't there anymore? What happens if you graduate? Or if you don't—" She stops herself.

I know what she's trying to say. *What if I don't get in?* What will I do then, when all my hopes of making things better are in the same basket marked ART SCHOOL? I rely on these things to make me happy—art, Prism, even Emery. Without them, I'm not sure what I would do.

That's why I *have* to get in.

"I'm sorry. I don't mean to be so moody. I just think about you here by yourself all summer and it's kind of depressing." Emery raises her eyebrows and gives me a gentle grin.

"I'll probably work extra hours at the bookstore once school is over. Trust me, I'm not going to be sitting at home with my mom feeling sorry for myself," I say. I'll probably be getting my portfolio ready for Prism. There won't be any time to be sad.

"God, your mom. Whenever I meet her she acts like the nicest person in the world, and then you tell me stories and I don't know. Have you ever wondered if she might be bipolar?" Emery takes another drink.

"I don't think that's it." Besides, even if Mom *was* bipolar, that's not an excuse. There are plenty of parents in the world with mental health conditions who don't treat their children badly.

"Well, I know where to get some lithium if she ever wants any," Emery says dryly. She never says it directly, but I'm pretty sure her dad is a drug dealer. She knows way too many names of prescription pills—even for someone with an interest in medical school.

It was never just art that bonded Emery and me as friends. It was our families, too. Because even though Emery is so much better at dealing with it, she knows what it feels like to have parents that aren't interested. She knows what it feels like to want to run away. She knows how badly—how desperately—I need to get into Prism, because she knows what it feels like to be afraid that staying in this town will feel the same as dying.

I make a face at her. "I would pay you actual money to be the one to tell my mom she needs medication."

Emery laughs and brings her hand to her mouth. "You don't think anyone's told her that before? Not even your dad?"

I shake my head slowly. "Not a chance. A sirloin steak doesn't try to reason with a dragon."

She tilts her head back and laughs. "What does that even mean?"

I laugh, too, even though it's too true to be *really* funny. Nobody can reason with Mom—not even Dad, when they were married. Maybe that's part of the reason he left. Because he couldn't get her to listen. Because he couldn't get her to care. About him, about me. Maybe he just wanted out.

And I know I should be mad at him for that, but I'm not. I *get* it. I want out too.

Emery's phone rings. "Oh, it's my mom. Give me a second?" She plugs her finger against her ear and speaks into the phone. "Hello?"

Their conversation seems serious from the start, so I pull out my phone and search the Internet for photos of Prism. It will make Emery feel like I'm not paying attention, and it will make me feel happy.

Because Prism is the most beautiful building I've ever seen in my life.

Huge glass windows in lopsided shapes, cube-shaped offices, color schemes like aqua and fuchsia and marigold, which have never once made it past my mother's beige limitations on interior design.

Prism is an enormous, colorful honeycomb, full of the most creative little worker bees in the history of the universe. Some people dream about going to Juilliard or Yale or Hogwarts, even. Because they're prestigious and magical and a dream.

Prism has always been my dream, ever since the day I googled art schools and saw how colorful it all was—the website, the campus, *and* the students. Plus, it's in New York, which is basically the art capital of the United States. I knew how much I needed it—to be a part of such a beautiful school and be taught by some of the greatest art teachers in the country. And I need it now, more than ever.

I picture my dorm room. I picture my roommate.

I bet we'd get along—both of us at a school because we love art so much we want to spend the rest of our lives doing it. How could we not get along?

She probably wouldn't even care that I'm half Japanese and don't fit in anywhere. In New York, people probably don't need to be told twice how to spell Kiko. They've probably met a thousand Kikos before.

It'll be my new beginning away from Mom and away from the memories and guilt I desperately want to escape.

I swipe through their website about clubs and societies and after-school activities. They have a forum section, too, where prospective students ask all kinds of questions about student life and whatever else they want to know.

And then I see it.

This post:

> *I have a question about the housing guidelines, as I just received my acceptance letter in the mail this morning.*

I don't read the rest. I don't need to. Because the post was written *yesterday.*

My eyes shoot up toward Emery. She's still on the phone, her eyes full of sadness.

I can't leave her. Not right now.

When she hangs up, she pushes her hands against her eyes and groans like she's full of tension and wants to get it out. "Why does family have to be so much work?"

"Anything I can do to help?" I have to make an effort to slow my voice down. My heart is beating so fast that I'm worried I won't be able to contain my excitement.

She looks up weakly. "Can you make my parents nicer people?"

"If I knew that trick, I'd have used it by now," I say.

Emery talks about her parents, and moving away, and how badly she wants to get into medical school, even if only to prove that she's different from the rest of her family. Eventually, she changes the subject to Gemma and Cassidy and how neither of them have big dreams to move away. And when she tells me about Cassidy's plan to hook up with one of her crushes before the summer is over, I can't hold it in anymore.

"People have been getting their acceptance letters into Prism," I blurt out. "I just read it on the forums. That means—"

"Go check your mail!" Emery squeals, pushing her empty cup aside. "Why did you wait so long to say something?"

I fidget in my seat. "I didn't want to just leave you."

"I would've left you." Emery smirks. "Your assignment this summer is to grow some serious ladyballs, Kiko."

I twist my mouth. "Why do people always use 'balls' as the epitome of bravery? Like, we have to 'grow balls' if we want to be strong."

"Because," Emery says too loudly, "saying 'grow some serious ovaries' doesn't really have the same ring to it."

A few people turn toward us and look at our table, and I feel my face flush.

"Oh my God." Covering my face with one hand, I stand up and laugh awkwardly. "Okay, I'm leaving. Good-bye."

"Text me as soon as you open that letter!" Emery shouts after me.

The drive home kills me. Every red light is torture. Every stop sign causes me physical pain.

People are already getting their acceptance letters into Prism.

That means . . .

I burst into my house like my body is literally on fire.

The TV is on, which means someone is downstairs, which means it's probably Mom. With the exception of Taro's fixation on the refrigerator, the three of us tend to migrate to our own spaces when we're inside the house.

Mom's perched on the couch like she's meditating, except her eyes are wide open and she's staring right at me.

"Did the mail come today?" I ask, breaking the ice that never truly goes away between us.

"It's on the counter," she says stiffly.

I can tell from her face—it's here. My letter from Prism is here.

I find the envelope with Prism's logo in the corner—three circles positioned like they're part of a bigger triangle. It's thin. That's a bad sign. I know it is. My gut knows it too, because now I feel like I haven't eaten in weeks and I'm about to fall to pieces. But more important, the envelope isn't sealed.

I turn to my mother. She looks 100 percent guilty. "You opened it? Why would you open my letter?"

"Because," she starts with a defensive laugh, "we weren't talking, and if it was good news I didn't want to have to be fake and suddenly happy for you. I needed time to prepare."

"Time?" I repeat.

"It came yesterday. Don't be mad."

WHAT I WANT TO SAY:

"Don't be mad? You opened the most important letter of my life yesterday and didn't even tell me. And you did it because you needed time to *prepare!*"

WHAT I ACTUALLY SAY:

Nothing. Because she said she needed time to prepare. And that means . . .

My heart thuds. And thuds. And thuds.

Oh my God. *Oh my God.*

I look back at the envelope. It's so thin. How can it be so thin if it's a "yes"?

I start to pull the letter out. I need to see the words. I need to—

"You didn't get in," Mom blurts out before I get the chance to read anything at all.

My heart implodes inside my chest.

She stands up, her arms folded in front of her. "I'm sorry, Kiko. But you didn't get in. I know you really wanted it, and even though

I'm still very upset with you, I do mean it. I'm sorry."

I don't even realize I'm crying until Mom turns into a blurry pink and peach blob. We stand there for a while, me leaking tears like a broken faucet and Mom pulling her arms closer and closer to her own chest.

Somehow I find the strength to move my feet, and when I'm alone in my room with the door closed and my thoughts drowned out with music, I open the letter.

I get as far as "We regret to inform you" and then the letter is in the trash can and my face is stuffed so far into my pillow that it practically absorbs into my red, screaming face.

I don't paint anything at all.

CHAPTER THIRTEEN

Everyone is talking about college at school. At least, that's how it feels. They're either talking about college or graduation tomorrow—doesn't anyone have anything else to talk about? It's not like everyone else hasn't had their letters for months. They've had plenty of time to share their college acceptance stories. I haven't been accepted anywhere, and I feel like my soul has been turned to ash.

"I'm so sorry, Kiko." Emery stares at me with big round eyes—eyes that say, "I don't know what to say or do to make you feel better."

Gemma and Cassidy keep looking around the cafeteria uncomfortably. I guess they don't know what to say either.

"Can we talk about something else?" My voice shakes.

Emery tells me about her graduation outfit. Gemma talks about getting her hair cut. Cassidy talks about kissing some guy from her English class.

I try to listen, but it's hard when "We regret to inform you" keeps pounding inside my head.

Ceramics class is even worse because Mr. Miller remembered how badly I wanted to get into Prism. When he asks, and I tell him I was rejected, I get to watch the disappointment color his face. It's only a drop of what I feel.

"Well, you can always reapply next year. I'm sure it was very competitive. What are you going to do now?"

It's a great question. *The* question, I guess.

What am I going to do now?

I have no backup school. I have a mom who has been encouraging me for more than a year to stay at home and go to community college—which, quite frankly, sounds only a *tiny* bit better than bathing in acid and letting a coyote eat my legs off. I don't have anything against community college; I just can't imagine spending another year living at home with Mom.

And *Uncle Max.*

I feel terrified. I feel completely lost.

Oh my God, what am I going to do now?

I stare at a blank piece of paper until I crumple it into a ball and stuff it beneath my textbook.

CHAPTER FOURTEEN

When I open the front door, I see Emery holding up two containers of Ben & Jerry's. She's wearing a minidress covered in cartoon cats and a smile that no one could possibly say no to.

"Half Baked or Chubby Hubby?" she asks, bouncing on her toes.

"Half Baked," I reply, stepping out onto the porch and pulling the door shut behind me. There's no point inviting her in—Mom's home.

I take the ice cream from her and we sit on the step, our legs stretched out onto the walkway. Emery's are so much longer than mine.

She pulls two spoons from her bag and passes one to me. We eat in silence, watching the street and letting the sunshine warm us.

"I really thought I'd get in," I say quietly.

"I know," she says.

I scrape my spoon against the ice cream, and cookie and fudge goo dribbles down the side because it's softening quickly in the summer air. I swipe my finger against the container before it drips onto my leg.

"Sorry. I didn't bring napkins," Emery says.

"Like I'd waste perfectly good Ben and Jerry's Half Baked?" I shake my head and press my finger to my mouth.

She laughs and takes another bite. "I kind of wish you were coming to Indiana."

"I can't follow you around the country," I point out. "Although to be honest, now I kind of wish I was too. God, I'm going to end up in community college. I'm going to end up *here*."

I feel like my organs are all made of stone and they're crushing me from the inside.

She shifts her body slightly so she's facing me, her eyes almost stern. "I know it's not your dream, but community college isn't the end of the world. I mean, maybe you could still take some art classes and apply to Prism next year. You're the best artist I know. I doubt it had anything to do with how good you were—they probably just had too many applicants."

"Maybe." I tuck my legs in so my heels are against the step. "The hardest part wasn't the rejection. It was having to see everyone's faces when I told them I didn't get in. I wanted Prism so bad, but I also wanted the proof that I could do it. Does that make sense?"

I keep picturing Mom's face. It was like she knew I wasn't going to get in. She knew and I didn't, and she might as well have stabbed me in the heart because that's how it felt to see how *she knew*.

Emery looks back toward the driveway. "You care too much about what other people think. I mean, so what if you fail? So what if it takes a few tries? You're following your dreams. It shouldn't matter to anyone else how long it takes you or what your journey is like—it should just matter to you."

"You sound like a doctor already," I say.

"I'm stealing some of the bullet points from my scholarship essay, but I feel like they work here."

I feel myself start to relax. Emery usually has that effect on me.

The door opens from behind us, and when I look over my shoulder I see Mom in white jeans and a striped tank top.

"Why are you girls sitting out here? Don't you want to come inside? I made a pitcher of iced tea." She steps back, holding the door open wide.

Emery and I glance at each other suspiciously. Mom never lets us invite our friends inside. Our house might as well be wrapped in yellow crime scene tape—that's how much of a big deal she's made over the years about keeping people away.

"Come on, before the flies come in," Mom says in her singsong voice.

Emery hurries after me and I lead her into the kitchen. The TV is off, and there's a large glass pitcher on the counter with three cups in front of it.

I set the ice cream down cautiously and sit down at the breakfast bar. Emery copies my movements, eyeing me like she thinks she's on a hidden-camera show.

Mom starts pouring tea into the cups, her blond hair pulled back into a high knot. "So, Emery, I heard you're leaving for college early. You always were so into your academics."

Emery nods, her fingers twisted together in her lap. "I'm in a hurry to start my life, I guess. The sooner I get my bachelor's, the sooner I can get into med school."

Mom smiles brightly. "You sound so much like Kiko. Always in such a hurry to fly away." She looks at me with all the blueness of her eyes, like she's not talking to Emery, she's talking to me. "It's not so bad to have to stay near home though. When I was younger, our parents couldn't wait to kick us out of the house. I wanted my kids to know that they could stay as long as they needed, so they could take their time and decide what they wanted to do with their lives."

I'm not sure what she's doing. I'm not sure what part of this is real. Maybe it's her way of apologizing about our fight, or sympathizing about me not getting into art school. I don't understand, because she never makes it easy.

I can't help it—I don't believe her. If she wanted to tell me this, why couldn't she have said it to me in private? Why did she have to invite Emery inside—which she *never does*—just to tell her how good of a mom she is?

"Kiko already knows what she wants to do though, don't you, Kiko?" Emery nudges me with her knee. She looks up at my mom. "She's so talented. Prism doesn't know what a huge mistake they've made."

Mom sips at her iced tea. "Everything happens for a reason, they say."

I pull my eyes away from her because talking about Prism— especially to Mom—is still too raw.

Emery straightens her back. "That's true—like running into

Jamie again after all these years. It's fate." She squints her eyes at me and pulls a goofy smile.

I feel my cheeks start to warm and distract myself with an obscenely long gulp of tea.

Mom sets her glass down carefully. "Jamie Merrick?"

I nod.

"When was this?"

"At that graduation party," I say.

Mom looks around the kitchen like she's distracted. "Well, I'm sure that must have been nice for you."

When Mom's back is turned to us, I shake my head at Emery to keep her from saying anything else. I don't want Mom to know anything else about Jamie. She likes to sniff out joy and squash it like a house spider.

I don't want my memories of Jamie getting squashed.

When Mom turns back to us, her eyes fall to Emery's forearm. "Are those tattoos?"

Emery doesn't pull her arm away like I would have—she pushes it closer to my mom. "Yeah. Want to see?"

"And your parents were okay with that?" Mom's mouth doesn't close, even when she stops speaking.

Emery shrugs. "They're kind of laid-back about body art. I mean, I'm salutatorian, so I guess they figured I can't be a complete mess if I'm getting straight A's."

Mom's giant soccer-ball eyes land on me next. "Do you have any tattoos? You better not."

"No." I snort. "I hate needles."

"You don't have any tattoos, Mrs. Himura?" Emery asks.

"She does," I hiss to Emery.

Mom points her finger at me. "But I didn't get it when I was underage. *And* I completely regret it because I was young and didn't understand that tattoos were forever."

"How did you not know they were forever? Isn't that like saying you didn't know ice cream was cold?" I raise my eyebrows.

Mom rolls her eyes. "You know what I mean. Sometimes when we're young, we don't understand the concept of forever. We live too much in the moment."

"Can I see it?" Emery leans over the counter.

"No, you most certainly cannot," Mom says, pouring herself more tea. When the glass reaches her lips, she adds, "It's not in a child-friendly spot."

Emery explodes with laughter, and Mom just watches her with a strange smile on her face. She looks proud—like she thinks she's won Emery over.

Except I know Emery. She laughs at everything. It doesn't necessarily mean anything.

I don't realize I'm scowling until Emery nudges me again and mouths, *What's wrong?*

I shake my thoughts away and try to enjoy my time with Emery, because there's not much of it left.

We drink more tea, eat way too much ice cream, and then Emery has to leave. I walk her to the door and she makes a face like we've just stepped into an alternate dimension and she has no idea how to react.

When I walk back into the kitchen, Mom is facing the doorway, her back to the counter. She's standing there, stoic and eerie, and there are tears streaming down her face.

My first instinct is concern. "What's wrong?"

Mom takes a few erratic inhales and wipes her tears away with her fingers. "Do you really hate me so much that I can't even get to know your friend a little better?"

"What are you talking about?"

"You looked so irritated that we were having a good time together. I was only trying to be nice."

"I don't care if you want to talk to Emery. You just confuse me. I mean, we had a huge fight. We weren't even talking. And you *never* let people inside," I point out.

Mom pulls her lips in and shakes her head. "I don't mind if the house is clean."

I grimace. I'm pretty sure she means she doesn't mind as long as it's her idea and on her own time. But I don't say that.

"It's hard for me too, you know." She's still wiping tears away.

I don't understand—she was smiling a few minutes ago. How does someone go from smiling to crying? I'm the one whose college plans recently imploded. Why is Mom acting more emotional than me?

"You guys always act like I'm not interested in you—but nobody is ever interested in me, and I don't get mad about it. You guys never want me around." Her face crumples like she's about to cry even harder, but the sob never comes.

"That's not even true. I do want you around. I invited you to my art show, didn't I?" *She's* the one who didn't want to be there.

She looks up at the wall, ignoring my question. "I wanted to be here today, hanging out with you and your friend."

Again—she wants to be there as long as it fits into her schedule. I don't know what to call that, but I certainly wouldn't call it "wanting to be around."

"I feel like you're embarrassed by me," she says, her eyes beginning to pool once more.

"You don't have to cry," I say, shifting awkwardly near the doorway. I'm not sure what I'm supposed to say; my second instinct is to feel bad for her. "I don't think those things at all."

"I feel like all my kids hate me. My parents never did a thing for me, and I don't hate them. I don't get it." She sniffs.

"We don't hate you," I tell her. The ice starts to thaw, just a little bit, just enough for me to forget that Mom makes the world feel dark.

"I want us all to get along," she says quietly. "I do love all of you. I mean it."

I nod. My third instinct is to hope—hope that this is some kind of turning point, or that her crying is some kind of sign that things will change.

It's strange—hope can make you forget *so much, so quickly*. That's why hoping is so dangerous.

Afterward, Mom gives me her credit card and says she knows I need clothes, so she wants me to order some new things as a graduation present.

I even manage to forget all about Prism until I'm lying awake in bed at night, realizing I haven't sketched a single thing all day.

CHAPTER FIFTEEN

When the ceremony is over, I sit on the steps of the auditorium with my scarlet-red graduation robes folded in a pile next to me. Emery is somewhere behind me, fluttering around like the social butterfly she's always been. I sit there, watching the cars disappear from the parking lot one by one, tapping my feet against the concrete and thinking about what I'm going to do with my life.

When I look back across the pavement, I catch sight of a familiar face.

Jamie's hands are stuffed in his pockets, and he looks like he hasn't decided if he's moving forward or backward.

And then he smiles, raises his hand, and waves.

I wave back, a little too excited, and my chest tightens the closer he gets to me.

"Congratulations." He's standing at the edge of the sidewalk a few feet away.

"Thanks. What are you doing here?"

"My cousin is in your class, remember?"

"Oh yeah. I knew that," I say. Rick is standing with his parents next to their car. He's still wearing his graduation robes.

Jamie brushes his finger against his thick brow. I get the feeling he's trying to think of an excuse to leave.

And I feel like I need to give him one. "I'm not sitting here by myself. I'm waiting on Emery," I say. "So, you know, don't feel like you have to come over and say 'hi' or anything."

"No, it's not—" He stops himself and studies me instead. It takes him a while to say anything, and when he does, he shakes his head like whatever he was thinking doesn't matter anymore. He sits down next to me, his long arms draped over his knees. "So, what's the plan? You off to college next?"

I flatten my mouth. "I was hoping art school, but I didn't get in. I'm still trying to come up with a plan B."

He pauses, holding on to his words like they aren't quite right in his head yet. "I'm sorry, Kiko. I know how much you always loved to draw."

I lift my eyes and follow the trail of his sharp jaw to his dark hair, which is just starting to curl above his ear. I've missed him so much. I've missed the way we were together. I've missed the way he always made me feel, like I was interesting and normal and funny.

Like I was someone worth being interested in.

He grins. "I still have some of your drawings, you know. The ones of us as different superheroes are my favorites." He laughs easily. "Do you remember Klepto Kiko? And Jamie Juggernaut?"

"Oh my God, *yes*!" I burst into a fit of laughter. My head rolls to the side and both my hands fly up to cover my face. I can hear

Jamie laughing too, and suddenly I really do feel like I'm six years old again and we're laughing the way we did when we thought we'd stay best friends for the rest of our lives.

When I thought I'd be in love with Jamie Merrick forever because we were perfect together.

"I can't believe you still have those. Or that you even remember that," I say dizzily.

He shrugs. "You still have that Batman key chain."

All the color returns to my face like a giant beet-red face punch.

Jamie nudges me. As in, actually touches me. I feel like I've been electrocuted, but in the best possible way.

"So," he says finally, "*Star Wars* or *Star Trek*?"

I laugh. I remember this game. *Our* game. "*Star Wars*, definitely. Batman or Superman?"

"Batman, definitely." He laughs. It feels so familiar. "Rogue or Storm?"

"Rogue. Gambit or Cyclops?"

"Gambit. Michelangelo or Raphael?"

"Neither. Leonardo all the way," I say seriously.

"Ahh," Jamie reacts, dragging out the sound. "I knew you were going to say that."

"It feels like we're kids. It doesn't feel like we're as old as we are," I say, and then I catch myself. I turn to him with stone eyes. "I didn't actually mean to say that out loud."

"I know," he answers simply. I don't ask him which part he's talking about because I know, too. He means all of it—what I'm feeling. He knows.

We've always known when it was just the two of us. We're two halves that got separated. We just fit.

But something went wrong. He moved away just before my parents' divorce, and even though I tried to stay in touch—when I *needed* to stay in touch—he seemed to forget all about me. I wish I knew why. Losing my best friend felt like losing half of my heart. It hurt. Sometimes it still hurts.

Jamie chews his lip, looking up at the clouds. "I'm sorry," he says, his eyes falling back to mine. "I'm sorry I wasn't there for you."

"It's okay. You were eleven." I shrug like it doesn't matter, even though it does. I missed him. I've never stopped missing him. "You don't have to apologize."

He looks like he's fighting for the right words, the right way to explain himself. "I don't want things to be weird between us."

Maybe that's what this is all about. Maybe he's been feeling guilty all this time. Maybe that's why sometimes he looks like he wants to run away from me.

Suddenly we don't make as much sense as we did before.

"Whatever you're feeling bad about, it doesn't matter. It was a long time ago." My voice is almost a whisper. "And I don't want you to feel like you have to talk to me just because we used to be friends when we were kids. I mean, I get it. We've grown up. We don't know each other anymore."

"No," he says quickly. "That's not it, Kiko. That's not it at all." He takes too much air through his nose, and it makes his nostrils flare. "Seeing you again . . . I know it's been a long time, and our lives are different now, but I don't . . ." He lets out a heavy sigh like he's giving up.

I don't know what he means. I don't know what any of it means. But I know I don't want things to be weird between us either. I know I want my friend back.

It's so quiet I can practically hear the thump of my heartbeat inside my chest.

A series of sharp honks sounds in front of us, and when we look up, Jamie's cousin is waving at him from the car.

"I have to go." He stands up, looking down at me like there are a thousand more words on the tip of his tongue that just can't be said. And then, because he really is giving up, he shakes his head and walks away.

I smell Emery's flowery perfume before she's even sitting down next to me.

"That," she says slowly, "was like watching a clown die at a children's birthday party."

My hands snap toward my cheeks automatically. "Was I the dying clown? Clowns are the *worst.*"

She shakes her head. "No wonder he didn't try to call you."

Something between a groan and a gasp escapes from my throat. "Hey!" I cry, play shoving her away from me.

Emery explodes into a fit of childish giggles.

Fighting hard to hide my smirk, I roll my eyes. "At least I get to say 'I told you so.'"

"What do you mean?"

"I told you he only offered to drive me home to be nice. It didn't mean anything." I fidget with my sleeve. "He's acting weird. It's like he's trying to avoid me but doesn't know how."

Emery sighs and rests her head on my shoulder. "For someone so visually oriented, you're totally blind."

I don't ask her what she means. I just sit with her, her wavy hair tickling my cheek, and I imagine that time is starting to slow down.

I'm not ready to say good-bye to my only friend.

I draw an invisible circle on the concrete with my finger.

CHAPTER SIXTEEN

When we get inside the tattoo parlor, I can see exactly why Emery always talked about this place like it was magical. It looks like they hired the Mad Hatter to decorate. There are lights hanging from the ceiling, and ornaments in all different styles and colors. Some of the furniture is modern and shaped like boxes and domes, and some of it looks like it came from a fancy British tea party. The walls are black and purple, and there is artwork from floor to ceiling on the entire wall behind the counter.

A young woman with a lavender pixie cut and silver earrings up and down her left ear greets us near the door. "Hey, Ems. I'm all set up in the back. You ready?"

Emery nods excitedly. "This is my friend Kiko. Kiko, this is Francis."

Francis shakes my hand firmly, showing off the full sleeve of tattoos on her right arm. "Emotional support, huh?"

"I'm nervous," Emery admits with a doe-eyed grin.

Francis motions us to follow her to the back, and Emery lies down on the bed. She lifts her shirt up to the top of her rib cage and motions to Francis where she wants the tattoo. Francis nods and turns to her counter of tools.

I glance around the room, still in awe of the change in scenery. I didn't imagine a place like this even existing in our quiet town. I guess I didn't know enough about tattoo parlors to imagine one at all.

There's a glass counter at the side with lots of different piercings for sale, and some rubber models of blank mannequin faces with silver studs in the ears, nostrils, eyebrows, and lips.

On top of the counter are three thick books. I move toward them curiously and see they're filled with pictures of tattoos. Most of them are drawings of common images—horseshoes, angels, stars, mermaids—but others are pictures of huge works of art after they've been tattooed onto actual people. I've never found tattoos beautiful before—not the way Emery does. But looking through the book now feels like I'm looking through someone's sketchbook. It's their art. Their story. Their passion.

I can see why Emery loves it so much.

When I turn back around, Francis has already started. I take a seat nearby, watch Emery's leg twitch now and then, and listen to the buzz of the ink scratching into her skin. She doesn't say a single word, but she winks now and then to let me know she's okay.

Francis looks the way I imagine I do when I'm painting, except she's way more stylish. She looks mixed, too, with dark skin and dark eyes. It's a rarity in this town, but I can't imagine anyone thinking she was weird-looking. She's *beautiful*. I wonder if Adam would've been embarrassed after kissing her.

And then I wonder if Francis would be dumb enough to let Adam kiss her to begin with. Probably not—she'd probably know he was a worm right from the start. She seems tough. Sure of herself. She probably couldn't care less about anyone else's approval of her.

No wonder Emery is always telling me Francis is her soul's muse. I think she might be mine, too.

I read through a pile of magazines, look up nonsense on my phone, and a few hours later Francis pulls away and the buzzing stops.

"All finished. You remember the rules? Try to avoid water and sunlight directly on the tattoo for two weeks while it heals. Showers are fine, but no baths or swimming." Francis scoots her chair back so Emery can slide off the bed.

"I remember," Emery says almost dizzily. She moves to the mirror, admiring the image of the pistol-wielding, gum-chewing girl that fills the small space above her hip and below her rib cage. "Oh my God, I love it."

"Well, you did draw it," Francis says, shifting her tools to the other counter.

Emery looks over her shoulder. "Yeah, but you did it perfectly. It's my favorite one by far."

"I hope you'll come and say 'hi' if you're back in town during the school holidays. And maybe leave some room free—I don't want to lose one of my best customers." Francis laughs and looks at me, her dark complexion making her lilac hair even more vibrant. "You shipping off to college too?"

I shake my head. "I don't know what I'm doing yet." It's the truth, even though I'm making it sound like it's my choice.

Emery stands perfectly still while Francis bandages her up. "Kiko is the one I was telling you about—the artist."

"Ah, right." Francis's husky voice cuts off at the end, and I know it's because Emery must have told her about Prism. "The beautiful thing about art is that you don't ever have to stop doing it. If you don't get into law school, you can't still be a lawyer. You know what I mean? But even if you have to wait on your dream school, you don't have to wait to work on your craft." She taps the side of her head like we're sharing the same thought.

Emery follows Francis to the counter and pays the bill, and when we step back out into the real world, I feel my eyes struggling to adjust. Real life somehow feels different than it did a few moments ago.

We drive to our favorite coffee shop, get our favorite drinks, and talk about Jamie and college and our parents, but mostly Jamie if I'm being honest.

She tells me she's going to miss me. I tell her I'll miss her, too.

When she drops me off at my house, I look over at her from the passenger seat. "Is this good-bye?" I ask.

"Can we not call it that? I hate good-byes. Besides, it's not the 1700s. We have phones. And e-mail. And Skype," she says.

I nod, ignoring the hard scratch in my throat. "Okay. Well, let me know when you get to Indiana. I want to hear all about your dorm room, and your classes, and, well, everything."

She smiles, and I can see her eyes glistening. "Be happy, okay?" She reaches across the seat and hugs me.

I don't find the note she hid in my bag until late at night when I'm looking for my good pencils.

DON'T FORGET, KIKO: LADYBALLS.

I don't even bother trying not to cry. I miss my friend already.

I draw a row of paper dolls severed in the middle and two friends promising to someday put them back together again.

CHAPTER SEVENTEEN

I'm sitting on the couch looking at the community college art program and trying not to spiral into a pit of depression when Mom looks at me.

"I like your hair today," she says.

My shoulders stiffen. Getting a compliment from Mom doesn't just mentally affect me—it's physiological, too.

"Thanks," I say, tucking some of it behind my right ear nervously.

She keeps looking at me. It feels severe, even if she did say something nice. "You should get bangs. Taylor Swift looks great with bangs."

I twist my face. "The last time I had bangs Taro told me I looked like a panda bear wearing a wig."

Mom laughs because she *always* thinks Taro is funny. "Well, I still think it would be a good style. She's so pretty—she kind of looks the way I did when I was your age. We have that all-American girl look."

I want to point out that I'm insulted she doesn't think I look

"American" and that the only way for me to look like Taylor Swift is to literally change every single feature on my entire face and body, but I don't. Because at least Mom is paying attention to me. At least she's trying to be nice.

After another few seconds of staring at me like I'm in an aquarium, she asks, "What are you doing?"

I let my phone fall in my lap. "Looking at other colleges. Why?"

She shrugs. "Because I'm interested. Have you given up on your art stuff?"

Your art stuff. Why is it so hard for her to just say art school? Why does she have to word it so it means so much less?

I shake my head. "No. I'm just trying to find other options."

She looks unsatisfied but stands up and moves toward the kitchen. I stand up too, ready to retreat to my bedroom because I feel a wave coming, but I'm not fast enough.

"Max is moving in tomorrow. Officially," she says casually, feeding fresh coffee grinds into her expensive machine.

My feet plant onto the wooden floors. I guess a weird part of me was hoping she'd change her mind.

"I know how you feel about him, but he's my brother, and he's not in a good place right now," she says coolly. "He needs me. Besides, he makes me happy. We laugh *so much* when we're together. Family is important. So be nice, okay?"

I swallow the painful lump in my throat. I don't like Uncle Max. It's not a secret. But *why* I don't like him is a secret to everyone except my parents.

The point is, she knows. She knows and she doesn't care.

Be nice. Like I'm the one she needs to worry about.

I give a curt nod.

Because there's no point in arguing with Mom about why she's so unbelievably wrong. She'll never see it.

Someone knocks on my bedroom door, but I don't pull my eyes away from the scales I'm painting onto the half dragon.

"I'm working," I call out robotically.

The door opens anyway. It's Shoji.

"Hey, there's a guy downstairs waiting for you and Mom is flipping out," he says. He's holding an Xbox controller in one hand.

"Oh," I say. Confusion floods me.

Oh!

I bet it's Jamie. It has to be.

Oh my God, Jamie is at my house.

I rush downstairs quickly. Mom is pacing in the front hallway like she's been pumped with adrenaline.

"What is he doing here?" she hisses.

I look at the door. It's still closed. "I have no idea. Is he still out there?"

Mom squeezes her hands at the air like she's trying to squeeze my brain. "I don't want anyone in the house. I didn't do my hair this morning, and the kitchen is filthy."

"He doesn't care about any of that," I say.

She growls. Like, actually *growls.* "I don't want people in my house judging me. Do not let him inside, Kiko."

I guess whatever mood she was in when she invited Emery in has passed. She's back to her old self and her old rules. Our house is once again wrapped in yellow tape.

And she wonders why I think she has ulterior motives when she's being nice. Even when she promises it's sincere, it only lasts for a short while. Sometimes I feel like I'm living with two completely different moms. Other times I know better—I know *her* better. Her mood swings aren't an accident; they're a reaction to whether or not she's getting her way.

With a sigh, I move toward the door. She scurries out of the hall to hide in the living room, probably listening to make sure I send him away.

I open the door. Jamie looks almost as flustered as I feel. I'm pretty sure he heard everything.

"Sorry," I say meekly. I step onto the porch and pull the door shut behind me. "What are you doing here?"

He laughs. It's an adorable laugh—a perfect blend of awkwardness and optimism. "I was wondering if you'd like to go to the fair with me. I drove past it this morning. All the games are rigged and the rides are pretty lame, but they have funnel cake."

"You're selling this incredibly well," I say.

He shrugs, smiling. "We all have our strengths."

I smile too. Maybe he really *does* want to be friends again. Maybe Emery wasn't completely wrong.

The skin at the back of my neck prickles. I can feel Mom back there, somewhere, spying on me.

"Let me grab my bag."

CHAPTER EIGHTEEN

The fair takes up a huge section of the mall parking lot. It doesn't look anything like the carnivals in movies. There's no grass, for one thing, and it isn't dark enough for any of the flashing lights to seem quirky or romantic. The loudspeakers are playing a horrible mix of pop songs from when I was in elementary school. All the stands are surrounded by chain-link fences, and the prizes look like they came from the reject crane machine pile.

But the air smells like toasted marshmallows and funnel cake and Jamie Merrick is here, so this is already one of the highlights of my life.

We play a game where you're supposed to throw these little red plastic rings onto glass bottle tops, but all the rings keep bouncing off.

We shoot air rifles at paper stars and barely get two of the legs off.

We throw darts at balloons that never seem to stick, but on the last try I manage to pop one balloon. It doesn't matter, though, because the carnival worker tells me you have to pop three balloons to win anything.

Still, I'm having so much fun I'm starting to get a headache. I'm not used to being around so many people. I'm not used to laughing so much. I'm not used to being so *happy*.

Jamie's been carrying a camera around his neck the whole time. The way it hangs over his checkered blue shirt makes him look like a tourist. Dark eyebrows, eyes like ice, and a fading tan—he looks like he comes from someplace completely magical.

He tells me he's majoring in photography and that one of his professors told him to take as many photographs as he could over the summer. He says even photographers have to practice.

I'm not surprised he decided he wants to take pictures for a living. When we were kids, Jamie was always playing with his dad's camera. I think one of the reasons we always got along so well was because we both saw the world as a series of moments that needed to be captured—we just captured them in different ways.

The flash of his camera startles me.

Jamie laughs from behind the lens. "That's what you get for zoning out. What were you thinking about?"

I reach for the camera. "Please delete that. I wasn't ready for a picture."

"Those are the best kind," he says simply.

I don't want him to have a stupid picture of me. What if he looks at it when he gets home and realizes what a weird face I have?

"Please delete it."

"If I show you the picture and you absolutely and truthfully think it's terrible, then I will delete it. But if there's even a part of you that recognizes what a good picture it is, I get to keep it. Fair?"

I nod, and he steps so close to me, I'm breathing in the cologne on his neck. He's so handsome. Like a European model and one of Tolkien's elves all molded together. It makes it so hard to concentrate.

Because he's not just good-looking—he's nerdy, and funny, and nice, and he actually seems to enjoy talking to me. And I'm just—

I look at the picture. My almost-black hair is flat against my head, and the tips of my ears poke through all the heavy straightness. My eyes—something between Mom's and Dad's— are staring past the lens and straight into Jamie's soul. They're dark, too, like my hair, and I'm so pale I look like a vampire. My nose—my grandma's nose—is too round, and my face is too round. My lips are full, except they're always crooked, as if my face never knows whether it's serious or smiling or about to speak. Oh my God, no wonder Mom has been telling me I've been going through a "funky stage" since I was ten. There are a million things wrong with my face.

"Please delete it." My voice is a whisper now.

Jamie is looking at me like he doesn't understand. He must not have looked at the picture well enough. Either that or he's so used to my weird face that a photograph of it doesn't even faze him.

His mouth starts to move. He wants to argue. He wants to ask if I'm kidding, if I really can't see what he sees. He wants to change my mind.

But I look at him with hard eyes, partly to hide how embarrassed I am, but also to remind him of our deal.

We had a deal.

He lets out a very small sigh. I hear his camera beep twice. "There. It's gone."

We walk toward the funnel cake stand. Jamie takes photographs of lots of things—kids eating cotton candy, a toddler crying when her shoe falls off, a couple hugging next to the fence. He doesn't show me any more of his pictures, but I have a feeling they're good. I can see the way Jamie's eyes move across the crowd. It's like the world is clay and he's shaping them within his mental frames.

As I'm watching him, I realize he's not talking to me. My chest starts to pound—not because I'm a needy person, but because I'm worried I've upset him. This is the problem with telling people "no"—I always feel bad about it immediately afterward.

"Are you mad at me?" I ask softly.

His camera drops to his waist. "Why would I be mad at you?"

"Because I made you delete that picture."

I see his jaw clenching. "That would be a ridiculous thing to get mad over. You know that, right?"

I shrug.

"Well, I'm not mad. I wish you didn't get so embarrassed over a photo—that was a really good one, by the way—but I'm not angry. It's just a picture, and if it bothers you, I can respect that. You don't have to feel guilty just because you didn't do what I would have liked."

I feel like he's telling me it's okay to disagree with him. It's a completely foreign concept to me.

"Can I ask you something?" Jamie reaches his hand across his chest and scratches his neck. When I nod, he asks, "What do you see when you look at pictures of yourself?"

I swallow. *Someone who looks too Asian to be pretty.* Because being Asian means I can never be as pretty as the other girls at school—the girls like Mom. I know this because people like Henry and Adam and Mom keep telling me I don't have the right face. I know this because when I look in the mirror, I see what they see—a girl who doesn't belong here. A girl who isn't good enough.

But I can't tell him that—he wouldn't understand.

"Okay. Well, what do you wish you saw?" He tries again when I remain quiet for so long.

Someone with bigger eyes. Lighter hair. A smaller nose. "Someone who looks more like everyone else," I say at last.

Jamie runs his thumb over the edge of his camera. "Do you know how many people would love to have your face? Yeah, you don't look like everyone else in this town, but that's special. You stand out because you're unique, and people literally never stop trying to be unique."

I twist my mouth. "But I don't want to stand out—not at all. I want to be normal. I want to feel like I belong in the same world as everyone else." If I looked like everyone else, it would probably be easier to make friends. I might even have a mom who cared.

That last part really stings.

"You might feel that way now, but it isn't like that forever. Wait until you see what the world has to offer besides this small town and your high school. People are different out there."

I'm assuming he means California. I'm not sure if I believe him. I can't imagine feeling like I'll ever belong anywhere. I'm either too white, or too Asian, but never enough of either.

And I'm weird. People don't react well to weird.

"Besides," he adds, "if you're worried you're not pretty or something, don't be."

He catches my eye. What does he mean by that? Does he think . . . ?

"My mom always said you were the prettiest girl in the neighborhood," he says. Why does it feel like clarification?

I roll my eyes. "Your mom hasn't seen me since I was nine. And I feel like you're making that up."

"Nope," he says triumphantly. "I'm not. Lying isn't my thing."

"Is it anyone's thing?"

"Probably. Everyone has a thing."

"I don't."

"Yeah, you do."

I go stiff. What does he think it is?

Jamie smiles without his teeth, but it's still the warmest, kindest smile I've ever seen. "You want to make everyone happy. Even if it's sometimes at the expense of your own happiness."

"Oh my God, I'm a people pleaser? That's the worst."

"I think compulsive liar is a lot worse."

"Or sociopath."

"Or serial killer."

"Or cannibal."

Jamie laughs and holds his camera back up to his face. "Yeah, any of those."

I stare into the lens. "Are you taking my picture again?"

"Can I?" he asks.

I wait. I think. And I nod.

I paint a carousel of mirrors and dragons, and inside one of the mirrors is the happiest girl alive, desperate to break free.

CHAPTER NINETEEN

It's hard not to be irritated about Uncle Max moving in. Besides the fact that deep down he's a terrible person, he listens to the worst music—nineties heavy metal. And he never closes his bedroom door, so I have to listen to the screams of an electric guitar from across the hall when I'm trying to paint. It's like creative cyanide.

I set my tools down, roll my chair toward my desk, and rummage through the top drawer for a set of headphones. I have a small pair that I almost always use, but Dad gave me a set of noise-canceling ones for my birthday years ago. It was around the time he and Mom were fighting a lot. Just before Dad's affair. Just before the divorce.

The headphones make me look like the generic alternative to an X-Wing fighter pilot, so I only wear them when I'm in my room. I connect the headphones to my iPod and roll back to my painting.

I'm at least four songs into my favorite playlist and a good hour away from finishing the piece when someone grabs my shoulder.

I jump, snap my eyes over my shoulder, and find Uncle Max

standing there. He hasn't shaved in days, and his eyes are blood-shot, like he hasn't slept all night.

He probably didn't. I'm not sure he was even home last night.

My chest tightens like there's a monster trying to stuff its hand between my ribs and squeeze my heart until it bursts. I feel like I'm sinking lower and lower into the ground, but there's nothing below my feet to keep me steady. I just keep falling, and something sick and weightless fills my stomach.

I slide the headphones off shakily. "What?" I manage to get out. I want to tell him he's not allowed in my room. I want to tell him I don't want him anywhere near me. But "what?" is the only word that escapes me. Because anything else will lead to confrontation. Anything else will give me a panic attack.

He runs his tongue along his molars like he has food stuck there. "You're going to blow out your eardrums like that, kiddo." He nods to my painting. "What are you making?"

My instinct is to cover the almost-finished canvas with my body. I don't want him looking at it—it's personal, and he doesn't get to be a part of what's personal to me.

But I don't move. I sit in my chair, frozen, with one hand still hovering over the painting and the other gripping the edge of the table.

There's cotton in my throat again. I swallow. "Did you want something?"

Uncle Max leans back like he doesn't understand why I'm so short with him. *Of course* he would pretend like nothing ever happened.

I mean, he denied it. And he may have fooled Mom and maybe

even Dad—we've never talked about it, so I don't really know—but he will never make me think I imagined it. I remember. I don't want to, but I remember.

"You know, you should try to be nicer to your mom." He folds his arms across his chest and leans back. His skin always looks like he rubs oil into it, but today it looks especially greasy. I wonder if I'm just noticing all the things about him that irritate me more than usual.

"I *am* nice to my mom," I say tersely.

He lets out a weak hum. "She says you've been giving her a hard time lately."

Of course she'd say that. The only way she gets out of being the bad guy for letting Uncle Max stay is if she makes *me* the bad guy instead.

He ignores the hurt in my eyes. "She feels underappreciated. And, you know, after everything that happened with your dad, you should really cut her some slack."

My shoulders twitch because I can't sit still. "What's that supposed to mean?" I'm terrible at sticking up for myself, but I can't help but defend Dad. Especially when Uncle Max is the one talking about him.

He shrugs like it's not that big of a deal. "I mean everything she had to put up with." His blue eyes are stained with yellow, like they've been poisoned over the years.

I don't stare at him for very long, and pretty soon my gaze is back at my hands. I just can't do it. It's intimidating. And I know who he's trying to blame—it's my fault that my parents split up.

They started fighting because of what I told Mom. Uncle Max moved out because it got too uncomfortable, and then Dad moved out because he wanted a new family.

It's my fault that our family broke apart in the first place, and Uncle Max knows it, just like everyone else in this house.

His hand rushes up like he's trying to catch a lightning bug. He clasps my shoulder too hard. "I'm right across the hall if you ever want to talk, kiddo. We used to be pals when you were younger. There's no reason we can't get back to that now that we're roomies again."

How does he do that? How does he sneer and speak to me like nothing happened? Like he thinks I don't remember? Like he thinks my parents don't *know*?

The monster squeezes tighter. I feel like I'm going to vomit.

I know nobody else ever talks about it because it's uncomfortable. It's the family secret everyone would rather have buried and forgotten about. Sometimes even I want that.

But pretending with me is a lot different from when I pretend with my parents.

Because it happened to me.

I don't realize how violently I'm shaking until Uncle Max pulls his hand away and stares at me like I'm an animal left out in the cold.

I sweep a small brush into a blob of cerulean gray and pin my gaze to the corner of the canvas until his footsteps leave the room.

I paint a monster with poisoned eyes swallowing up the sun so the whole world goes dark.

tell Emery all about Jamie, because if I keep talking about the things that make me happy I can trick myself into forgetting about the things that don't. She's happy for me, but she's also overwhelmed with school. I have to remind myself not to text her too often—it's hard breaking the habit, but I know she's busy starting her new life. She's on a scholarship—her future depends on her getting good grades, and I can hear in her voice it's not as easy as it was in Mr. Miller's classes.

And even though I know I miss her, sometimes I forget I do at all because I've been too excited about being friends with Jamie again.

It feels so familiar. It feels like it did all those years ago, when I had such a clear understanding of happiness. It wasn't muddied and confusing like it is now. Maybe that's just part of growing up—things aren't black and white, hot and cold, happy and sad. They're complicated. Feelings are complicated.

With Jamie, everything feels simple. I need simple. I need a friend.

I text him: Lucky Charms or Cap'n Crunch?

He texts back: Cap'n Crunch, if it's peanut butter.

I write: I'd pick Cap'n Crunch no matter what.

He writes: Want to come over?

I write back: Okay.

I feel like I need to bring something with me, so I rummage through the kitchen cupboard. I find a package of chocolate chip cookies that have been there for months and a bottle of kiwi-flavored water that Mom hates.

Jamie texts me his cousin's address.

When I show up with the water and cookies, he shakes his head in the doorway.

"Who brings flavored water to a house party?" His hair is a deep toffee color under the porch light, but his eyes are still the brightest blue I've ever seen.

The skin on my forearms buzz with nerves. "House party?" I repeat.

The girl from the party appears behind Jamie. The one with all the lip gloss. "Hey, stranger." She's wearing a pale orange crop top and a leather miniskirt, and the bulk of her hair is swept to one side.

I take a step backward automatically. "Sorry. I didn't know you had company. I can come back another time."

Jamie scrunches his eyebrows. "What's wrong with now?"

The girl moves away from the door. I think she's trying not to make me feel more uncomfortable, but it's not her fault. I live my life in the small space between "uncomfortable" and "awkward."

I'm still walking backward without even realizing it. "I should go home." I look at my hands, and suddenly I'm moving toward him. Thrusting the water and cookies into his chest, I say, "Here. You can keep these for your party."

When I reach my car door, I realize Jamie's followed me. He looks confused, and *of course* he is. Normal people don't need to prepare for social interactions. Normal people don't panic at the sight of strangers. Normal people don't want to cry because the plan they've processed in their head is suddenly not the plan that's going to happen.

I'm not normal. I know this. And now Jamie is going to figure it out too.

Because I'm not the girl who wears crop tops and short skirts and looks like one of Taylor Swift's best friends.

I'm the girl who brings kiwi-flavored water to a house party.

"I don't understand. Why won't you come inside?"

"I'm not really good at parties. Or people," I say squeamishly.

"We ran into each other at a party."

I shut my eyes as tight as I can. "That was different. Emery wanted me to go, and then I couldn't stay at home because of— well, it doesn't matter; I just needed to get out of my house. But then your girlfriend—" *Oh my God*, I'm talking way too much. I peel my eyes open.

Jamie's lips are pressed together and his eyes are wide—the biggest I've ever seen them. "So you'll go to a party full of strangers when you're distressed, but you won't when a friend asks you to hang out?" He studies me for a moment. "Kiko, that doesn't make any sense."

I shrug because what else am I supposed to do? Of course it doesn't make sense—feeling this way doesn't make sense. But if I could fix myself and turn off the anxiety long enough to feel normal, I would have a long time ago.

He looks flustered. I *feel* flustered.

"Look, I was exaggerating when I called it a house party. It's just Sarah, her sister Missy, and this guy Alfie I used to play soccer with when I was a kid." He pauses. "You see more strangers every time you're at work."

"But they don't expect me to talk beyond showing them where things are sometimes. At work I'm just a cashier. They don't expect me to be—" I let out a breath.

"A human being?" Jamie blinks at me.

I feel my entire body getting hot. I feel like I'm being interrogated. I feel offended.

"I'll talk to you some other time," I say stiffly.

Jamie's hand catches my arm. "Hang on. You're angry—why are you angry?"

I bite my lip because I'm worried I'm going to start crying like a weirdo. I'm not used to having to vocalize how social anxiety makes me feel. Emery was used to it—she didn't make me explain myself.

I think of what she'd say if she were here.

I think of her note. The words she left behind to remind me to be brave.

"I feel like you're pressuring me. I told you I didn't want to go inside, and now you're making me feel bad about it," I say. The words surprise me when they come out. For a brief second I feel strong—brave—but then I'm overcome by an intense wave of guilt.

He shifts his jaw and lifts his shoulders. "I'm not trying to pressure you. I just don't understand."

I feel my knee lock and unlock like a nervous tick. I wish it wasn't so hard to tell people what I'm feeling. A long time ago, it wasn't hard for me to tell Jamie anything. I wonder if it will ever be like that again. "I'm not asking you to understand."

Jamie pulls his neck back and shakes his head. "Why are you making it so difficult for me to hang out with you?"

My stomach somersaults and I feel something swell inside my chest. It isn't long before my throat tightens and my head starts to spin. I don't know how to answer Jamie's question.

His blue eyes soften. "Look, I'll be right back. Don't leave, okay? Please?"

When he disappears back into the house, I really, *really* want to drive away. It's uncomfortable between us now. It's not like it was when we were kids—now it's complicated.

But I don't leave because he has eyes like gems that make me want to stay, even when he says the wrong thing.

Jamie comes back with his iPod and some headphones. He's still holding the kiwi water and cookies I brought.

"Will you sit with me?" He lowers himself onto the sidewalk, twists the bottle of water open, and pulls out a chocolate chip cookie from the package. A crooked smile appears in the corner of his mouth.

Suddenly I don't want to leave as much as I did before.

I sink down onto the concrete next to him, mostly because being closer to the ground makes me feel steadier.

He holds out the cookies. As soon as I take one, my eyes start to water. I blink as hard as I can.

We both crunch and chew into the humid night air. When I'm finished, I dust the crumbs from my fingers and blink again to make sure the tears are gone.

His hand falls to his lap. "Sarah isn't my girlfriend, by the way. Our parents are still friends, so we hang out whenever we're in the same place."

She's not his girlfriend. That's . . . "Oh. Okay."

He fountains the bottle into his mouth and swallows like he's in pain. "This is the most disgusting thing I've ever tasted."

I can't help it—I laugh so loud that the sound bounces off the street and fills my own ears. For a second I'm stunned by the noise, and I can hear it in my head long after it's quiet again.

I clear my throat and hope he doesn't see all the redness burning through my face.

"If this is what you drink at your house, you should definitely come inside." Jamie scratches the side of his head. "We've got water. And soda. And pink lemonade. All three of which are better options than this twisted form of torture you brought to my cousin's house."

Part of me wants to say yes. Why is it so hard? It's just as difficult as saying no, when it should be *so much* easier.

But the more I think about going inside, the more my heart feels like it's going to burst.

"I can't," I say to the street.

"You can't or you don't want to?"

This time I look straight into Jamie's eyes. "I can't."

A sad kind of acceptance washes over his face, but it disappears quickly. "Here." He holds out an earbud.

I put it in my left ear, and he puts the other in his right.

Drums. Violins. A keyboard.

"What is this?" I ask.

Jamie doesn't look at me. His head is tilted back and his arms are crossed over his knees. "Wilco. Do you like it?"

"Yeah. It's relaxing."

"I listen to a lot of Wilco when I'm taking photographs. And The Smiths."

"I don't know them."

"You will. We might be here for a while."

I rub my fingers along my shins. "You can go back to your party."

"Of course I can," he says. "But I want to hang out with you. That's why I invited you over."

We listen to two more Wilco songs, and when Jamie puts on The Smiths, I start to forget where I am. The almost-black sky is painted with stardust, my left ear is full of guitar strums, and every time Jamie taps his thumb against his knee to the beat of the music, I fall more in love with him.

The earbud drops to the concrete and I am on my feet. I'm not in a position to be falling in love with anyone. And especially not Jamie Merrick, who I've loved practically all my life, who could probably crush my heart with two fingers and a half smirk.

I'm supposed to be coming up with a plan. I'm supposed to be figuring out what I'm doing with my life. I'm supposed to be finding a way to get out of this town for good.

"I should go home," I insist before any words tumble out of his partially opened mouth. "But thank you. For sitting with me, and for Wilco." *And for trying*, I want to say.

Jamie gets up and wraps the earbuds into a tight coil. "Okay. No problem, Kiko." His face looks strained because he doesn't understand me. He doesn't know how to fix me.

He doesn't know I don't *want* him to fix me.

Prism was going to make everything better, but now that it's out of the picture, I know I have to work through the clouds in my head all on my own. Otherwise the next time I lose what's important to me, I might not have the strength to come up with another plan.

Hearts aren't meant to be broken an infinite amount of times.

I drive home without looking at him again, even though I really, really want to.

I paint Jamie sitting on the sidewalk, watching the stars, listening to Wilco, with a ghost sitting beside him.

CHAPTER TWENTY-ONE

Y ou can't get so disheartened when someone doesn't act the way you want them to. Even Mr. Darcy wasn't perfect. And just because someone makes you feel uncomfortable doesn't make them your mom."

Emery always has the best advice, even when it's compacted into five minutes because that's all the spare time she has between classes.

I text Jamie a GIF of a Pikachu making a weird face.

He texts back a GIF of James Franco smiling and mouthing the words "It's okay."

And just like that, we're back to normal again.

When I get home from work, the acrylic tubes are still on the desk, but not the way I left them. I know because when I have a new painting idea, I always line them up a certain way to get a feel for the color scheme. But they've been pushed to the side, like someone was looking for something.

It wouldn't be strange if I was used to people coming in my room and touching things, but nobody comes in here. Mom would probably rather die than admit she's seen a painting of mine, and my brothers don't bother because all the video games and food are in other rooms.

I'm not trying to be a jerk when I immediately blame Uncle Max, but I can't help it. Who else would come in here?

"You shouldn't accuse people of things when you don't have any proof," Mom says from the couch. She looks irritated that I've interrupted her TV show.

"But you said you didn't go in there, and I'm telling you, somebody was in my room." I feel like she's treating me like a whiny little girl. But I have a history with Uncle Max. I have a history with him coming into my bedroom.

Why doesn't she ever seem to get this?

"Is it really that big of a deal? Maybe he was interested in your drawings."

WHAT I WANT TO SAY:

"You're already a crappy mother for letting him back in this house. If you let him in my room, you'll be the world's *worst* mother."

WHAT I ACTUALLY SAY:

"It's a big deal to me. It's my *stuff*."

Mom rolls her eyes dismissively. "Well, what exactly is it you want me to do?"

I shrug. *Just be my mother*, I think. "Just tell him not to come in my room," I say.

She looks at me like winter has inched through the house and we are freezing from the inside out. With the remote control attached to her hand, she raises her arm toward the TV and mutes the sound.

"I really need to talk to you."

My chest thumps with excitement. I wish it didn't. Disappointment always, always follows excitement.

Mom leans forward. "Are you gaining weight?"

I blink. "What?"

Her blue eyes are full of very real concern. "I don't want you to get upset, but your face is looking rounder than usual. Now that you don't have to walk around school, I'm wondering if maybe you aren't getting enough exercise. It's important, you know. For your health."

"I've only been out of school for a week. I doubt my face is rounder after seven days of not walking to class." My words are all right, but my voice is shaking so bad I'm positive she's never going to hear them. I close my arms around myself protectively.

"Don't be sensitive about this," she scolds. "I'm only saying it because I love you."

I don't know what else to say, so I shrink back upstairs and lock myself in the bathroom.

When I look in the mirror, I don't see a fat girl. But after five minutes of pinching my skin and studying every angle in the reflection, I see the fattest person in the world.

I paint a girl in a circus freak show with wide, stumpy legs and a face shaped like a perfect circle.

CHAPTER TWENTY-TWO

When I drive Shoji to tae kwon do practice, I ask him if he thinks I'm fat.

"Obviously not," he says, staring at his empty hands. He must have forgotten his book today.

"You can't tell if I've put on weight?"

His head falls to the side. "Why are you asking me this? You sound like Mom."

I grimace. That's the last thing I want, so I stop talking immediately.

The car pulls up to the building, but Shoji doesn't move right away.

"Are you going away for college?"

My eyes widen in surprise. "I want to. I don't know though. I didn't get into Prism."

"Yeah, I know, but are you still moving out?" He's watching me impatiently.

"Probably." I have to. Staying here isn't an option—it *can't* be.

Shoji is still for a while. I wonder if this is about my room—maybe he wants to swap after I've gone. I have the bigger closet by a long shot.

"Do you think Dad and Serena would let me move in with them?" His voice is floating somewhere high above us. I barely hear him.

"You don't want to stay with Mom?" I ask quietly. I always knew Shoji preferred Dad, but I never realized it was enough to want to move out.

He looks at me with careful eyes—desperate eyes—but the light in them vanishes quickly, like a window being slammed shut. Shoji doesn't want me too close—he's protecting his heart too.

Shoji clicks his seat belt and jumps out of the car. "Never mind," his voice clips as quick as a paper cut. "I'll see you later."

I watch my little brother jump up the stairs and disappear behind the glass doors. The car engine rumbles and the bass of the stereo makes the seat vibrate, but I don't drive off.

Shoji feels what I feel—the urgency to get away. Because being around Mom is like swimming in poison. It kills your soul, slowly, bit by bit.

It's one of the reasons art is so important to me. It's my light-house, guiding me through the storms.

But eventually that lighthouse is going to wear out. Eventually the storm will reach it.

I can't let my soul die to the point where I lose my art. I just can't. Shoji protects himself by being invisible, but I'm not good at that. Not when it comes to Mom. Because it hurts too much when she doesn't look at me the way I need her to. I don't know how to turn that off.

I have to get away. I don't want to stay here, I don't want community college, and I don't want to live with Dad and Serena, even if they are the nicest. I just want to *go*.

I lean my head against the headrest, trying to think of a way to change my future so it stops feeling like an empty hallway that stretches forever and ever.

I draw a little mouse so afraid of the world that he hides in the dark until he goes blind.

CHAPTER TWENTY-THREE

can't find my new brushes. Or the twenty-dollar bill I left next to the receipt, which is also missing.

Mom tells me I'm being dramatic when I tell her I think Uncle Max is stealing from me. I don't think it's dramatic at all. He doesn't have a job, but he goes out every night and comes back with drunk eyes and bad breath, if he even comes back at all. He must be getting the money from somewhere.

"I want to put a lock on my door." I'm looking at Mom seriously, but she's smiling like this is the funniest conversation in the world.

"No. It's my house, and nobody is locking me out of the rooms I pay for." She's flipping through a catalog from some hipster-looking clothing store. I seriously doubt she'll buy anything—I think she's just judging the models and playing her "Who's prettiest?" game.

"I'm going to be eighteen in a month. I think I should be allowed to have a lock on my door." *Especially since Uncle Max is sleeping across the hall from me,* I want to add.

"I said no. Drop it." She stops flipping the pages and holds up one of the glossy images for me to see. "What do you think of this sweater?"

It's a black-and-white patterned kimono with tassels.

"Are you going to a music festival?" I ask dryly.

Mom squints her eyes at me. "Don't be mean." She stares at the picture again. "I think I'd look super cute in this."

"If I can't have a lock on my room, I'm going to move out. I don't trust the people living in this house," I say.

She lets the catalog flop onto the kitchen counter. "Can't you see I'm trying to have a nice conversation about clothes? Why do you always have to be so negative?"

"Can't you see I'm trying to have a conversation about somebody *stealing my money*?" I feel like a vein is going to burst from my neck. It's not easy for me to say what I'm thinking, but I'm trying anyway because it's important. I need her to know how uncomfortable I am with Uncle Max being in my room. I need her to understand. Why can't she see that? Why doesn't she care?

"God, Kiko!" Mom marches to the living room and shoves her hand into her oversized purse. She comes back with her wallet. "Here." She flings a twenty-dollar bill at me, which I ignore and let fall to the floor.

"I don't want your money." I dig my hands into my ribs.

"What is it you want from me, then?" Her voice is shrill and sharp.

WHAT I WANT TO SAY:

"For you to be the mother I need."

WHAT I ACTUALLY SAY:

"Permission to put a lock on my bedroom door."

Rubbing her temples with her peach fingernails, she shakes her head. "You can't have a lock. If you want to keep your stuff safe, find a better hiding place. Or better yet, go talk to Max and you can clear up this entire misunderstanding."

I don't tell her I shouldn't need a better hiding place in my own home. I don't tell her talking to Uncle Max won't bring back my stuff. I don't tell her Uncle Max would never admit to stealing from me.

She's not listening. She never listens.

I leave her and her twenty-dollar bill in the kitchen.

Taro comes into my room while I'm painting and flicks my ear.

Flinching, I pull my chin toward my chest.

He snickers. "Your boyfriend left this for you on the porch." He tosses a shoe box on my desk. It's wrapped with an obscene amount of Scotch tape. On the front are the words: FOR KIKO.

"I saw him pull up outside, so I know it's from him," Taro states. He adjusts his thick plastic glasses. "Are you going to open it?"

"Not in front of you," I say with a laugh.

Taro looks offended. "Why not?"

"Because it's none of your business." I blink at him. "Do you want something?"

He laughs. "I want to know what's in the box. What if it's a bomb?"

"You're an idiot," I say.

He starts walking toward the door but stops. "Someone took some money out of my room too."

"Seriously?" I feel my chest start to tighten. "Did you tell Mom?"

"I don't tell Mom anything. I'm a lot smarter than you." He laughs again, but this time it sounds sad. "I'm only telling you so you don't think I did it."

"I didn't think you did."

I don't know what else to say to him. Taro never sounds sad. I'm not sure I realized he *could* be sad. He's been smirking and avoiding feelings for as long as I've known him. And I don't know why he suddenly cares what I think about him. He's never cared before.

Has he?

I honestly don't know. I understand my brothers even less than I understand Mom. It never occurred to me Taro might understand a little bit about *me*.

He scratches his nose with his knuckle, laughs uncomfortably, and leaves me alone with the shoe box.

A rush of excitement builds, and I'm no longer thinking about what it means to have brothers who never talk to you but somehow still *know* you—I want to know what's inside the box. I saw at the tape with a pair of scissors until the lid comes free. It's full of photographs.

They're all from the fair. Some of them are black-and-white and some are colored. They're candid and beautiful. When I look through them, I can smell funnel cake and fresh doughnuts. I can hear the blend of laughter and screams. I can hear the popping of balloons and air rifles, and I can hear the *clink* of glass bottles and plastic rings. I can almost feel Jamie next to me, looking at things the way I do—with too much focus on what's least important, which to us is the most important of all.

The very last photo is the one of me. It's colorful and rich. I'm barely smiling, but my eyes are content. My ears still poke through my hair, and my nose still seems too wide for my face, but I don't see the ugly version of myself I normally do. I see what Jamie wanted to capture. I see what he wanted me to see.

And it's not terrible.

I paint a girl confronting the monster under her bed, who really isn't so scary after all.

CHAPTER TWENTY-FOUR

At work, I text Jamie:
Black or white?
Lasagna or spaghetti?
Day or night?
And he texts back:
Black.
Lasagna.
Day.

I tell him I'd pick the exact opposites, and it doesn't make me feel like I'm disagreeing or hurting his feelings. It just feels like we are being ourselves.

I draw a bird and a fish falling in love.

CHAPTER TWENTY-FIVE

Something stirs me while I'm sleeping. I don't know if it's the loud breathing or the footsteps, but when I open my eyes I'm as alert as I'd be in the middle of the day. There's light spilling in from the hallway, washing over me like a harsh spotlight.

I can hear him. I can hear Uncle Max.

Fear replaces my blood. It's everywhere, all through my body, and it's taking away my ability to move. I can't roll over. I'm not sure I want to. Because if I see him, everything will be real.

I wish I could turn to dust and disintegrate into the dark air like I don't exist at all. It would be easier that way.

If he touches me, I'll scream. If he comes any closer, I'll force myself out of the bed. But right now I don't move an inch.

He's breathing with his mouth open—they sound like the snores of a drunken man, even though he's obviously awake.

Awake but definitely not sober.

I think he's reaching toward me—I can feel the air shift because it feels like someone is pulling off an entire layer of my skin—so I stiffen all my joints and squeeze my face into the pillow.

What do I do? What do I do?

The footsteps pad away, and the door closes silently. Beneath the door, I watch as the light vanishes and the house goes still.

Alone, I sit up, choking on my own fear. I don't think—I grab my bag, my phone, and my keys and slip through the house, and before I know it, I'm driving down the road with panic in my throat and no idea where I'm going.

I end up at Jamie's cousin's front door because I don't know where else to go.

Instead of knocking, I call him. Because if I knock, he might think it's an emergency and get scared. I mean, it's my emergency, but it's probably not a real one. Not in comparison to a fire or a burglary. I don't know what to call what happened tonight. I just know I'm about ten seconds from vomiting all over Jamie's porch if I don't sit down and rub the frantic pain drilling through my head.

"Hello?" he croaks sleepily.

"It's Kiko. I'm sorry I woke you up, but I don't know where else to go." *Oh my God,* I'm crying. I definitely didn't mean to start crying.

"Are you okay? Where are you?" His voice is loud. I'm pretty sure he's not in bed anymore.

"I'm at your front door." *Oh my God,* this is so embarrassing.

There's shuffling through the phone and then shuffling behind the door. The lock clicks, and suddenly Jamie is there in his shorts and shirt, and his hair is everywhere—literally everywhere—and his blue eyes look as panicked as my heart feels.

"What happened?" He's scanning me like he's searching for wounds. I guess *that* would be an emergency.

But I don't have any injuries. I have an anxiety attack. If I tell him that, he'll probably be irritated I woke him up and whatever illusion he has of "Kiko, his childhood friend" will be replaced with "Kiko, the weird sleep interrupter who doesn't understand what an actual emergency is."

"My uncle," I start, but I stop myself. I've never said it out loud—not since I told Mom the truth all those years ago. I don't want to say it again. Partly because I'm too confused to acknowledge it, but also because I don't understand what "it" is. My fingers wipe at my cheeks clumsily. "I'm sorry."

Jamie looks into the street like he's checking for someone. "Are you alone? Did someone hurt you?"

I shake my head quickly. "No, it's nothing like that. I . . . didn't know where to go. I can't go home."

"Here, come inside."

I'm not sure where I get the energy to move my feet, but I follow him into the living room, and suddenly his arms are wrapped around me and he's squeezing me against his chest like he's afraid I'll fly away. I melt into him and the tears keep pouring.

I cry until my chest is sore, and then I breathe and breathe and breathe, and finally I'm not crying anymore. I don't want to look up and let Jamie see what I mess I am, so I stay buried in his shirt.

"Do you want to talk about it?" He keeps holding me.

"I can't," I admit.

"Can you call your dad?" he asks.

I pull away, but I don't look up. "No. It's . . . complicated." Because if I stay with Dad, I'll have to tell him everything. I'm pretty sure he's still trying to forget what happened the first time. I don't want to ruin another marriage for him—not when he has two little babies to take care of and he's so happy with Serena. What I'm feeling seems to hurt everyone else more than myself. I can't tell Dad. I can't tell anyone.

My body starts drifting away from Jamie's, but he doesn't stop me. He's looking at me like I'm breakable—like I'm made of thin glass and one nudge too hard will shatter me into a trillion tiny pieces.

"I'm sorry. I don't know why I came here." I should've gone to a motel. What was I thinking making this Jamie's problem?

"I do," he says seriously. "I don't know what happened, but I know you shouldn't be alone right now. You can stay here, okay? As long as you need to."

I wipe my face again. "I don't think your aunt and uncle would like that."

"They're still in Florida for Rick's graduation trip. I've got the house to myself until they get back, so I'm the only one who has to know. Besides, they wouldn't mind. They're cool—they'd understand."

"I need to find an apartment." I can't stay here forever—we both know it. This might buy me a night or two, but I can't permanently live on someone's couch.

Besides, Jamie will go back to California before the summer is over, and what am I going to do then? I'll be all alone.

"We'll figure that out when they come home. Until then, you're safe here." He puts his hands against my shoulders. I'm still not looking at him. "It's going to be okay. Okay?"

I nod. What else am I supposed to do? Mom is going to *kill me* when she finds out I snuck out of the house. I have no way of proving Uncle Max was in my room, just like I had no way of proving he was stealing my things. But I can't go back there. It's not safe. *I don't feel safe.* Mom will never understand that. She'll never choose me over Uncle Max—not when he agrees with everything she says and tells her how wonderful she is all the time. She has friends and enemies and nothing in between.

I don't fit in Mom's world.

Jamie makes me a bed on the couch, but I'm not tired, so we sit together and watch a movie.

Except I guess I was *really* tired, because the next thing I know it's morning and my head is on the pillow and I'm covered up to my shoulders with a blanket.

Jamie is fast asleep on the floor next to me.

CHAPTER TWENTY-SIX

Mom doesn't call me until after two p.m. I guess that's when she finally noticed I wasn't home.

"I'm not staying at the house anymore. Not unless you make Uncle Max leave." My voice shakes. I'm in the upstairs bathroom talking to her because I don't want Jamie to hear. It's embarrassing enough that he saw me sobbing. There was probably snot all over his shirt and everything.

Strangely enough, she's not as mad as I thought she'd be. She just sounds irritated. "We can talk about this at the house, Kiko. Come home."

"Is Uncle Max there?"

"He's sleeping." *Of course* he is.

"Well, I don't want to be in the same house as him. I'll talk to you when he's gone."

She hangs up the phone.

I find Jamie in the kitchen. His laptop is set up on the breakfast bar with a USB cord plugged into his camera. When he sees me, he straightens his shoulders. "Everything okay?"

"She wants to talk at the house."

"Is that what you want?"

I shrug. "I doubt she'll listen to me. But I might go over later." *When Uncle Max goes back out to drink,* I think.

Jamie nods and points to the screen. "I'm just transferring some photos off my camera. I was planning on taking some shots at the mall. You interested?"

"Yeah, okay. What's at the mall?"

"People." Jamie laughs.

I could never take photographs the way Jamie does. He captures strangers like he's invisible. And he sees the best possible version of them—it's the way I imagine things in my head, but the only way I can make it real is to paint it. To me, ideals don't exist in real life. I have to make them up.

But Jamie sees them everywhere. Imperfection is his ideal, because it's real and tangible, and he knows how to translate it into a frozen moment in time that will be beautiful forever.

I could watch him take photographs all day. The way his left eyebrow digs lower than the right. The way the sides of his mouth curl down and then up again. The way he doesn't blink until he takes the photograph, just in case he misses the perfect moment. The way he looks at me with a wide smile after he captures what he wants to, because he doesn't live in the moments of his photographs—he lives in the moments right here, with me.

I'm so in love with Jamie Merrick I want to run straight into a wall and squash into a flat pancake because loving him feels like a cartoon.

When he's finished taking pictures, we wander to the food court and get giant cinnamon rolls the size of our faces. Jamie lets me look through the digital copies on his camera.

"These are amazing." I feel dizzy looking at them. He's so talented. *Way* more talented than me. He'd never have been rejected by Prism.

"I want to see your paintings," he says. "I bet they're amazing too."

Laughing, I eat another bite of cinnamon roll. "Your expectations are already way too high. I'm not that good. Not like you."

"I doubt that." His blue eyes sparkle. I forget to chew for at least three seconds.

Clearing my throat, I drop my eyes. Somewhere inside my bag, my phone vibrates. It's a text from Mom.

He went out. Come home so we can talk.

I take a deep breath and glance up at Jamie. With the exception of when he's looking at his camera, he's barely taken his eyes off me since last night.

"Will you come with me to my house?" I don't want to face her alone.

"Of course I will."

I text Mom back: **Okay. I'm bringing Jamie.**

We're already back in the neighborhood when she finally texts back: **I bought dinner, so I hope he likes Italian food.**

CHAPTER TWENTY-SEVEN

Mom's wearing a cream cable-knit sweater, even though with the humidity it feels like it's ninety degrees outside. Her makeup is done and her hair is perfect, and she's wearing the vanilla perfume she always wears when she goes out, but never when she's inside the house.

There's something strange about her smile, but I can't figure out what it is. I try not to pay attention—Mom is always analyzing the way people perceive her. Every time I talk to her it feels like I'm taking a test. Most of the time I fail before I even open my mouth.

I hope Jamie doesn't notice. I don't want him to feel as weird as I do.

"Hey, Jamie," she says enthusiastically. "The last time I saw you was at Taro's birthday party. Do you remember that? It was years ago."

Jamie gives a polite smile, but his eyes flicker back and forth like he doesn't want to look directly at her. I'm not sure why.

Maybe her smile is too intense for him, too. "Yeah, I remember." He looks at me. "It was the day that old guy yelled at us for going in the Jacuzzi because we were too young or something."

I grin. I remember too. After we got yelled at, we decided to spy on him from up in the nearby trees. In our game, he was an evil space pirate, and we were the half-robot half-human rebels who were trying to save the world.

Except we forgot what game we were playing after a while, and we ended up sitting in the tree for the rest of the pool party playing our "one or the other" game and trying to master the art of whistling. We completely missed the birthday cake, which Mom was really mad about. She said we were supposed to be there for the pictures—for the memories. I guess she didn't care that we were making our own.

Mom crosses her arms and pushes a hip out. "You and Taro were such good friends. Sometimes I felt like you were my third son."

My teeth press together. Jamie Merrick was *my* best friend, not Taro's. You see? She even tries to take *my best friend* away from me.

Jamie pulls his lips into his teeth in a tight smirk, but he doesn't say anything. I'm not sure he notices what I do.

"I hope you two are hungry," she says, leading us into the dining room.

There are at least four giant containers of pastas and two massive meatball subs on the table, not counting the empty packaging that my brothers already cleared out. It's way too much food.

"Are you having a party or something?" Jamie asks as she slices the sub in half and passes it to him.

Mom laughs melodically. "I thought you guys would be hungry, that's all. This place is so good. Make sure you try the eggplant parmesan. Kiko, I got that for you, because you're a vegetarian." She's watching me, and her blue eyes look like they were pulled out of a doll—unmoving, always smiling.

It takes a lot of control not to give away what I'm thinking. She's probably made an active effort to pretend I'm not a vegetarian hundreds of times over the last two years, but now that there's company, remembering a personal fact about me makes her look thoughtful. So *of course* she mentions it.

"Thanks, Mom." I hesitate when she passes me a plate of food. It feels like I'm making a deal with the devil. Nothing nice Mom does is for free. I just won't know what it will cost me until it's too late.

I take the plate. Maybe bringing Jamie here was a bad idea. I just didn't want to come back here alone.

She asks him about college, and California, and whether he has a girlfriend—*it's so uncomfortable*—and eventually she asks how his parents are doing.

Jamie nods through a bite of meatball sub. "Mm-hmm. They're good." He keeps chewing. And chewing. I've never seen anyone chew for so long just to get out of saying anything else.

Mom watches him carefully for a while, her eyes half closed and the same partial smile stapled to her face as a disguise. "Well, I'm sure your parents must be so proud of you. You seem like you turned out to be a very nice young man."

I cringe through another mouthful of breaded eggplant. Jamie laughs gently. When she tries to come across normal like this, it's *so weird.* And I know weird—I'm probably the very definition of weird—but when people come to the house, it's like she turns into some suburban housewife cyborg. Everything she says is nice and thoughtful and makes her look like the greatest mom in the world.

Nobody ever sees what I see. Nobody ever knows what I know.

At least, nobody who lasts. Anyone who figures out what's beneath her pretend skin gets shoved straight into enemy territory. It's why she and Dad never speak. It's why I'm her least favorite. It's why the only long-term friends she has are the ones she never sees—the ones that get too close eventually figure my mother out. She doesn't keep anyone around who could potentially crush the pretty exterior she wears to hide all the ugliness.

They start talking about photography—like Mom knows anything about photography!—and it doesn't take long before she starts telling him how she used to model.

"It was such an exciting time in my life," she gushes. "If I hadn't decided to get married and have kids, I probably would've ended up in Milan or Paris."

"That's cool." Jamie pushes his plate farther away, but she keeps scooping more pasta onto it.

Mom's boiling over with energy, and she's trying to shove it down our faces like she is with the Italian food. "You know, I sacrificed a lot to have children. Being a mother is truly one of the most selfless jobs you can do."

Jamie pushes his chair back. He's probably just trying to get away from the food, but he could also be trying to get away from her desperation for a compliment. "Do you mind if I use your bathroom?"

"Not at all. It's right around the corner on the left." Mom points down the hall.

"Yeah, I remember. Thanks."

When he disappears, Mom rests her head in her hands and stares at me. "He turned out super handsome, didn't he? He's got nice teeth, nice eyes, good skin. And he's very tall." I hate her checklists. She does it with every person I've ever brought to the house. I feel like she's letting me know if they pass her approval test because of the way they look and not because of the person they are.

I don't realize I'm shaking my head until she scoffs.

"What? I'm trying to be nice," she says defensively. When I don't say anything, she folds her arms flat against the table. "Are you mad that I'm talking to your friend?"

"What? No." I'm frowning. She's already in control of where this conversation is going, but I don't know how to take it back.

"I know you don't want me to be a part of your life."

"I never said that."

"I know you'll laugh if I say this, but I'm really an amazing person."

I *do* laugh. And I press my fingers against my eyes because I don't know what is going on right now. "Good for you, Mom. I have no opinion on this."

"Yes you do," she snaps. "That's why you want to get out of the house so badly. Because you hate me. It's almost like you're jealous of me."

WHAT I WANT TO SAY:

"I want to leave because you make me feel small and ugly and unlovable, and because you're letting Uncle Max—*Uncle Max*, the reason Dad *left us*—live across the hall from me, and you won't even let me put a lock on my door to keep him out!"

WHAT I ACTUALLY SAY:

"I am not jealous of you!"

Her eyes float around the room. "So what do you and Jamie talk about? How horrible you think I am?"

"*Oh my God*, Mom. Why are you doing this?" I ask stiffly. "I came over here to talk to you about how I'm moving out. Why are you making this all about you?"

"I never make anything all about me," she snaps. "I'm sitting here, trying to have a nice time. I bought you guys all this food, I'm trying to get to know your friend, and you're acting like I've committed some kind of crime. I'm not some evil dictator."

This conversation is spiraling out of control. I don't even know what edge to grab ahold of to steady myself. My mind feels like it's been caught up in a violent twister.

"I'm not suddenly going to be in a good mood because you bought pasta. And for the record, I never asked you to buy dinner. And I'll pay you for it, because I don't want you feeling *put out*." My knuckles crack under my thumbs.

"I don't want your money." Her face is like stone.

"I'm in a bad mood because Uncle Max came into my room

last night, drunk, and I don't feel safe. If you don't kick him out, I can't live here anymore." My chest is throbbing. My breathing is quick. My throat is tightening.

"You're not an adult. You have to live here," she says simply.

My hands shake. "Then I'll call child protective services, or something. I'll tell them what happened. I'll get a restraining order."

Mom laughs. "You're such a drama queen."

Tears burn my eyes. "This isn't funny. I'm serious."

Her face freezes over. "I can't believe you'd even threaten that. Do you know what that would do to our family? This is a private family issue. You're being unbelievably selfish right now."

"Selfish?" My skull is pounding.

"Your words could ruin someone's life. Did you ever think about that?"

I stand up, my whole body convulsing with anger. "You care more about Uncle Max than me. The only reason you don't want me to leave is because people might ask questions and then you'll look like a bad mom."

She leans back. Our eyes radiate into each other's. I can't believe I actually told her what I was thinking. I got all the words out without tripping. It feels powerful.

And terrifying.

Because I told her how I feel. I told her what I'm really thinking, without worrying about how I should say it, without distorting my actual feelings to avoid making her angry. I feel like I've thrown my armor away, and I'm standing in front of her completely exposed. I'm vulnerable and unarmed, but I've told her the truth, and somehow that gives me a sense of strength I've never felt before. Maybe I don't need weapons or armor if I have the truth.

I brace myself for Mom's reaction.

"Do what you have to do. Put yourself above your family." It's not permission. It's a taunt loaded with malice.

"I'm not telling anyone," I choke. "But I am moving out."

She closes her eyes and opens them again like she's looking at the world for the first time—so innocent and pure. "You obviously need time to cool down. So go ahead—*go and feel like a grown-up*, if that's what you need. I'll forgive you when you come home, because I'm your mom and I love you."

Inside my head, I'm screaming. I step away from the table and my eerily still mother. When I reach the bottom of the stairs, Jamie is sitting there with his hands clasped together.

I smear my tears away with the edge of my sleeve. "Sorry."

He shakes his head and swallows. "I didn't want to interrupt. I didn't know where to go."

"I'm going to pack a bag," I say with a weak voice. And then I try to smile, but it just feels sad. "I guess you'll get to see some of my paintings, if you want."

He nods, and I lead him upstairs.

Jamie looks through my canvases and my old sketchbooks. He studies the pictures I've hung on the walls and the unfinished pieces wedged under books. All the while he doesn't say a word. He just investigates on his own like he's in an art gallery.

I pack a duffel bag of clothes and toiletries. I pack Emery's note. I pack two of my sketchbooks, and I even pack my unfinished portfolio full of photographs of all my paintings. I look around. I'll never be able to fit everything in one bag. There are too many canvases and art supplies and books.

I'm aware I haven't thought this through. I know Mom's probably right—I'll come back home eventually. Because all my stuff is here. Because I don't have a long-term plan.

But I need to get out of the house before Uncle Max gets home. I don't care if he was drunk or if he doesn't remember it—if I stay, I'm saying "I'm okay with this" when I'm absolutely not.

I pack my best pencils and feel a horrible ache in my heart when I leave all my acrylics and brushes in the corner.

"These paintings are incredible." His voice is so clear. It's the light in all the darkness.

I look at the canvas in front of him. It's a girl floating on top of the water, surrounded by fireflies and water lilies.

I meet Jamie's eyes. "I didn't get the lighting right on that one."

"Kiko, I'm serious. You are unbelievably talented."

I scratch at my arm because I don't know how to respond.

"Thanks," I say to my duffel bag. I yank the zip and seal away the compacted version of my life I'm going to be living with.

"Are you going to take any of these?" He's still by the canvases.

"There's no room. I still don't know where I'm going." I feel rattled. I'm afraid Uncle Max will come home and yell at me for upsetting Mom. I'm afraid to look at him at all.

We go back to Jamie's house. I don't tell my mother good-bye.

I draw a girl on a train, surrounded by empty seats.

CHAPTER TWENTY-EIGHT

I'm looking at apartments on my phone, getting more and more disheartened by the cost and the fear of the complete unknown, when Jamie groans from the other side of the room.

"My cousin is at Harry Potter World right now," he says, flicking his thumb over his phone screen. "He keeps sending me pictures to make me jealous. That place is amazing."

"I want a Harry Potter wand so bad." I sigh. "Like, I want to show up and have the wand choose me."

"Would it impress you at all if I told you I totally did that?"

"Yes. It absolutely would."

"Well, I did. And I tried butterbeer."

"You're kind of the coolest person I know right now."

"It doesn't come naturally. I actually have to try really hard."

I burst into a fit of laughter. He's trying hard to keep his mouth flat.

"You live in California. At least you can go to a theme park whenever you want," I say. "The most exciting place we have here is an outdoor shopping mall."

Jamie's face lights up. "You should come to California with me. We could go to Disneyland or Universal Studios. You know, to celebrate graduating high school."

"What are you talking about?" I roll my eyes. "I can't go to California. I need to find an apartment." And then I pause. My brain starts to piece something together—something that makes me nervous and excited and terrified all at once.

An idea. A beautiful idea.

I look up at Jamie. "Do you think," I start, "I don't know, maybe . . ." Should I really ask him this? Have I lost my mind? "Do you think I could look at art schools in California? Maybe some of them are still accepting late applications. Plus, California is cheaper than New York."

My heart thumps like a bass drum. I can't believe I'm actually considering this.

When I catch the curiosity in his eyes, I raise a hand. "I don't want that to seem weird, like I'm trying to follow you across state borders. It's just, well, it's someplace new, you know? A fresh start." At least I'd know someone in California. Navigating through a new city wouldn't be so scary if I had a friend there. Plus it's hundreds of miles away from *here*. "I could go on a trial basis, for a couple of weeks. To see what the schools are like. What the area is like."

Jamie's eyes widen before snapping away from me. He looks

like he's struggling to say what he wants to, like all the words racing through his mind have just screeched to a halt on the tip of his tongue. Oh my God, he probably thinks I'm being ridiculous. He's probably trying to think of a polite way to tell me I've lost my mind—that I can't move to California to be closer to him. That we've only recently started to be friends again. That it's too soon. That he doesn't want me there.

My face gets hot, and I'm watching his eyes move around the room so quickly that I'm already trying to find a way to take back everything I've just said.

His gaze meets mine, and his mouth opens into such a huge smile that I feel the entire room get brighter. "You could stay at my house," Jamie says, and everything inside me turns to air and happiness. "Until you figure out what you want to do or whatever. You know my parents already, so it wouldn't be weird." His blue eyes are wild with electricity. I think mine are like that too.

His dark lashes flutter just once before his pupils freeze like a cat in the street. We don't have to speak, because we already know.

We're picking up where we left off all those years ago.

Is that why it doesn't feel fast? Is that why it feels so natural?

I know I should be thinking about this more. I know it's reckless and unplanned and I'm choosing California because having Jamie there feels safer than being alone, but I don't care.

It feels good to hope.

I swallow. It's like a dream. I mean, not the first dream of being accepted into Prism, but it's a perfect backup. It means I could spend more time with Jamie. We could be best friends again.

Jamie's hand closes over mine. Sparks ignite in my core. I forget to breathe.

"Jamie." My voice creaks. "I want us to be friends again." I don't mean it to sound indifferent, but it does. I don't know how to use the right emotions when I speak—I'm just not good at speaking, period.

He pulls his hand away like he's retreating.

If me and Jamie keep looking at each other with sparks and electricity and magic, there won't be any turning back. I'll be in love with him forever, and he'll know it. And then there's the chance I'll lose him, and I don't think I could handle losing Jamie. Not again. Not when I feel like I have so little control over my life as it is. There's Mom, Uncle Max, Prism, and even the kiss with Adam—I'm suffocating beneath the weight of life inexperience. I don't want Jamie to turn into the thing that breaks me.

He's too important to me. Our childhood friendship is too important.

His expression softens. "Me too, Kiko." Maybe I'm reading into everything. Maybe the sparks only exist in my head. Maybe he just wants to be friends too. "We *are* friends."

The lump in my throat plummets to my stomach. "Okay. Cool."

He raises a brow. "Friends and temporary roommates?"

I grin. "Yeah. Okay. Let's do it. Let's go to California together."

We're both giggling with excitement now.

Even though I feel sick, I try not to let it show.

Because disappointment always follows excitement.

I draw a boy and a girl swimming through a sea of stars.

CHAPTER TWENTY-NINE

I call the bookstore and tell the manager I've had an emergency. I don't explain why, but I say I need to leave the area for two weeks. She tells me she can give out my shifts to some of the part-timers, but that I'll have to use up my vacation days. I tell her that's fine.

Of course it's fine. I'm going to California with Jamie Merrick. I'm going to look at art schools and see the ocean for the first time. I get a break from Mom and Uncle Max. I'm going to find a new dream.

It's more than fine.

I follow behind Jamie out of town in my own car. I don't say good-bye to Mom. I don't even tell her where I'm going.

She doesn't call, either.

It takes a few hours to cross the first state border. The sights amaze me because somehow I never realized how ginormous the world really is. There's so much earth everywhere. It's like all the people migrated to these pockets of lights and noise, and they left all these miles and miles of nature completely untouched.

We keep our phones on speaker when we're driving, so it sort of feels like we're driving together. We play our game. We listen to Wilco, and The Smiths, and lots of other bands I've never heard of. We stop for lunch. Jamie laughs at how I go *exactly the speed limit* and not one mile per hour over.

We pull in for the night at a small motel in the middle of nowhere. We ask for a room with two beds. I try to pay for half of the cost, but Jamie keeps pushing my hand away. When he's in the shower, I sneak the money into his suitcase. When I wake up in the morning, it's back in mine.

We cross another state border. And another.

Jamie says we'll be in California by the next evening. We find another motel, but this time when we ask for two beds, the man at the front desk shakes his head.

"Sorry, we've only got queen rooms left." He taps his finger against the mouse button. He knows we'll take it anyway—it would take a while to find another motel.

I shrug at Jamie. "It's fine."

I try to pay again, but he won't let me.

When we're in the room, I set my bag at the foot of the bed and twist my hair.

"I want to pay," I insist. "I can't let you pay for everything. It isn't fair."

"I would have had to pay for these rooms anyway. Taking your money would make me feel like I was trying to get you to pay for half of my trip," he says. "Besides, you need your money for art school."

It doesn't make me feel better. "No. I want to pay. Please. I don't want to be a burden on anyone." My cheeks burn. I still have the money in my hand.

"It's not being a burden. Let me do something nice. What's the big deal?"

"I don't want to owe you more than I already do," I manage to say.

My words don't sit well with him—he looks like I've said something hurtful.

But he doesn't understand. I'm already going to California because it's easier to be with Jamie than to be alone. I couldn't have gotten this far if he wasn't here with me—if he wasn't letting me stay with him and his family. It doesn't feel right to accept his money, too.

I know he's not Mom—I know he wouldn't hold it over me for the rest of my life. But he's already doing me a bigger favor than he realizes. And people run out of favors eventually.

I don't ever want Jamie to regret letting me follow him to California.

He takes the money. "Just so we're clear, you are not a burden, and you don't owe me anything. You never have."

By the time we shower and crawl into bed, I have ice in my lungs from my short, quick inhales that refuse to calm down. I'm worried he's mad. I'm worried I've offended him. Why is it so hard to have a disagreement with someone that doesn't mean anything? Do all disagreements have to mean something? How do people ever say no without fighting?

Oh my God, are Jamie and I fighting?

Jamie rolls over so he's facing me. "Hey," he whispers, like he can read my mind.

I roll toward him. Both of us are on our side, looking at each other in the darkness. I've been close to Jamie when he hugged me, but this feels even closer. It feels intimate.

He pauses. "What's going on in your head right now?"

I fight to keep my shoulders from shaking. I can't help how fast my heart is beating—when the anxiety starts, I can't stop it. It has to run its course.

"I feel bad that we're arguing on our second day together."

"That wasn't an argument, Kiko."

"It feels like it."

"It was a minor disagreement, *maybe*. But nothing serious enough for you to be having a panic attack."

I know he's right. Of course he's right. But that doesn't mean I can just reprogram the way my emotions work. Fixing me isn't like fixing a loose screw or a little bit of rust. I'm like a giant mess of problems, all linked together and tracing back to my childhood. Back to when things got so complicated.

"Does it feel like a big deal to you? When we don't agree on something?"

"Yes," I say.

"Why?"

I think carefully.

WHAT I WANT TO SAY:

"Because disagreeing with my mom is the reason she doesn't like me. I don't want it to be the reason you don't like me either."

WHAT I ACTUALLY SAY:

"I can't really tell when people are mad at me."

"It's okay to say no to people, Kiko. Everyone does it. And trust me, they don't feel bad about it. Do you think I would have felt bad if you had kept your money? Or if you had let me keep that first picture of you at the fair?" He props his head up with the heel of his hand.

I keep my head flat against the pillow because I still feel dizzy. "I guess not."

He raises his brow. "You know, if someone is going to be mad at you just because you didn't let them have their way, you're better off without them."

My breathing slows. The ice in my throat begins to thaw.

He watches me quietly, his breathing quick. It doesn't matter that it's dark—I can still see his jaw clench and his lips twitch. "Why did you call yourself a burden?"

I pinch my fingers together nervously, but I can't find the words to explain myself.

"You're the opposite of a burden." He sighs. "I wouldn't do something nice and have there be strings attached to it. Especially not with you."

I nod. I feel like I should thank him for being so nice to me. But then I feel embarrassed that "nice" feels like such a foreign concept.

"I've never been around someone who"—he pauses—"reacts the way you do. You didn't used to be like this."

I know he isn't finished talking, but I can't stop myself. "Things were easier when we were kids. The scariest things we had to worry about were nightmares and horror films. It's different now."

He's quiet. "What are you so afraid of?"

People. Uncle Max. The truth. Never really being loved. Disappointing everyone. Disappointing myself. Feeling guilty for the rest of my life.

"Not doing the right thing, I guess," I say at last. "It always seems like the only way to keep everyone else happy is to do something that makes me unhappy. I don't know how to grow out of that."

"Maybe you don't have to try so hard. Maybe you'll grow out of it without noticing," he says.

I tilt my face toward the ceiling. "Maybe," is all I say.

"Can we make a deal?" he asks in the darkness. "I'll try to be more patient with your anxiety, and you try not to overthink everything."

"That's fair," I say.

"And about what I was saying before—about the way you react. Even though I find it frustrating, it's still a million times better than not having you in my life."

I don't say anything, but I don't need to. Jamie's hand finds mine beneath the blanket. He curls his fingers over mine. It feels like holding my hand next to a campfire. Warm. Cozy. Peaceful. It's how I think home should feel.

I don't pull my hand away. I just fall asleep.

I dream we wake up, still holding hands.

CHAPTER THIRTY

Jamie's parents don't look the way I remember them. His father, Brandon, had black hair the last time I saw him. I remember because I used to think he looked like Elvis Presley. Now his hair is full of salt and pepper, and he's not as tall as I remember. Not even as tall as Jamie.

Jamie's mother, Elouise, looks sort of the same, but narrower. It's like someone squeezed all the extra water out of her, and now she's small and thin and *so tan*.

She doesn't greet me right away. She watches me the way you'd watch a stray animal you've never seen before. With distrust and hesitation. I wonder if she looks at all the girls Jamie brings home this way.

I wonder how many girls Jamie has ever brought home. And then I wish I hadn't wondered it, because now I can't get it out of my head.

"Gosh, you've sure grown up," Brandon says with an earthy chuckle. His arms are around me before I even realize it. When he pulls away, his bottom lip is pulled back and his chin is dimpled. "I can't believe this is the same girl who used to make clubhouses out of our couch cushions."

Jamie smiles next to me and scratches his fingers at the back of his neck. "Okay, Dad, not so close, geez."

Brandon lets go of me. "Well, it's not like you came over to give your old man a hug." He folds his arms around Jamie.

Elouise steps toward me. She walks like a dancer—graceful and balanced. "Hi, Kiko. It's nice to see you." We hug each other awkwardly—I don't know whether to go right or left and I guess neither does she—and we pull away quickly.

"Thanks for letting me stay," I say with as much appreciation as I can possibly find. Jamie didn't tell them what happened at home—he just told them I was coming to look at colleges.

She eyes her husband like she's scolding him. Brandon notices, but he keeps grinning anyway. "It's no problem," she says at last, turning on her heels. "You two must be hungry. Your dad made burgers."

"Kiko's a vegetarian," Jamie says. "Sorry. I meant to tell you that on the phone."

Elouise looks over her shoulder curiously. "Is she?" She looks at me for an extra second before disappearing into the kitchen.

When Brandon is out of earshot, I whisper to Jamie, "Are you sure it's okay that I'm here?"

"Positive." He picks up our bags. "I'll show you the guest room."

Something feels off. I don't think Elouise is happy about me staying. But I don't argue with Jamie. I just follow him.

Because at this point, where else would I go?

Elouise makes me a grilled cheese even though I tell her I don't mind eating coleslaw and chips. This makes Brandon laugh, although I don't know why. When we're finished, Jamie and I clear the table and put all the leftovers away. His parents go off to watch TV, and we sit outside on the deck because it's so warm and beautiful, and I can see the ocean from his backyard.

"You have a really nice house," I tell him.

Jamie is typing away on his laptop. "I'll tell my mom you said so. She designed it."

"I don't think your mom likes me very much," I admit.

He looks up. I expect him to look surprised, but he isn't. "No. She likes you just fine."

I narrow my eyes. "I don't believe you."

He grins. "Lying isn't my thing, remember? Honestly, it's not you." He pauses. "Her and my dad are probably just fighting about something and they're trying to hide it. Dad's better at it, clearly."

I remember how bad my parents used to fight right before they split up. They never tried to hide it in front of us.

Jamie might not see me as a burden, but maybe his mom does. My mom never let anyone come over toward the end of my parents' divorce. The house was a constant war zone. Elouise might not want an outsider intruding on her private life either. I've got two weeks here—I need to make absolutely sure I don't outstay my welcome.

"Hey, can I borrow your laptop when you're done?" I ask.

Jamie spins the laptop toward me. "I'm done now."

I look up art schools in the area, narrow it down to three, and tilt the screen back to Jamie.

He grins. "You're not wasting time."

"I'm growing ladyballs," I say.

Jamie half chokes, half snorts. "What did you just say?"

My cheeks burn. "It sounds a lot better when Emery says it. Never mind."

He laughs, and I look back at the screen.

Three schools that are still accepting late applications. Three schools with a good painting program. Three potential new dreams.

I study the applications, print out directions, and stay awake for hours after I'm in bed, staring at the ceiling and wondering if this is all really happening.

I ask Jamie to come with me because I get anxious going to new places. I know I need to be stronger, but . . . baby steps.

We visit the Glass Art Institution of Southern California first. It's beautiful, inside and out. There's curved windows and most of the building looks like boxes stacked on top of each other. The outside is all white, and the inside is like a futuristic space station. Gleaming, polished, and so modern. There are paintings and framed photographs all over the walls and glass boxes full of pottery and sculptures spread out all over the floor space.

I'm nervous to visit the art rooms in case we get in trouble for interrupting a class, but it turns out I didn't need to be nervous at all. The entire side of the art building is glass—you can see everything that's going on right from the sidewalk.

It's pretty quiet inside. A few people in the pottery room, another person working on a stone sculpture on their own. The painting room is completely empty. I wonder if it's always so quiet, or if it's because it's summer.

We visit Blue Phoenix next. It's so busy we have to park across the street. The outside is cream and blue, and looks like a generic building. The reception room is full of artwork, but it isn't as crisp and clean. It feels more like someone's bedroom with every inch of wall space covered. I don't mind it though—it makes me feel more comfortable. It makes me feel less nervous.

Their work spaces have the same feel. Even the half-finished projects left out on various easels make me feel calm. I might have a chance of getting into a school like this. They might accept someone like me—someone who can paint, but not quite well enough to get into Prism.

But it doesn't feel *right*. Not like how Prism did the first time I saw their website.

When we step onto Brightwood's campus, I don't even feel like I'm in California. It's green everywhere, and people are sitting under the trees sketching in the afternoon sun. The woman at the front desk is drinking her coffee and laughing with one of the students. The walls are olive green and full of the brightest artwork imaginable.

It's a happy school. It makes me happy.

I tell myself I need to forget Prism. Comparing it to every other art school is never going to turn out well because Prism is *the* art school.

If I let Brightwood be Brightwood all on its own, I might actually like it.

"Can I help you?" the woman asks.

I step toward her meekly. "I'm just looking around. I was thinking about applying."

"Very cool." She smiles and slides a drawer open. "Here's a map of the campus." She passes me a sheet of paper. "Feel free to wander around. There aren't many classes going on right now anyway. But if you see anyone working, we don't mind at all if you watch from the windows; just please don't interrupt them. Some of the professors here can be a little moody." She wiggles her fingers in the air like she's casting a spell and giggles.

"Thanks," I say with a small smile.

When I turn to Jamie, he's smiling too.

"What do you think?" he asks.

"Maybe" is all I say.

All of the rooms downstairs seem to be for pottery. The second floor is graphic design and photography. And the third floor is drawing and painting.

I look through one of the windows from the hallway and see five students surrounding a table full of objects—a jar of marbles, a horse-shaped piñata, a mannequin head with a neon-blue wig, and lots of other oddities. They're all sketching furiously like they're being timed. They probably are—I hate timed sketches.

I never feel like I get to say what I want to say. Maybe because it takes me a long time to sort out my thoughts, even with art.

Some of the rooms are barren except for the drawings and corkboards all over the walls. Some of the rooms are full of desks and whiteboards. Some of the rooms are full of students.

All of the rooms are full of color. All of them feel like home.

Oh my God, maybe this is it. Maybe this is where I'm meant to study.

Maybe.

It's easy to look around with Jamie beside me. I don't feel like I'm going to get yelled at when he's around. It's like he's protecting me from being so painfully out of place.

Jamie makes me feel safe, and right now I need him more than ever. A month ago, I'd never dreamed of driving across the country to look at colleges without even being invited. I don't have the courage to step outside of my own element. And my element, quite obviously, is being alone and invisible.

I tell myself I need to thank him, when I'm not busy drooling into the windows and hyperventilating over the oil paintings and watercolors and canvases as big as my garage door.

Eventually we head for the door. We can't stay here forever; otherwise I totally would. On our way out, the woman at the desk stops me, her hand waving in the air like she's hailing a taxicab.

"Here," she offers, handing me a small magazine. "There's a list of all the local art events inside. There's a student gallery coming up if you want to check it out." She flashes a bright smile. "You never know. They could be your future peers."

In the car, I flip through the pages. There are events happening almost every week throughout the summer, but the student gallery isn't until August. I don't know what my life will look like in August.

I turn another page. It's an ad for a local art show with a white background and simple, black writing.

> *Hiroshi Matsumoto*
> *Milk and Stardust Exhibit*
> *Open to the public*
> *June 27, 4:00 p.m.*

At the bottom of the ad is a photograph of a man with his arms folded behind his back. His dark hair is pulled back behind his head, stretching the skin across his cheekbones. He's wearing a loose white shirt and a half smile, like he's in on a joke that nobody else seems to realize. Behind him is the most beautiful painting I've ever seen.

A girl with black hair, small eyes, and her arms raised to the sky is bursting from the sea, and pale blue feathers sprout from every inch of her clothing. When I look closer, she has feathers growing from her hair, too, like a mythical creature from the ocean transforming into a bird.

It's so beautiful I can hardly breathe.

"What is that?" Jamie asks from the driver's seat.

I feel the air escape over my lips. "I have no idea. Something amazing."

He's grinning. "Well, when is it? Do you want to go?"

I bring my eyes to him and feel like feathers are bursting from my skin. "It's in two days." I want to go. I *need* to go. But not alone. I'd be too nervous to go to an event alone, where I don't know a single person, in a city I've never been in before, without anyone to hide behind. "Will you go with me?"

Jamie doesn't even hesitate. "Of course I will, Kiko."

I press the magazine to my heart and close my eyes.

I draw a girl—no, a bird—no, a star splitting into a thousand pieces—and then I don't draw anything at all, because all I want to do is close my eyes and dream of painting for the rest of my life.

CHAPTER THIRTY-ONE

Elouise trades a triangle of toast for her car keys and curls her fingers in the air. "I'm going to work. Put the dishwasher on when you're finished?"

Jamie flips his thumb in the air and keeps chewing. "Mm-hmm."

His mom smiles at him, then me, and then she's not smiling at all—she just looks sad. She hurries out the door.

I scrape my fork against the scrambled eggs. I made breakfast for everyone, but Elouise only ate half a slice of toast. Maybe she hates my cooking. Maybe she doesn't think making breakfast makes up for intruding into their family home for two weeks. Maybe she doesn't want me here.

"It's too early for that," Jamie grumbles across from me. The skin beneath his eyes is puffy from too much sleep, and he's wearing a blue and gray plaid shirt and jeans that fit him way too good. It's unfair—jeans shouldn't fit *anyone* that good.

I frown, but I've already forgotten his comment. I'm still thinking about the jeans.

"You're thinking," he says seriously. "Or . . . analyzing. Nothing is going on right now, you got that? Everything is cool." He opens up his eyes like he's trying to hypnotize me into believing him.

Laughing, I shake my head. "You don't even know what I was thinking about. It could've been something good."

"It wasn't. You had that look in your eyes. Like a startled deer, or someone who's just been given bad news."

I pull my hands away from the table and shove them into my lap. "I'm sorry. I'm worried your mom is mad I'm here."

He sets his fork down. "She doesn't mind you're here. I told you that already."

"I know you did." I rub my lip with the back of my finger. "But she looks sad all the time. I feel like it's because of me."

"It's not you." Jamie shifts his jaw thoughtfully. "It's my dad. They're not getting along right now. It's part of the reason I went to stay with my aunt and uncle again." His eyes dart away and back again because his words have slipped through by mistake.

"Again?" I repeat.

Jamie has been back home before.

I never knew. Now I know it's because he didn't want me to.

"How many times have you been back to visit your aunt and uncle?"

He shifts forward and shakes his head. "A few, but it's not what you think."

Does he even know what I'm thinking? Do I even know what I'm thinking?

Jamie ran into me at a party by accident. If we hadn't seen each other, I would never have known he was in town, and he would've never come to see me. We're sitting here together because we bumped into each other and remembered we were friends.

Maybe he's thinking he felt sorry for me. Maybe I'm thinking I don't like what that means.

"I don't want you to think I didn't want to see you." His eyes are like two shiny crystals. "It's just . . . complicated."

We watch each other like two people who used to know each other and now don't know what to say.

Jamie opens his mouth, but my phone goes off next to me.

"It's my mom." Pushing myself to my feet, I grab my phone, pull my shaky gaze from Jamie, and walk toward the guest bedroom.

"Hello?" I close the door behind me.

"Umm, hi." There's an uncomfortably long silence. "How's *Cal-i-for-nia*?" She drags out each syllable like she's being completely sarcastic.

I breathe out of my nose. "It's good. How did you know I was here?"

"You could have left a note or something. I had to find out from Taro."

I start to ask how he knew, but then I decide I don't care. "Did you need something?"

"Can't I find out how my only daughter is doing? I'm worried about you. I gave birth to you. I will always care about you, no matter how many times we fight."

"Okay. Well, I'm fine."

"What have you been doing?"

"I don't know. Looking at schools and stuff."

"What, so you're moving there now? Are you coming back home?"

"I haven't decided yet. And I told you, I'm not living in the same house as Uncle Max." My heart starts to beat faster and my throat closes up.

"Max didn't take your money. I asked him."

I roll my eyes even though she can't see. Because *of course* he isn't going to admit it. Why would he? It's my word against his, and I've already moved out.

"Look, I want to ask you something, but don't get mad. Did you take some money out of my purse to pay for California?"

"What? No," I growl into the phone. "Of course I didn't. I have a job, remember? I don't need your money, and I certainly wouldn't steal it. Why would you even ask that?" *Thud. Thud. Thud.*

"I think I'm missing money too." She laughs uncomfortably. "I'm only asking, okay? You don't need to get so upset."

"Umm, did you ask Uncle Max?" My voice is too loud because I can't help it.

"I knew you were going to say that." Her voice is almost melodic.

I sit at the edge of the bed and grab a fistful of quilt. "Did you seriously call me to find out if I took money from you?" I'm breathing so quickly the air is hurting my nose.

Mom groans loudly. "You are making this a way bigger deal than it needs to be."

WHAT I WANT TO SAY:

"It hurts my feelings that you think I'd steal from you."

WHAT I ACTUALLY SAY:

"I have to go."

"Well, all right. Call me later, okay?" Mom says in her cheeriest voice.

"Bye," I say. My heartbeat doesn't slow.

When I return to the kitchen, Jamie is clearing the table. He looks up at me thoughtfully, his left hand balancing two plates and his right hand holding the tub of butter.

I cross my arms to hide how shaky my hands are. I don't want to talk about Mom, and I don't want to talk about why Jamie didn't want to see me. "I'm going to apply to Brightwood."

His smile is brighter than the sun.

I return a little bit of his warmth so he won't ask if anything is wrong. After we clean up, Jamie lets me borrow his laptop. While he watches TV, I fill out the online application and try to imagine what it would be like to never go home again.

I draw a girl living on the edge of a crescent moon, staring down at the earth and not missing it at all.

CHAPTER THIRTY-TWO

Do you think aliens are a lot more advanced than humans, or do you think they'd look at us and think we were the Japan of the universe?"

Jamie's hands are behind his head and he's only slightly propped up by a wooden lawn chair.

Laughing, I stare up at the broken pieces of glass decorating the night sky from my own chair. "I doubt we're the Japan. It's impossible that another planet out there doesn't have better robots than us already." My arms are folded around my knees.

He hums. "We are pretty behind on the artificial intelligence. I was at least expecting some kind of robot butler by now."

I grin. "Robot chef or robot housekeeper?"

"Housekeeper. Who likes cleaning?"

"But a chef could make you a sandwich at literally any time of the day. Like you could wake up at three in the morning and ask it for a snack."

"Or you could *never clean again for the rest of your life.*"

I shrug. "I know how to clean. I don't know how to make butternut squash risotto with truffle sauce and fried gouda cheese."

Jamie rolls his head toward me. "Is that a real thing?"

"I don't know. It sounds good though, doesn't it?" I'm grinning. And hungry. Brandon started making enchiladas but had to run back to the store when he realized they were out of cheese. Jamie and I are the only ones home.

"If you could travel back in time to any point in history, what would you pick?"

I blink at him lamely. "I'm half Asian, a girl, and I believe in aliens. Pretty much every lifetime before mine would have sucked for me."

He raises his brow and pulls his hands to his chest. "That's a good point. I thought you were going to say medieval times or something because you like all those fantasy games, but you're right—they would've arrested you for heresy or something."

"And burned me at the stake." I shrug. "I wouldn't even last in medieval Japan—they'd just be wondering why the weird not-really-Japanese-but-not-white-either-looking girl was wearing pants."

Jamie's face steadies. "Why do you always refer to yourself as weird?"

Surprised, I scrunch my nose. "I don't know. Because it's true?"

He sits up and grips the metal of the chair. "You say it like it's a bad thing. Like you think 'weird' is all you are."

It gets quiet. We just breathe to ourselves, and while Jamie watches me, I watch the crickets leaping away from the stone fire pit next to us. The light breeze tickles the palm trees, and I can hear the crackle of the ocean from down the coast.

"I want to show you something." His voice slices across the air, stirring something in the pit of my stomach.

"Okay," I say.

I follow him upstairs, where he leads me to his room. The walls are painted dark blue, and there are oversized black-and-white movie posters crammed close together like a Tumblr grid. *Blade Runner. Back to the Future. E.T. The Empire Strikes Back.* It's sci-fi heaven.

To top it all off, his room smells like him—like the ocean and warm sand and crisp leaves. It makes my brain spin in a thousand rapid circles.

Jamie pulls out a small frame from his desk drawer and hands it to me.

My fingers press against it, but he doesn't let go. "There is a fairly good chance you're going to think it's creepy I still have this, but just . . . Well, please don't think it's creepy, okay?"

Frowning, I take the frame from him and look down at the picture inside the glass.

At first I see two kids with teeth that are too big for their faces, with huge smiles and giant nostrils because they were both staring down into the camera lens when the picture was taken.

And then I realize it's me and Jamie. It's a photograph from a lifetime ago—a snapshot of what our friendship was like. Two wildly happy children with our faces close together and our arms around each other's necks because sometimes we felt like one person.

"I don't even remember taking this," I say softly.

Jamie scratches his forehead and takes a deep breath. "I don't want you to think I didn't think about you. When I went back there, I *always* thought about you. I always wanted to talk to you. I missed you, Kiko. And I don't want you to think I moved away and forgot about you like you didn't matter."

The room feels warm. It's hard for me to concentrate. "I don't understand. Why didn't you visit me?"

"It's hard to explain." There's frustration behind his eyes. "It wasn't because of you, I swear. I just . . . couldn't be around you."

I don't know what I'm supposed to feel. I'm not sure if his words are supposed to be comforting or hurtful. "Then why did you keep this picture?"

Jamie goes still. His eyes are ice and mine are fire. Why can't we meet somewhere in the middle? "Because I missed you."

He swallows. I swallow.

"And because I think you're beautiful."

My heart explodes from my chest and my body fills with starlight and hope. I don't realize he's stepped closer to me until I feel his fingers trail along the top of my shoulder. My body zaps to life.

He tilts his chin down, his blue eyes locking onto mine with urgency. I can't pull my gaze away, or my shoulder away, or my body away. I'm frozen, but this time I want to be. Jamie is trying to hide his breathing, but it's the only sound I can hear. He smells like spearmint chewing gum and the beach. I want to reach up and touch the softness of his chocolate hair. I want to trace my fingers against his jawline. I want to press my hand against the muscles that protect his heart.

I want to be more than friends.

Somewhere below us a door closes and the echo of footsteps bounces through the house.

"Guys? Are you upstairs?" Brandon calls out.

Jamie's hand drops and he takes a step back. "Yeah, Dad. We'll be down in a second."

I take a step back too, and press my hand on the shoulder his fingers just left. I hold the frame out in front of me. "Thanks for showing me this."

He pauses before taking it, not wanting to leave the brief world we built together but knowing we have to. I can't stay up here when his dad is downstairs making enchiladas and probably waiting for us—it's too weird.

When I walk downstairs and look over my shoulder, I see Jamie standing at the top of the stairs, watching me like there's so much more he wants to say but can't. He runs his hand over his collarbone and follows me anyway.

Whatever it was, it will have to wait.

I draw a black heart exploding in every direction, and inside is a girl made entirely of light.

CHAPTER THIRTY-THREE

Mom texts me: When are you coming home?

I text back: Is Uncle Max still there?

It takes her an hour to respond: Can you call me tonight? I want to know how you are.

I'm going to an art show. I'll call you tomorrow.

Okay. I love you.

Okay.

CHAPTER THIRTY-FOUR

Hiroshi Matsumoto doesn't look anything like his photo in the magazine. He looks like he's been electrocuted, for one. His black hair is wild and points in every direction, like someone who drove for hours with all the windows down. His warm ivory skin is free from a single imperfection, like a porcelain doll behind a glass case. And he's shorter than the average person, but not short enough to be considered "short." Like me.

I'm also pretty sure he's wearing a dress. Or the longest shirt in the world. I can't quite decide.

Pacing back and forth like a ghost haunting a museum, Hiroshi never makes eye contact with any of the people here to appreciate his paintings. He simply floats by them with peculiar disinterest.

It makes me nervous. If he isn't interested in his adoring fans, he isn't going to want a single thing to do with me.

I don't have to look far for Jamie—he's one step behind me, admiring a large painting of a flock of black swans pulling a carriage through the air. Inside the carriage is a voluptuous woman spilling over the edges with her hands up in the air like she's on a roller coaster.

"These paintings are hilariously random," Jamie notes.

"They're amazing," I correct with my head dipped low and my voice quiet. I'm afraid someone will hear me.

"Did you see the frog one?" Jamie asks with a grin. "It's just a giant green frog—I'm not kidding—wearing a top hat."

"But they're so good," I gush dizzily.

"What are you supposed to call this kind of art?" Jamie looks genuinely curious, even if he does think the paintings are silly.

"Pop surrealism is what the art people keep calling it." His voice is mellow and soft, but it sounds like the only noise in the room. Hiroshi blinks at the painting on the wall like he's not entirely satisfied with it. When he leans toward me, I can smell vanilla and smoke. "I'm not sure it's supposed to be called anything though, really. It's just my own brand of nonsense."

Oh my God, Hiroshi Matsumoto from the magazine is talking to me.

"Oh, hey, you're the artist," Jamie says with blissful innocence. "Really cool gallery. I liked the frog."

My face is burning—literally burning—and I think I'm going to pass out when I watch Jamie and Hiroshi shake hands.

"And your name?" Hiroshi watches me with small eyes the color of cocoa powder.

"Kiko," I manage to whisper. My breath hiccups nervously.

"Ah, a cousin of mine," he says with a mischievous smile. "I thought you looked part Japanese."

"My dad's side," I tell him.

"Mine too. And my mother's." He's chuckling slowly. Everything he does seems slower, like he's in complete control of time and makes it match his pace instead of the other way around. He looks back at Jamie. "What about you?"

Jamie laughs easily. "I'm the odd one out, I'm afraid. My mom's family is German, and I think my dad's family was Scottish or something, but it was so long ago nobody knows for sure."

"And do you speak German?" Hiroshi bounces on his toes.

"I can barely speak English." Jamie scratches his head with a grin.

Hiroshi's laugh is like a song. "I always ask, because people always ask me if I can speak Japanese. I try to beat them to it." He looks over his shoulder at some of the other people waiting to speak with him. I get the feeling he's trying to avoid them. "Do you both go to school around here?"

I shake my head like a frightened rabbit.

Jamie nods at me—he's trying to be encouraging, but it's not working. I don't know how to talk to strangers, and especially not ones I admire. He pulls Hiroshi's attention from me to break the silence. "I do, but Kiko lives in Nebraska." He pauses thoughtfully. "She's actually here visiting to look at art schools for the fall."

Panic floods my body. He wasn't supposed to tell him that. Now Hiroshi's going to think I'm an artist. He's going to wonder if I'm any good. He's probably going to assume I'm better than I am. And I'm a complete amateur compared to him.

This is so embarrassing.

"Art school, eh? And what's your flavor?" Hiroshi presses his lips together in a tight smile.

"Acrylics," I say meekly. "But not like this. I mean, I'm not as good. As you, I mean. I'm not as good as you. At all." Oh my God, I can't speak English either. I look at Jamie, my eyes begging for him to save me, but he doesn't seem to understand that I'm drowning.

"We all start at the same place, but you're completely in charge of where you finish," Hiroshi says. "You can be as good an artist as you want to be. You just have to practice and work hard. I'm sure your parents have told you this, yes?"

I'm frozen. My parents don't talk to me about art. Will he know this without me saying it? His serious eyes tell me he does.

Hiroshi presses his hands together like he's praying and rests his chin on the tips of his fingers. "My parents told me art was what lazy people did when they just wanted to work on the side of the street. They wanted me to be a doctor. So when I had two daughters, I told them they could be anything they wanted, even if it was a painter on the side of the street. And do you know what? One of them is in medical school and the other wants to be a surfer." He laughs. "We all have to dream our own dreams. We only get one life to live—live it for yourself, not anyone else. Because when you're on your death-bed, you're going to be wishing you had. When everyone else is on theirs, I guarantee they aren't going to be thinking about your life."

Jamie pulls his phone out. "She's *really* good. She just doesn't realize it. Here, look."

I don't know what's going on. Hiroshi is leaning in to Jamie, looking down at the brightly lit screen while Jamie swipes again and again and again. Each time, Hiroshi stares thoughtfully, grunting to himself the way a dog does when it's having a dream.

What are you doing? I manage to mouth. Seriously, Jamie, *what are you doing?*

Jamie shakes his head at me like he doesn't want me to ruin whatever moment they're having. I make the mistake of leaning forward and looking at his phone.

They're pictures of my paintings. Pictures of my portfolio. *On Jamie's phone.*

And Hiroshi Matsumoto is looking at them.

Can I please die now?

I feel my body shrinking and shrinking. I've shriveled up into a small, frightened child. Why would Jamie show him those photos? Why did he even have them on his phone to begin with? Has he completely lost his mind?

I hold my breath and try not to vomit while I wait for Hiroshi to look back at me. I'm sure he will, eventually, to say something along the lines of, "Good effort. Just keep working hard." Something to confirm I'm nowhere near as good as I'd like to be. Words to remind me I'm not good enough for Prism and their superstar art program.

When Hiroshi looks back at me, a black strand of hair hanging at his temple, he doesn't say anything. He just stares at me like he's only just noticed me, even though we've been talking for at least five minutes.

A tall woman with a short bob taps Hiroshi's shoulder. "Sorry to interrupt, but there's a Mr. Bolton here to see you."

Hiroshi nods. "Okay, I'm coming." He looks at me and Jamie

and gives a wrinkled smile. And then, just to me, he says, "You should bring your portfolio to my studio sometime. Those art schools like their recommendations. I'll see what I can do."

I think my brain might actually blow up. I nod frantically, like a bobble-head strapped to a rock crawler.

Hiroshi floats away like a phantom, the hem of his white dress trailing behind him.

"Oh my God, what just happened?" I hiss in Jamie's direction.

A smirk appears. "I think he was impressed."

I blush. "Why did you take photos of my portfolio?"

"Because I wasn't sure if you'd ever let me see it again. You're so private about your art—you panic if you think anyone is watching you draw in your sketchbook."

"Well, that was super embarrassing." And a huge violation of my privacy, I want to add, but I don't because my tongue is fighting with my brain and really I'm just hearing Hiroshi's words on a continuous loop. I clear my throat, and then I'm unable to contain my happiness. "And awesome. And seriously the coolest thing that's ever happened to me in my life." Hiroshi Matsumoto wants to see my portfolio. And write me a recommendation. And help me get into art school.

Jamie doesn't hesitate—he takes my hand in his and squeezes. "You deserve it, Kiko."

Now I want to die for all the right reasons.

I draw twins with black hair all tangled together who have only just realized they look exactly the same.

CHAPTER THIRTY-FIVE

It turns out Hiroshi Matsumoto is kind of a big deal.

He worked as an illustrator when he was younger, but he's been painting for the last twenty years and has a huge online following. Images of his work are all over social media, and he has an online shop full of prints that appear to be incredibly popular.

Now I'm more nervous than excited.

Because not only is he a professional artist, but he's kind of famous. What if he realizes he made a mistake? What if he changes his mind? What if he forgets he even asked me to come by in the first place?

I look over at Jamie in the driver's seat. He pulls into an empty parking space and turns off the engine.

Meeting my eyes, he frowns. "What's wrong?"

I pull my hands away from the portfolio resting on my lap. My palms are sweaty. My chest feels tight. "I think we should go home."

"What are you talking about? We're already here. His studio

is, like, thirty feet away." He sounds impatient, which makes me feel guilty.

The sun shines through the window. I try to keep my eyes on something other than Jamie and my portfolio, but all the passing strangers out for an afternoon stroll are making me nervous.

Jamie closes his hand over mine. He's been doing that a lot lately. It only adds jitters to my nerves. "He's already seen some of your paintings. You don't have to be so nervous."

My hand trembles beneath Jamie's. He doesn't understand what's happening inside my core. He doesn't realize there are earthquakes and tsunamis and volcanic eruptions destroying my brain and my heart and my soul. I am terrified of Hiroshi rejecting me. I'm terrified of *anyone* rejecting me.

I nod anyway because Jamie keeps squeezing my hand like he's trying to reassure me. I guess I feel like I have to reassure him, too, even though it's kind of a lie.

We stop at the door because even though Jamie insists the address is right, we're looking directly into a small café.

Shrugging, Jamie pulls the glass door open and a bell shakes above our heads.

A petite girl with shiny black hair and eyes more like mine than Jamie's looks up from the counter and smiles. She steps toward us and reaches for the menus, but Jamie shakes his head.

"I think we're lost. Is there an art studio around here?" he asks.

She puts her hands on her hips and purses her lips. "Oh, it's upstairs. The entrance is at the side of the building." She pauses. "Is he expecting you?"

I clutch my portfolio to my chest. "He told us to stop by."

The girl nods. "Okay, well, I'll take you up there." She unties her mint-green apron and hangs it on the wall. We follow her back outside and down a small alleyway next to the building. There's a door leading to a steep set of stairs, and at the top is a wide landing and a large metal door.

When the girl pushes it open, I feel the cold hit my face like I've walked into the frozen food aisle at a grocery store.

"Dad?" the girl calls. "You've got company."

Hiroshi Matsumoto appears from around the corner. His hands are covered in flecks of brown and red paint, and he's wearing a gray T-shirt with a Coca-Cola image on it and black pants. There's paint all over him, but some of it looks like it's been there for a long time.

I feel sick. I bet he doesn't remember us. I bet he's going to be mad that we're interrupting his painting.

Tucking his shoulder-length hair behind his ear, he walks toward us almost giddily. "Kiko, Jamie, so nice to see you two again."

Wincing, I look up at Jamie. He's grinning at me like he wants me to know I've been worrying for nothing.

"I see you've met my youngest daughter, Akane. She's going to college in Michigan this fall." Hiroshi stands next to her, and I can totally see the resemblance. They both have high cheekbones, happy eyes, and big, comfy lips. She's basically a tinier female version of him.

Akane clasps her hands together, showing off her yellow and

blue nails. "Nice to meet you." She looks back at her father. "I have to go back downstairs. Frank isn't here yet to take over the counter."

Hiroshi nods. When she disappears, he sighs sadly. "I can't believe she'll be moving away soon. She is the only employee we have who shows up on time." He chuckles like he's made of the frothy sea.

"Is the café yours?" Jamie asks.

Hiroshi squints. "Technically it's my wife's, but we all pitch in when we can. She believes families who work together stay together." He shrugs. "But both our daughters are going to college out of state, so I think she's got that all wrong." He holds his painted hands open. "So! Let's see this portfolio."

For what feels like an entire excruciating hour, Hiroshi looks through every image in my portfolio. He studies every photograph of every painting, and he spends an awful long time on each drawing. I brought my sketchbook too, in case the portfolio wasn't enough, and he spends even more time looking at that.

"These are very good," he says finally. "The subject matter here is very intriguing. And the way you manipulate shadows is very impressive, especially for someone so young." He looks up thoughtfully. "Where are you applying for school?"

"Brightwood," I answer nervously.

He nods. "Brightwood is a good school. What made you pick it?"

I look at Jamie even though he can't help me with this one. I wish I didn't need so much reassurance, but I'm not good at talking to new people. I'm not good at talking to old people either, to be honest.

Jamie looks down at my sketchbook like he's studying it too. He wishes I were braver. I can see it in his eyes.

I wish I were braver too.

I gulp. "Well." My voice quivers. "I wanted to go to Prism, but I didn't get in. And I don't want to live at home with my mom, so I came out here to look at schools, and I really liked Brightwood—even though it's not Prism—and I applied because maybe I could get a job out here and go to school and not need any help." I run out of air and my voice catches.

Hiroshi nods slowly, and then I realize he's staring at Jamie. They look like they're having a silent conversation. Maybe Hiroshi is wondering why I bring Jamie everywhere with me. Maybe he's going to figure out I don't know anything about independence because I can't go anywhere new without having a panic attack. Maybe he isn't going to want to help someone so small and sad.

Jamie presses his fingers against the middle of my back and leans in like he's coaxing a puppy out of hiding. "I'm going to go downstairs and get a cup of coffee. I don't really understand any of this art stuff, and you guys would probably be more comfortable without me hovering." He laughs gently and his blue eyes sparkle. "Meet me in the café when you're done?"

I nod because what else am I supposed to do? I can't beg him to stay, and I certainly can't say out loud that I feel wobbly and unbalanced without him nearby. It would probably freak him out.

"Tell me about this one," Hiroshi says just before the door falls shut and we're the only two left. He's pointing to one of my sketches—the one of a girl with no face.

"I don't know," I say quietly.

"Why did you draw it?"

Because when I look at myself, the face I see and the face Mom sees and the face Jamie sees aren't the same face. I might as well be a white canvas because none of us seem to agree.

But that's too much to explain to someone I don't know. It's probably too much to explain to anyone. My shoulders rise and fall like they don't understand his questions.

"Why are you applying to Brightwood when you want to go to Prism?"

A scratchy feeling rises in my throat like I'm coughing up sandpaper. "I didn't get into Prism," I repeat. Heat radiates across my face.

"You didn't get in this year, but what about next year? Or what about reapplying with a new portfolio? Maybe you simply need to show them the right work. Art is like that—it speaks to people in different ways at different times. Maybe what you thought was your best wasn't really your best. Maybe it was just the work you were least hard on yourself about." His brown eyes flicker left and right like he's analyzing me.

I want to sink to the floor and cry. It's too much staring. I hate the spotlight.

Hiroshi turns a few more pages of my sketchbook. "Do you ever paint your sketches? I don't see any of your acrylic pieces in here."

"No. They're just doodles, really."

"I think you should paint them. Give color to what you want to say." He brushes his inky-black hair away from his eyes. "How long are you in California for?"

"A couple of weeks, I think." I hesitate because I'm not sure how much I'm ready to say out loud. "I'm not ready to go home yet."

He closes the folder gently and straightens his shoulders. "I'll tell you what. Why don't you come back tomorrow morning and you can paint here. You can pay me for the supplies you use, but you can use the studio for free. Work on something new—maybe something from your sketches. We'll see if we can't put together a portfolio that tells the world who you truly are as an artist."

My heart feels lighter somehow. "You want me to paint here? With you?"

"Sure." Hiroshi waves his hand around. "There's plenty of space. And I'll promise to write you a very good recommendation letter as long as you promise something in return."

"What's that?"

His eyes fold closed. "I want you to reapply to Prism with your new work and with my recommendation letter."

I feel my eyes begin to burn and I press my tongue against the roof of my mouth to force my jaw to stop moving. "Why?" is all I manage to get out.

Hiroshi lifts his chin up and suddenly he seems an entire foot taller. For a second I see my father, but it passes quickly. "Kiko, I think other people can see you more clearly than you can see yourself. As an artist, you have to know what's inside you if you want to get it out on the canvas. It hurts me to think someone as talented as you is holding themselves back without even realizing it." And then he flexes his fingers and shrugs matter-of-factly. "Besides, my daughters have no interest in art. I never got to teach them anything about paintbrushes or oils. This will be fun for me."

"Thank you," I say with a closed-up throat. He doesn't see how my skin is crumbling off me like it's old and dead, revealing something glowing and wonderful underneath.

Or maybe he does. Maybe he sees how badly I need this— maybe he's giving me this chance because he can see that without art, I'm nothing.

I draw the sun teaching the moon how to shine.

CHAPTER THIRTY-SIX

Mom doesn't say anything when I tell her about Hiroshi. I should know better by now than to have any expectations—she will never have the reaction I want. Not about anything I care about.

I shouldn't even have brought up my art in the first place. I mean, all she asked was "Why didn't you call me?" and "What have you been doing?" I could have just said I was busy. I didn't have to elaborate.

But there's something about my mother, and when she hooks you into a phone call, it's already too late. You're going to tell her your whole life story if it's what she wants out of you.

"Did you hear anything I just said?" I ask.

"I think it's very weird he would ask you to go back to his house like that."

"It's not his house, Mom. It's his studio. And it's to paint."

"I don't know. Are you sure he's even legitimate?"

I snort. "What does that mean? He's a real artist, if that's what you're asking."

"I don't get why a grown man would want a teenage girl hanging around his place if he doesn't have ulterior motives."

My blood gets hot.

WHAT I WANT TO SAY:
"I can't believe you're going to insinuate Hiroshi is some kind of child predator when Uncle Max is still sleeping across the hall from my bedroom."

WHAT I ACTUALLY SAY:
"He's not like that. He's nice. He's like Dad."

Mom laughs wildly. "Oh, well, that makes everything so much better."

I don't respond because it's impossible to make her see reason when Dad's name appears on her target.

"Have you talked to your father lately?" she asks coolly.

"No. Why?"

She tuts into the phone. "See? He can't even get in touch with his own kids. It's so pathetic."

"I don't want to talk with you about Dad. Seriously."

She goes quiet for a while. "He chose to leave. I hope you don't blame me."

"I've never blamed you. I know he cheated—you told me that already."

"Yeah, well . . ." Her voice trails off. I can hear the TV in the background. "I feel like you resent me because of your dad, and I'm the one who stayed to take care of you guys."

I want to tell her that staying to take care of us is sort of the deal you make when you have children. I want to tell her that I resent her because of Uncle Max and not Dad. I want to tell her I don't want to talk about any of this because I'm trying to get out of the black hole she keeps sucking me back into.

But I don't tell her any of it. I close my eyes and say, "That's not true, Mom."

And then she squeals into the phone and tells me about some weird outcome of a reality show about hoarders.

I call Emery afterward. She completely freaks out when I tell her I'm in California with Jamie.

"Why didn't you tell me sooner?" she cries into the phone. "This is amazing!"

"It happened really fast, and I guess I've just been so busy," I admit.

"I think I've been replaced." She says it like it's a joke, but I'm suddenly aware there might be some truth to it. I mean, she hasn't been *replaced*, exactly. It's not like I've traded one friend in for another. But Emery always made going out and doing things easier. She was my social crutch. She made me feel less afraid of the world because she was always nearby if I needed someone to hide behind. I used to worry I'd feel lost without her, but I don't. And I wonder if it's because Jamie came into my life right when she was leaving for college.

I tell her about everything else that's been going on, including how often Mom keeps trying to call, and she tells me about school and how she's been so busy she hasn't had time to go to a single party. She tells me Gemma and Cassidy got into a fight because both of them hooked up with Adam. Hearing his name doesn't make me as uncomfortable as I thought it would, which weirdly puts me in a better mood.

But even with all the news, I keep thinking about her words. Have I replaced her with Jamie? Have I gone from depending on one person to depending on another?

I don't like how it makes me feel, so I tell myself it isn't true.

After dinner, Brandon asks us if we want to play charades. I look panicked because making faces and throwing my hands around in front of a group of people sounds like an actual nightmare I've had more than once.

Jamie suggests we play Pictionary instead.

He's thoughtful that way. And amazing. And so good-looking it kind of hurts my chest.

Elouise has about the same enthusiasm for Pictionary as I had for charades, but it doesn't take Jamie very long to convince her to play.

Holding a glass of deep red wine, she sits on the chair farthest away from Brandon. He's so busy looking for two markers in the side table that he doesn't notice.

Jamie comes back with a whiteboard from the office. It's still covered in neon-colored Post-it notes in the corner. He pulls them off one by one and sets the board up next to the fireplace.

"Kiko, you want to go first?" he asks.

Brandon tosses me a marker, which I don't catch because I'm uncoordinated as well as unprepared. "Two creative types on the same team? Seems rigged to me."

From the partially reclined chair, Elouise clenches her teeth and pulls her eyes closed for a very long blink.

Jamie notices. He looks like he's regretting convincing his mom to play.

"How about girls versus boys?" I offer meekly.

I feel Elouise open her eyes toward me, but she doesn't say anything.

Brandon slaps his knee. "All right, yeah." He points to his eyes and then to Jamie. "We got this."

I move toward the whiteboard, and Jamie passes me the game cards that came from their old Pictionary box.

Dropping like flies.

I tighten my mouth and look apologetically at Elouise, and then spend sixty seconds doodling something that resembles an ugly waterfall. She doesn't guess it.

Jamie gets "*Planet of the Apes*" and Brandon guesses before half their time is up.

Then Elouise gets "sunburn" and I guess right. She high-fives me.

The boys miss the next one, which irritates Brandon and makes Elouise smile.

After three more turns each, Elouise and I are leading by four points. She's so happy, we may as well have won the game already. I think she finds it bizarrely satisfying to see Brandon getting so worked up.

Jamie slumps down next to me on the couch and shakes his head like he knows I have the better teammate. I laugh.

"One more, one more," Brandon urges.

"We've been beaten. Let's call it a night. I'm tired." Jamie yawns.

Elouise wiggles in the chair to our left like she's doing a victory dance. She raises her glass in the air. "Good job, Kiko."

"Thanks." I grin. I've never seen her so happy, and certainly never toward me.

Brandon growls and covers his face in his hands. "I can't believe this." He pulls his hands away, laughing loudly like he's forgotten any rules about volume. "I should have known Kiko would be good at board games. Do you remember that time at Charleston Grove when—" His face falls immediately. His jaw clamps shut.

Elouise stands up and leaves the room.

Brandon waits about two and a half seconds before he gets up and follows her to another room in the house.

"What just happened?" I'm watching Jamie carefully because he looks startled. I feel like I've seen into a door I wasn't supposed to. I know where Charleston Grove is—I'd been there a few times as a kid. They have live music and festivals, and lots of families take picnics there. But I have no idea why it would upset Elouise so much.

Jamie rubs his neck like he has an itch. Muted shouting starts from his parents' bedroom.

"Do you want to go for ice cream?" Jamie asks almost desperately.

We get into his car, but he doesn't drive to get ice cream—he drives to the neighborhood park. When I look over at him, his blue eyes darkened by the lack of lights, he looks stoic and frightened.

"Are you okay?" I ask. It feels weird, like we've traded places. I'm usually the one who looks scared. I'm usually the one who looks like the world is about to split in half.

"I don't want to lie to you. I don't. But what's going on with my parents—it's not my story to tell." His voice cracks in the dark. When he turns his head, I know he's looking at me, even though his expression is lost in the shadows.

"Is it about me?" I ask softly. When he doesn't move, I add, "If your mom hates me, I'd rather know. I don't want to stay in her house if I'm making your parents fight."

"It's not about you, okay?" Jamie's voice is loud—borderline shouting even.

It doesn't feel good to be yelled at by anyone, but especially not Jamie. I turn away from him, but I can see his body relax in the corner of my eye. He's caught himself.

He reaches for my hand but finds my knee instead. "I'm sorry." I feel his finger move in small circles. Okay, maybe he meant to find my knee. "Look, I know it's not fair, but can we not talk about this anymore? I don't know how much time we've got left, and I'd rather talk about superheroes, or Hiroshi, or Brightwood, or . . ." His fingers stop moving, but they don't leave my knee.

"Or what?" The noise comes from me, but it doesn't sound like it. My voice is all high-pitched and raspy and far, far away.

"Or we don't have to say anything," he says, his voice smoky. "Can we just . . . sit for a while?"

I look down at my hands. I wish I knew how to help, but how can I when he won't tell me what's bothering him?

I've always felt like I desperately needed to say my feelings out loud—to form the words and get them out of me, because they've always felt like dark clouds in my head that contaminate everything around them. But maybe Jamie feels better keeping his words in. Maybe it's how he keeps his own clouds from growing.

When I look back up his eyes are soft and his lips are parted, and then I understand. He doesn't need to share his feelings—he needs the company. Because sometimes when the world doesn't make sense, it just feels better if there's someone around to make it a little less lonely.

Jamie is always trying to be what I need. Right now I want to be what he needs.

"Okay," I say, settling into the chair.

He nods back, and it feels like enough for now.

We listen to the radio for twenty minutes, and then we drive back to his house and find his parents in separate rooms pretending as if nothing happened.

I draw two warriors with swords made of starlight, pointing their weapons at each other and drawing lines in the sand.

CHAPTER THIRTY-SEVEN

On the first day with Hiroshi, Jamie sits in the café while I sketch in the studio. On the second day, Jamie wanders around the shopping center while I paint shards of broken cerulean glass onto the stretched canvas. On the third day, Jamie drops me off and goes back home while I paint a woman with milky-white skin and even whiter hair. On the fourth day, I take my own car and I drive myself.

It feels like a big step, doing things on my own. It's scary, but it makes me feel stronger, somehow. I feel like my feet are heavier than I realized and if the wind blows I won't be knocked over. Except it's not my feet that feel strong; it's my heart.

Hiroshi stands behind me, his hands clasped behind his back and his neck dipped low. "Mmm. Don't be afraid to make mistakes. When you're too careful with color, you're holding back. Don't hold back. Say what you want to say."

With a palette balanced in my left hand, I press the tip of my brush into the gray splotch of acrylic paint. When I sweep the color along the hem of the woman's torn dress, I know I'm being too careful. I can't help it—I'm not as wild with a brush as Hiroshi is. He seems to splat paint all over the canvas and somehow it becomes exactly what he wants. It's like someone scattering puzzle pieces all over a table and putting them together two-by-two all over the place.

I start from the corners and work my way in. It's the only way I can be prepared for the bigger picture.

Hiroshi grunts. "No. This isn't what you want to say."

"I'm trying." I stuff my bottom lip into my mouth and slouch in the stool.

"It's not your technique; it's your subject." He picks up my sketchbook and flips through to some of my older drawings. The girl with wings. The girl blending into the trees. "These are pieces of your soul, Kiko. Not this." He waves his hand at my work in progress. "This is merely practice."

I set the palette down on the table, rolling the brush between my fingers. "I don't understand."

He makes his hands into fists and holds them close to his chest. "I want you to tell me a story. Tell me anger. Tell me sorrow. Tell me happiness. Just tell me something that matters to you."

My eyes drop to the floor. I can taste salt on my tongue—I bet my tears somehow sucked back into my eyeballs and made their way down my throat. The last thing I want to do is start crying in front of Hiroshi because he told me I'm basically wasting my time with this painting. Maybe he's expecting too much. Maybe I'm not good enough to paint the way he does.

Pressing my eyelids together, I breathe slowly and think about how I feel when I sketch. My heart quickens as I sort through my memories, and I try to find the trigger I pull when I think about drawing. I can't help it—I think about Mom.

She stands in front of me with a half smile and exhausted eyes. She's so tired of me; it feels physically painful to be caught in her line of sight. Her blond hair rests on her shoulders in perfect waves, and her arms are crossed together like she's wearing her armor. My mother—always ready for battle. And then there's me, standing across from her, desperate for her approval, suffocating with the weight of the past and ridden with anxiety that reminds me *I'm just not good enough.*

I look up at Hiroshi. He's still waiting on a story.

I swallow. "When I was little, I drew this picture for my mom. A girl in a boat, fishing for stars. It was probably terrible, but I had just learned how to shade with colored pencils, so I thought it was really good. I put it in an envelope and left it on her desk. She kept piling things on it—mail, shopping lists, magazines—and I kept checking on it, to see if she had opened it yet. She hadn't, but I didn't want to ask about it because she always made me feel like I was being too needy. One day I went to look for it but it was gone, along with the stack of papers my mom had been collecting. So I finally asked if she had seen it. She said it must have gotten thrown out with the trash." I clear my throat and fake a tight smile. "I believed it was an accident for a long time, but a few years after that I tried to show her something else I drew—I can't remember what—and she made this really weird face and said to me, 'It's a lot better than that one you drew of the boat and that girl fishing.' That's when I realized she had lied to me. She had opened the envelope. She just didn't want to admit it, and I still don't know why."

My eyes are watering and my throat is dry, but I'm using up every bit of strength I have not to let my emotions take control.

Hiroshi raises his fists above his head and releases his fingers like they are fireworks exploding into the room. "There it is! Your story. Your soul. Now paint it." He goes back to his canvas on the other side of the room.

I take a minute to calm down, and then I set the brush on the palette, move the unfinished painting to the floor, and open up a blank page in my sketchbook.

I draw for hours. I'm so consumed by the deliberate pencil marks that I don't notice my phone is ringing until Hiroshi taps me on the shoulder and makes me jump.

It's Jamie, wanting to know when I'm coming home because he wants to go see a movie with me. I tell him I'm leaving as soon as I've finished the sketch.

"It's important," I say.

"Okay," he says.

I draw a woman wearing an elaborate dress, twirling like she's made of light and sun. And then I draw a shriveled girl trapped within her shadow. She doesn't want the light—she just wants her mom.

CHAPTER THIRTY-EIGHT

We watch a movie about superheroes, which is normally exactly the kind of movie that Jamie and I would gush over for hours together. But I'm acutely aware that I'm the only one gushing. And the only one talking about their day. And the only one saying more than four words at a time.

Jamie didn't eat any popcorn, either.

"I'm sorry I was gone most of the day," I say when we're walking along the street right outside the theater. "I didn't think I was going to be so long, but I had to start over with my painting."

"Oh, it's fine." His hands are stuffed in his pockets like he's hiding something he doesn't want me to read.

"Were you not hungry?" I ask.

"Huh?" He looks at me for only a split second.

I shrug. "You didn't eat any popcorn. Usually that's *my* thing—to think so hard I forget to eat." I doubt my smile is infectious to anyone at all, but I try one anyway because I want Jamie to cheer up.

"Oh. No. I was just watching the movie."

My feet stomp together. "Seriously? Jamie, what's wrong? And don't tell me it's nothing—I have an honorary degree in trying to keep my feelings a secret."

This cracks his temporary shield a little bit. The corner of his mouth turns up. "Is that so?"

I bounce my chin up and down and scrunch my nose. "Yup."

Jamie raises his shoulders but keeps his hands pressed in his pockets. "God, I really don't want to complain to you about it, because I know your home life sucks." He glances at me apologetically. "No offense."

"None taken."

"I just mean that I know things aren't easy for you. Not that you ever tell me why, or what happened." He pauses. He's talking about Uncle Max. "But I can tell, you know?"

I nod. "So what's on your mind?"

"I think I may be making things with my parents worse. I mean, it's obvious to everyone but them that they should just get divorced. But for whatever stubborn reason, they're trying to make it work." His brow furrows. "No, that's such crap. 'Make it work.' What does that even mean? They're not actually trying to make anything work; they're just staying in the same house together making each other more and more miserable. Making *me* miserable." He shakes his head.

"Maybe they're staying together because being a family is important to them?" I offer.

"If family were so important they wouldn't be fighting in the first place." He catches himself. "I shouldn't be talking about this. It's their problem, really."

I shrug. "You're allowed to vent about how it makes you feel."

"I guess. Anyway, I'm sorry. It's just been a long day." He starts to walk again, so I imitate his pace.

"What did you mean when you said you think it's your fault?"

He pushes his tongue into the side of his mouth and pulls a hand out to fidget with his neck. "It's nothing." And then he laughs into the humid air. "It's funny. You came here to get a break from your family, and now I kind of want a break from mine."

When we get to the car, he turns toward me and takes both my hands in his. My skin tingles.

"Kiko, I don't want you to go back to Nebraska." The blue in his eyes looks like a pottery glaze. "Stay with me. Stay in California. You don't have to move back in with your mom and your uncle."

I blink, my chest rising and falling because I'm struggling to breathe normally. "I've only just applied to Brightwood. I might not even get in."

"But I mean, even if you don't get in, stay here anyway." He presses my hands together between his. "I know you said you want to just be friends. And I am your friend, and I'll always be your friend if that's still what you want, but . . . I care about you, Kiko. I just want to be close to you. I feel like we wasted so much time already."

There's air between us, and something else, too. Something heavy and important—something I don't understand.

He wants me to stay in California. My heart wants to explode like red confetti all over the sidewalk. I want to say "yes" to the dream.

But something stops me. There's something crawling through my mind like a black insect, causing me to doubt. Because I'm not ready for red confetti and happy endings—I wish I was, but I'm not. I can barely drive to new places alone, or talk to strangers, or walk into art galleries without someone practically holding my hand.

If I can't figure out how to live on my own—how to *do* things on my own—how am I supposed to live at all? I don't want a crutch. I don't want someone who feels like they have to take care of me. Someday in the future, my dependency would suffocate him. It might even end up suffocating me, too.

"If I did that, I'd be dependent on you. I need to figure out where my life is going. I need something that is mine. Otherwise . . ."
Otherwise I'll never fully break away from what my life has always been. I'll always be attached to it, like a branch that's growing farther and farther away but it doesn't matter because its roots are a part of the tree's roots. I need to be my own tree.

I don't want to go back to Nebraska, but the truth is, I have no idea what I'm going to do. I don't know what I *can* do; I don't know what I'm capable of accomplishing all on my own. I don't know if I'm strong enough to start a new life away from what are equal parts toxic and familiar.

I need to be strong enough to move away on my own, to pull Mom's hooks out of my heart, to forget about Uncle Max.

I need to be strong enough to carry all the guilt of what happened to my family because of me.

That's a lot of strength. I don't know if I can carry so much weight, but I know I have to try. If I don't, someday it will destroy me.

Jamie's eyes are so pure and honest. "I want to take care of you. I want to make sure you're okay."

If words could be a dagger to the soul, these would be the ones.

My forehead crumples, and I hold his hands back firmly because I need him to listen. "Thank you for wanting to look out for me. But I don't want you to take care of me." I close my eyes and imagine the words I want to say. It surprises me when I actually say them. "I want to take care of myself."

I'm not trying to push Jamie away. In fact, there isn't even a small part of me that's happy when he lets go of my hands. But I feel like I've spent most of my life wishing for someone else's approval, or relying on their reassurance that I'm living my life the right way. And somewhere along the way, I forgot to care what I thought about myself.

I feel trapped beneath all the things that make me think less of myself. If my life were a video game, I would have hit the reset button a long time ago.

Art school is my reset button. And I need to push it by myself. Otherwise I'll end up in the same cycle as I was before.

But I don't know how to explain all of this to Jamie.

He presses the palm of his hand against his eye like he's

exhausted, but something tells me he's trying to wipe away his emotions.

"It was a stupid thing for me to say," he says with a short laugh. "I don't know what I'm even talking about. I'm just tired, I think. I'm sorry." He pulls his lips in and releases them again. "I shouldn't have said anything. It was a dumb idea."

My brain feels frantic, but there's nothing clever or humorous or even disarming that I can think of to say. Every thought I have seems like it would only make Jamie feel worse. Every thought except one.

I like you too, Jamie. I want to be with you too.

But I can't tell him that. Because I am barely holding my head above water. If I think for a second it will be easier to rely on Jamie than myself, I'll stuff my head back under the waves and never come up for air again.

Until he breaks up with me. Or changes his mind. Or meets someone else.

It's too much pressure. I can't ruin *us* with *me*. I just can't.

We don't listen to any music on the drive home. We're too busy listening to our own thoughts.

I draw a boy with a flashlight searching for hope in the dark.

CHAPTER THIRTY-NINE

Mom texts to ask how I'm doing, what I've been doing. And I don't know why I do it, but I send Mom a picture of some of my sketches. I guess there's a weird part of my inner child that just can't seem to let go of the idea of a mother who cares.

It takes her a few hours, but eventually she does text back. Except she doesn't say anything about my drawings—she sends three photos of her from when she was younger and asks which one I think is the prettiest.

I'm starting a blog, she texts. **I want it to be beautiful.**

I tell her I like the second photo best, and then I delete the entire conversation. Because even if I can't unsend the drawings, I can at least pretend like I didn't send them in the first place.

It hurts less this way.

I draw a girl shrinking into the grass until she's hidden by a bed of flowers that are all so much prettier than she is.

CHAPTER FORTY

I'm sketching out some faces, thinking of the perfect color for the hair and eyes, when Hiroshi takes a seat next to me.

He places his elbows on the wooden table and lets out a hum.

I feel myself begin to shrink. "They're just practice. I know I can do better."

"They're superb," he says, but he's still frowning.

I tap my pencil against the edge of the sketchbook, anticipating a "but."

He motions his finger over the faces. "Where does this image come from?"

"My head?" I answer like it's a question.

"Yes, but where? Why did you decide on this exact face over any other?"

I look back down at the drawing, rotating his questions in my mind like I'm searching for their hidden agenda. "I don't understand," I say at last. And then I blink. "I just thought it looked good."

"So this is the face you decided would be beautiful. This is the face that made sense to you." He nods.

I shrug. "I guess. Yeah." It's the face I've always drawn—it's just become more detailed over the years.

"But why? Who told you this was beautiful?"

I stop holding back. "Magazines. TV shows. Everyone at school." I set my pencil down and shove my hands between my knees.

"So beauty to you is what's palatable to everyone else? You're drawing what you think everyone wants to see?" he asks gently.

In a tiny voice, I say, "I guess it never occurred to me to draw them any other way."

I look around the room. Hiroshi's paintings are everywhere, all of them with different faces, all of them with *unique* faces. They have such varying degrees of color and shape and style. They represent the whole world.

My eyes fall back down to my sketchbook. The faces I draw rarely change, like they come from cookie-cutter molds. None of them ever look like me.

"Beauty isn't a single thing. Beauty is dreaming—it's different for everyone, and there are so many versions of it that you mostly have no control over how you see it. Do you understand what I'm saying?" Hiroshi smiles, pats the table, and walks back to his own canvas.

Everything about him is stylish and cool and otherworldly—the way he speaks, the way he walks, the way he paints. Sometimes I can't believe Hiroshi Matsumoto is a real person. He's so comfortable in his own skin. Even if I lived to be three hundred years old, I still wouldn't have his confidence. It's his gift—a gift he's trying to share with me through art.

I stare at the faces for a long time, and when I'm sick of them I shut my eyes tight and let my imagination take over. I think of so many faces—Emery and Susan Chang and Francis from the tattoo parlor and Akane and Mom—and then I let everything blur together until I'm daydreaming about beautiful quirky strangers I've never met before. They have freckles and tans, light hair and dark, crooked features and curves, and they are all exactly as they are meant to be.

I open my eyes, find a blank page, and leave the cookie cutters behind.

I draw face after face after face after face . . .

CHAPTER FORTY-ONE

M om's voice is weird today. She's talking to me the way she talks to strangers—with her nice voice.

I look at Jamie and point upstairs. I don't like talking on the phone in front of people—it makes me uncomfortable, and I feel like everyone is listening.

He smiles and points to the TV. He and Brandon are watching a cop drama I've never heard of.

"Have you heard anything back from the school?" Mom asks. She's trying to sound nonchalant, but I can tell she wants to know the answer. She's rarely interested in me; it's not hard for me to tell the difference when she actually is.

I close the guest bedroom door and lean against it. "Not yet. Their website said it usually takes four weeks to respond, so it will probably be a while."

"I see." She pauses. "Is anyone there? I thought I could hear someone in the background."

"Not anymore. I'm upstairs."

"Do they have a nice house?"

I perk up. "Yeah, *really* nice."

"Is everyone nice to you? Do you guys talk a lot?"

"Just a normal amount, I guess. Why?"

"Can't I be curious? They're taking care of my only daughter. I have a right to know." She sighs dismissively. "It's so hot here. I should be getting some sun, but I'm so busy with work and my website."

"Mmm," I grunt into the phone.

"So, what do you guys talk about?"

I move around the room anxiously. She's leading into a question—I can feel it. "I don't know, Mom. Normal stuff."

"Like what?"

"The weather. Food. If the water pressure is too high."

"Do you talk about me?"

And there it is.

"No."

"I find that hard to believe."

"Why?"

"Because I know you tell everyone about how horrible you think I am. You know, I hope you at least keep *some* things private."

Anger swells in my throat. Hurt floods my chest. "That's not true—I don't talk about you. And if you're talking about Uncle Max—"

She tuts into the phone, interrupting me. "You mean to tell me you drove all the way to California without telling Jamie how miserable you think your life is?"

It's hard to hold the phone up to my ear because my hands are trembling like it's below freezing in this room. "Actually, yeah. I haven't talked to Jamie about you at all. I didn't even tell him about Uncle—"

"God, Kiko." Mom groans. "Enough about Max and the money."

My palms sweat. "I'm not talking about the money."

She ignores me. "Well, I don't trust you. I have this gut feeling you guys have been trying to drag my name through the dirt over in *Cal-i-for-nia*."

"Why do you keep saying it like that?" I snap.

"I'm saying it completely normally. Stop being so sensitive."

"I have to go to the studio." My knees feel like they're made of jelly. It's impossible to stand still.

"Okay. Well, I love you, even if you hate me."

Normally I'd correct her. Normally I'd convince her that I don't hate her. But I'm too angry and I don't care if she thinks I hate her. She's probably only saying it because she wants me to fall back under her spell anyway.

"Bye." I hang up the phone.

When I reach the bottom of the stairs, I see Brandon's head pop up from the other side of the couch.

"Was that your mom?" When I nod, he asks, "How's everything at home? Your brothers okay?"

"They're fine." At least I think they are—Mom doesn't usually talk about them unless she's complaining, but that's normal, so I just assume everything is normal with my brothers, too. I walk closer to Jamie, who pushes his body forward suddenly so he's leaning away from the couch. "I'm going to head over to the studio."

"Okay," he says, his fingers flexing.

Brandon is staring at the television screen, but he's still talking to me. "I heard your dad got remarried."

I'm sure Jamie's jaw clenches.

"He did," I say. "They had twins a little while ago. Two girls."

Brandon's eyes find mine. "Oh, really? Wow. That's great. Good for him."

Jamie suddenly shoots up from his seat. "Actually," he says a little too loudly, "I'll drive you over there if that's cool. I could use a coffee."

He's out of the house so fast I barely have time to process what just happened. When I ask him about it in the car, he shrugs and tells me it was nothing. I want to believe him, because it's Jamie, and because I don't think he would lie to me, but it's obvious he's hiding something.

But he doesn't talk. Neither of us does.

Hiroshi notices I have something on my mind. Something different than normal.

"I hope this is the emotion you've brought with you to paint today," he remarks.

It's taking me forever to blend the right amount of white and yellow paint because I can't stop thinking about Jamie's shifting jawline and my mother telling me how she doesn't trust me, even though *I never talk about her*. At least not in the way she means.

I talk about me, and that's different. It feels necessary.

It's my story, after all. Maybe I need to make sense of things. Maybe I *need* to talk about it. And telling my story isn't the same thing as breaking her trust.

I don't want to talk about Mom to anyone, if I can help it. I'd prefer if she just didn't affect me anymore. I'd prefer if I hardly had to think about her at all. Not because I hate her or anything, because I don't. But thinking about her hurts me; talking about how she makes me *feel* hurts me.

What I want is for the hurt to stop. I want a mother who thinks more of me than she does. Who recognizes that I'm a better person than the version of me she has in her head. I just want her to know me, and be interested in me, and care about me without it being because she thinks she's supposed to.

And maybe—*just maybe*—I want her to think I'm pretty, too, even if it's just a little bit and even if it's just in my own way. I know I don't have her blond hair and blue eyes. I don't have her long legs and her delicate nose. And I want her to tell me that it's okay. That being pretty in a different way to her is *okay*. Because pretty is important to Mom. I want to be important to her too.

And then I don't think—I paint.

I paint my mother shimmering like a pearl, her arms allowing—no, expecting—the world to worship her.

CHAPTER FORTY-TWO

Hiroshi invites me and Jamie to dinner. I'm worried Jamie won't want to go because he doesn't act the same around me lately. He's . . . grouchy. And irritable. And he snaps at me when I ask him if he's okay.

I feel like I've hurt him somehow, and I'm not sure how to make it better.

But not only does Jamie agree to go; he actually seems excited about it. He even wears a white shirt with a suit vest over it like he's catching the tail end of a wedding. When I ask him why he's so dressed up, he laughs and asks, "Why not?"

I'm underdressed next to him, with my hair in a ponytail and my jeans flecked with gold paint. I'm living out of a suitcase—packing a nice dress wasn't a priority.

Akane greets us at the door. "Come in. Come in. Make yourselves at home." She's wearing a red tank top and a white skirt. "Leave your shoes by the door, please."

Their house smells like oranges and nutmeg. The floors are

dark wood, and all of the fixtures seem to be the same brushed metal. To my surprise, none of the artwork around the house is Hiroshi's. They are all abstract and blend perfectly with the color theme of each room.

Hiroshi looks happy to see us. He introduces us to his wife, Mayumi, who is a decade older than him, which I think is all kinds of awesome, and his oldest daughter, Rei, who is so pretty up close that I can't believe she isn't a professional model.

They're all so nice and happy, and they treat Jamie and me like they've known us for years. Mayumi makes the mistake of referring to us as boyfriend and girlfriend three times. Neither of us corrects her, which definitely hasn't gone unnoticed.

We eat vegetable ramen for dinner, which Hiroshi made specifically because of me. Afterward Mayumi brings out mochi ice cream, which is so good I make an actual noise when I eat it.

"I can't believe you never have mochi before," Mayumi says. Unlike Hiroshi, she speaks with an accent. "Rei and Akane love since they were children."

I shrug. "I've never had ramen like that either. We've only ever eaten the stuff from the foam cup."

She makes a noise like she's about to faint. Everyone at the table giggles, even me.

When we're finished, I offer to help clean up, but Mayumi shoos me out of the kitchen.

"Spend time talking. You our guest," she insists.

On my way back to the living room, I feel a rush of fresh air envelop my skin. The wide, sliding door to my left is open, exposing the square deck overlooking the hills.

I step into the evening warmth. Hiroshi's house is so close to the water I can practically taste the salt in the air. I feel it on my skin—my face feels tighter, as if all the salt has found its way to every crevasse and pore. It makes me feel calm, but I don't know why.

My fingers rest against the edge of the balcony. The ocean sends another wave toward the sand before pulling it back again. Over and over again it does this. It's hypnotic. It's beautiful.

All my life I've felt lonely, and it has always left an ache inside me, like there's a supernatural presence crushing my heart within its fist. Looking out at the ocean, I don't know how anyone could be anything but lonely. There's nothing out there to see—just water and space. But it feels good. If lonely can ever be something good, this is it. This is Kiko at peace with the world. This is Kiko not in the middle of a raging war with her mother. This is Kiko just being Kiko.

I decide I am in love with the ocean. I'm totally counting it as a legitimate relationship, because if I ever felt this way about another aspect of nature, it would absolutely feel like cheating.

Jamie's voice breaks my thoughts from the wide, open-planned space behind me. When I turn around, I see him talking to Rei. They're both smiling, moving their hands around enthusiastically and talking to each other like they've known each other for months. It looks so easy. Social interactions make sense to Jamie. He understands the rules.

"Do you surf?" Hiroshi steps onto the decking with his bare feet and gray, loose-fitting clothes.

"No. I don't know how to swim."

"Don't they teach you to swim in school?"

I shake my head again. "They teach us softball and stuff, but not swimming." And thank God for that. I'd die if I had to wear a bathing suit in front of anyone.

Hiroshi frowns and his eyes completely disappear. "That's terrible. Everyone should learn how to swim." He moves next to me and drums his fingers at the banister. "Akane is a very good swimmer. She can teach you."

I glance back at his youngest daughter standing near Rei and Jamie. She's slim and cute and has sleek black hair that looks like it's been soaked in conditioner. If I went swimming with her I'd look like a beluga whale next to a mermaid.

"It's okay. I don't really like the water," I say.

Hiroshi points his finger in front of him like he's using it to focus on me. "I can see you, Kiko. You love the water. Why are you trying to hide yourself?"

I'm not prepared to answer such a very big question.

He leans against the railing. "My father never wanted me to paint. In fact, he only wanted me to do what he himself approved of first. Because you see, to my father, my purpose in life was not to follow my dreams. It was to bring him happiness. He had a very strong understanding of what I needed to do in order to make him happy. And if I wasn't making him happy, well, then, what was the point of having children?

"I wasted a lot of time trying to be the son he wanted because I thought failing him meant that I was failing in life. Anytime he was unhappy, I thought it was my fault. If he was angry at me, I felt to blame. He always found a way to make me feel as if I had let him down in some way." Hiroshi straightens his back. "At his funeral, I overheard some people referring to him as 'Starfish.' I asked them why they gave him that nickname, and they told me it was because he always had to be the center of attention. Like the legs of a starfish, all pointing to the middle. He thought he was the center of all things." Hiroshi laughs. "All that time growing up, I thought I was the only one who could see. I thought nobody understood the way he was. I thought I was the problem. But some people are just starfish—they need everyone to fill the roles that they assign. They need the world to sit around them, pointing at them and validating their feelings. But you can't spend your life trying to make a starfish happy, because no matter what you do, it will never be enough. They will always find a way to make themselves the center of attention, because it's the only way they know how to live."

I feel like all my blood has drained away and I am left standing and empty.

A sense of clarity washes over me, and all the images I've collected of my mother over the years start to morph into something different. For the first time in my life, I really *see* her.

The mother I've always wanted isn't real; she's a dream. And not every dream comes true. Sometimes a wishing star turns out to be just a lump of rock that crashes into a planet and kills all the dinosaurs. Mom's not a shooting star—she's a *starfish*.

And for the briefest, smallest moment in time, I feel like I don't have a mother at all.

Hiroshi pulls himself away from the balcony and places a hand on my shoulder. "Don't live to please the starfish, especially when their happiness is at the expense of yours. That is not love. That is narcissism. There's an entire ocean out there, Kiko—swim in it."

After he goes inside, it takes me a while to move. When I look over my shoulder, I see Jamie watching me with the same adoring smile he has from the first time I met him.

Jamie is not a starfish. Not even close.

I draw a very small fish swimming in the ocean and realizing it's filled with planets and stars.

CHAPTER FORTY-THREE

When Mom tells me she's kicked Uncle Max out of the house, I think she's making fun of me.

"I'm serious, Kiko. I'm so mad at him." She's talking really fast, like she's building up to an explosion.

"But . . . why?" Has she changed her mind? Is this her way of trying to get me to come back home?

"He's been taking money from me." Mom scoffs into the phone so loud I can practically hear the spit hit the speaker.

I try not to let my chest rise, but it's really, really hard not to. "You caught him stealing?"

"I've been noticing money has gone missing from my purse for weeks, but at first I thought it was me being forgetful. But then I found all this stuff in Max's room. New clothes, a new watch, a *ton* of cigarettes. He doesn't have a job—there's only one place he could get the money." She spits again. "I can't believe my own brother would be so horrible to me. After everything I've done for him. It makes me so sad."

I lie back on the bed and drop my hand to my chest. It would have been nice if she'd just believed me the first time, but I guess this is better than nothing. At least he's out of the house.

"Don't you think so? Don't you think it's terrible?" She wants validation—an acknowledgment that she's been wronged.

"Yeah, it sucks." I pause. "Is he gone for good?"

"Oh, for sure. I will never forgive him for using me like this. I don't even care if we never talk again." I don't know why, but she laughs.

I sit up irritably. *This* is the proverbial straw that broke the relationship between Mom and Uncle Max. *Clothes and cigarettes.* Not what happened when I was a kid. Not what happened a few weeks ago.

Mom's listening for a reaction from me. She has to know what I'm thinking, right? She must know how infuriating this is for me.

"So," she starts, "are you going to come home now? You don't have to worry about your stuff going missing."

"I'm doing pretty well out here," I say truthfully. "I was thinking it might be good for me to stay. I might get into Brightwood."

"This all seems really dramatic. I don't understand why you just won't come home."

"I was never going to live at home forever," I point out.

"Yeah, but Taro and Shoji don't help with anything around here. They never take turns cooking or cleaning. I have to do everything by myself. It's not easy, you know—to feel like you spend your whole life with people walking all over you. I want you to come home. I need someone to talk to."

Oh my God, is there a compliment buried in there somewhere? "Are you trying to tell me you miss my cooking?" I ask. *Or that you actually miss me?* I think.

"I mean, it's nice to have someone cook for you," she says. I count the silence for five seconds. "You can send me pictures of your drawings, you know. I am interested."

"I sent you pictures before, remember?" I feel like there are bugs crawling over me and I keep fidgeting to fight them off— tiny little anxious bugs that are trying to eat me alive.

"I was busy before," she insists. "I had a lot on my mind with the whole money thing. But I promise I'll look at them this time."

I want to challenge her, or suggest she's making it up, or point out how she's never been interested in my entire life. But I don't.

Because as a daughter who craves her mother's love, I consider this a win.

I text Mom pictures of all my newest sketches as soon as I hang up the phone. I can't help myself—I get hopeful and excited over the possibility of Mom thinking I've done well at something.

Five hours pass. I paint with Hiroshi. I get coffee with Jamie. I sketch on his parents' balcony.

Mom never writes back.

Carrying two glasses of water, Jamie puts them on the glass coffee table and sits in the chair next to me.

"What are you drawing?" He's wearing shorts and a white V-neck shirt. The sides of his dark hair sit just above his ears, but he's pushed his bangs away from his eyes. It kind of reminds me of James Dean, which can only ever be a good thing.

"I'm practicing faces," I reply, closing my book to hide the unfinished doodles. "Did you take any pictures today at the beach?"

He smiles. "I did. The weather was perfect for it—slightly overcast, but nice enough that there were actual people around to photograph."

"Sorry I've been spending so much time with Hiroshi," I say. "I hope it's not rude, staying at your house and not really being around. I just want to finish this painting, and I don't think I'll ever get an opportunity like this for the rest of my life."

"You don't need to apologize. I'd do the same thing." He rests his head back.

I pick up the glass of water and draw lines in the condensation.

Jamie stares at his knees. "Do you want to go somewhere tonight?"

The cold glass fights against my hands. "Go where?"

"To a party. Rei invited us."

I didn't know he and Rei were in touch. "When?"

"A little while ago. She texted me."

They exchanged numbers? Did I miss something? Do they like each other?

My heart drops.

He taps his finger against the armrest. "I know you don't like parties, so it's not a big deal if you'd rather not go."

Does that mean he wants to go alone? So he can see Rei alone? Would he rather I just stayed home? Does he like Rei? *When did this happen?*

I'm pretty sure I look like I'm going to throw up. "Oh. Right. Well, I can just work on my sketches. I don't mind."

There's sadness in his eyes, except it's almost like he was expecting it.

I squeeze the glass of water in my hands and try to imagine the cold reaching the flush in my face. Jamie pulls out his phone and starts texting.

Staring at the still water, I ask, "What time are you leaving?"

He puts his phone down and frowns. "I'm not."

"But I thought—"

"I'm not going to go to the party without you."

"Why not?"

"I want to spend time with you. Don't you know that I—" He stops himself and shakes his head. "Never mind. We can watch a movie or something." He shrugs like it doesn't matter, but it doesn't hide his frustration.

It makes me feel horribly guilty.

I make a decision. I'm going to do something for Jamie. I'm going to be the one giving up something for him. "Let's go. I'll be fine."

He blinks. "Are you sure?"

"Mm-hmm. Positive."

The anxious bugs start to envelop my skin, and once again I'm so nervous I feel like I'm about to pass out.

For Jamie, I try to ignore it.

Rei's apartment is on the third floor. The living room looks like a dance studio, with a big open space, exposed brick walls, and metal overhead lighting. The kitchen is tucked away behind a row of counters to the right, and an L-shaped leather couch sits in front of a wide television on the left. One of Hiroshi's paintings—squirrels having a tea party—hangs between the two back windows.

Rei waves us inside the room. She's wearing a white dress and her hair is in a long braid.

"Wow," Jamie says, looking around. "This place is awesome."

She nods and makes a face. "Thanks. My parents bought it as a rental, but I get to keep one of the rooms for when I'm back here visiting." She laughs. "I'm pretty sure it was Dad's last-ditch attempt to get me to stay in California."

I try to avoid the crowd nearby, but Rei practically ushers us toward them.

"Here, I'll introduce you to everyone. This is my part-time roommate, Aubrey. And that's Troy, Liam, Monica. . . ." She lists off every person in the room, but I lose track after the first few names. I'm too busy trying not to make eye contact with people while giving off the illusion that I am.

Jamie smiles and shakes everyone's hands. It's so natural that it makes what I'm doing seem *so much worse*.

"So are you the one who has been painting with Rei's dad? Man, you're like the luckiest person alive," a stocky boy with red curls says, his face swollen with awe.

WHAT I WANT TO SAY:

"It's amazing. I can't believe he's actually taking time out of his day to help me. I'm learning so much. It's the greatest thing that's ever happened to me."

WHAT I ACTUALLY SAY:

A string of incoherent, clustered syllables.

"What was that?" the boy asks again, his pudgy fingers locked around a can of soda.

Jamie's eyes dip to the floor. It happens so fast that I'm sure he's hoping I didn't catch it, but I did. He's embarrassed for me. Or *of* me. What's the difference, really? Everyone else is watching me, waiting for me to speak. All I want is for someone to start talking about themselves—for someone to talk about anything except me.

"Are you an artist too?" Jamie asks the redhead.

"Oh yeah." His shoulders settle, and his body relaxes. "I'm in illustration." He tells Jamie about his classes and his dream job. My brain is too fuzzy to pay attention—I feel like Jamie has just saved my life.

The conversation shifts from school to mutual friends to inside jokes I'm not a part of—relief rushes over me. I can breathe again.

Rei asks if we want anything to drink—I say no, and Jamie asks for any kind of soda—and it somehow becomes just the two of us again.

"You doing okay?" he asks thoughtfully. When I nod, he adds, "You can uncross your arms, you know."

My arms limp to my sides. I wish he wasn't drawing attention to me—I wish he could ignore my awkwardness the way Emery used to. Pointing it out makes it so much worse.

He lowers his head. "You kind of look like you want to be anywhere but here."

My back stiffens, and defense rushes through me. "I'm trying. Maybe give me a little credit? This isn't easy."

"I just wish you didn't look so uncomfortable."

"I was fine. Now I feel like I'm ruining your night."

"Can you please not overthink this?"

"Can you please be a little more patient with something I have no control over?"

There's fire between us. Our bodies are stiff; our words are so specific. I don't know when the tension started—days ago, maybe—and it's finally starting to bubble over. We stare at each other like we're about to go to war, until both of us realize almost at the same time that neither of us wants to fight.

"Truce?" Jamie lifts his brow.

"Truce," I repeat.

"Look." Jamie puts his hand against my back—my skin buzzes—and he leads me in front of him. "Do you honestly think anyone here is at all bothered that you aren't the most talkative person here?"

I look around. Everyone is either smiling, or talking, or drinking, but none of them are looking at me.

"I guess not," I say quietly.

Jamie shifts so he's in my line of sight. "Don't think about everyone else. Don't even think about you. Just relax. Pretend it's just you and me."

His hand locks around mine. I don't know why I was ever wondering about him and Rei—he doesn't hold Rei's hand; he holds mine.

We spend the rest of the night in our own little world. Other people occasionally visit, but they don't stay forever, because we are the creators. We make the rules. We are a team.

I honestly don't know what I'd do without Jamie. I need him.

But as much as I like Jamie, as much as I might even love him, needing him is something else entirely. Needing him is scary.

Because needing him means losing him will hurt so much more.

I draw a girl in love with a snowman at the beginning of spring.

CHAPTER FORTY-FOUR

When Hiroshi gets a call about one of his paintings, I slip away to give him some privacy and find an empty chair in the back corner of the café. Akane sees me and brings a vanilla latte over without me asking.

"It's on the house," she says, falling into the chair across from me. "So my dad isn't getting on your nerves yet?" She smiles. "He can be a little intense sometimes when he's talking about art."

"Not at all," I say. "He's awesome. I can't believe he's letting me hang out with him."

She laughs. "Trust me, I think you're the one doing him the favor. You're like the adopted daughter he always wanted."

I look away, embarrassed.

She doesn't seem to notice. "It's good for him, having people around. I don't know how he'll cope once Rei and I are both in school again." She plays with the tips of her hair like she's checking them for split ends. She's comfortable around me, and even though I've known her only a little while, I'm comfortable around her, too.

Maybe it's because I don't feel so different when I'm around her. When I look at her, I don't see someone living in a different world. I see someone living in my world—our world. Maybe it's because she looks like she could be my family, and that makes her *feel* like family.

Is that why Mom and I don't understand each other? Because we don't look like each other? Maybe when Mom looks at me, she sees someone from a different world too.

I wish she had made room for me. I wish she had tried to fit me in, even if I didn't match the rest of her house.

Isn't that what parents are supposed to do? Try? Or is it supposed to come naturally? And if it doesn't, what does that mean?

I don't know. Maybe I don't want to know.

"Do you have any siblings?" Akane asks casually, her words breaking apart my thoughts.

"Two brothers," I say. "And two half sisters, but they're only a few months old."

She nods in the same slow-motion, peaceful way Hiroshi does. "Are you guys close?"

"Yeah." I pause. "I mean, no." I pause again. "I mean, we used to be, when we were little. I think. To be honest, I'm not sure anymore." Is it possible to be really close and still feel like complete strangers?

"Sounds complicated."

"I guess it is." I shrug. I don't think of my brothers in terms of close or not close—we just *are*. We were raised by the same parents, rejected by the same mother, abandoned by the same father—even if he did have a good reason. Even if it was my fault.

I suppose if I had to think about it, my brothers know more about me than anyone else does. Even more than Emery or Jamie.

But I'm not sure if knowing about feelings and experiences is the same thing as being close.

Being close feels like it requires more effort.

Akane brushes her hair out of her eyes, and I notice a small tattoo on her wrist. She catches me looking at it and waves her hand. "Oh no. It's not real. Mom would *kill* me. It's just pen."

"What is it?"

She holds her wrist toward me. "It's the sun goddess, Amaterasu. My dad drew it for me on a napkin years ago. There's a whole story about her hiding in a cave and turning the world dark. It's kind of an analogy for depression, I guess."

I look back at her in surprise. "Sorry," I say, unsure if I've opened a door I'm not supposed to.

She shakes her head, pulling her hand away. "It's fine. I'm not embarrassed or anything. I mean, why should I be? You wouldn't be embarrassed if you were diabetic, would you? Or if you had a heart condition?" She smiles and shrugs matter-of-factly.

I wish I could see things the way she does, like it's okay to be different. Like it's normal to be weird or nervous or anxious or sad. I wish I could tell people when I'm uncomfortable, and just shrug afterward like it doesn't matter.

Akane is braver than I am, and maybe it's because she has Hiroshi. And Mayumi. And Rei. Maybe that's been the secret ingredient all along—*family*. Love. Acceptance. Self-confidence.

Seeing the beauty in who she is and where she comes from.

Maybe that's what I'm missing.

"How did the sun goddess overcome it?" I ask.

Akane runs her finger over the fake tattoo. "Well, they trick her into coming out, and when she sees her reflection she's overcome by how beautiful she is, and then she's happy again." She laughs. "But I like to think of her seeing her own beauty as her seeing her own strength. That maybe she needed a little bit of help at first, but the ultimate power lay inside her, you know?"

I nod. "It's beautiful."

"Yeah," she muses. "My dad's pretty cool, even if he is intense."

The door opens, and a customer approaches the counter.

Akane stands up and taps at the table. "Gotta get back to work. Let me know if you need anything else, okay?"

But I don't need anything else. I feel like I have the world, and even though Prism isn't in it, Hiroshi is. His family is. His *art* is. He's filling a void I never knew was there, with his stories and his family and his paintings and the kindness he never seems to run out of.

And somehow, right now, that feels more important than art school.

I draw a girl breaking apart the sun until one star becomes a hundred stars, because she wants to cover the world in beauty.

CHAPTER FORTY-FIVE

Jamie makes a playlist of Billie Holiday and The Velvet Underground—one of my favorites and one of his favorites. He sits at his desk, editing his most recent photographs. I sit on his bed, sketching different kinds of dresses.

A few months ago, if someone had told me I'd be sitting on Jamie Merrick's bed listening to a mash-up of our favorite music together, I would have laughed until my lungs exploded.

As long as nobody was watching, of course.

But things are different now. I've since found out dreams really can come true.

Jamie pulls his mouth to the side and his right cheek dimples. "What do you think?"

I look at his computer screen and see a picture of me. He took it when we were at the beach earlier. I was standing at the edge of the water, waiting for the waves to come in so the sand could swallow up my feet. I like how it feels—like I'm not going anywhere, and that's okay.

Jamie is noticeably surprised when I don't pull a face. To be honest, it surprises me, too.

"I like it," I say honestly. I'm not looking at the camera. I'm looking somewhere over my shoulder, probably trying to find Jamie, who moves around so silently when he's taking photos it sometimes feels like he's not there at all.

But I look peaceful. Peaceful is good.

He nods a few times before he smirks. "Let's see yours."

I turn my sketchbook around, and this time I *do* make a face. "I'm trying to figure out what I want the woman in my painting to wear. I'm adding all the details onto her dress tomorrow."

"Are those tentacles?" he asks with a quizzical brow.

I shut the book and laugh too loudly. "It's stupid. Forget it."

"No, it's not," he insists. "Is she some kind of sea creature?"

I shrug. I don't know how to tell him she's a human starfish without telling him *everything*. It's a conversation I don't know how to have without baring my entire soul. "They're only sketches. I haven't decided what I'm going to do yet."

Jamie looks back at his computer screen, tapping his finger against the edge of the keyboard in time with the music. After a few minutes, he turns back to me, his eyes overflowing with blue concern. "Is the woman in your painting supposed to be your mom?"

It takes me a while to answer. When I do, my voice doesn't waver. "No. The painting is about how she makes me feel. It's not about my mom—it's about me."

There's something hidden beneath his brow that tells me he wants to ask more, but he doesn't. He goes eerily quiet, and I have no idea why.

Hiroshi doesn't stop smiling when he sees the clothing ideas for my painting.

"These are wonderful. The details are so thoughtful, so visually interesting." He pauses before snapping his brown eyes to mine. "Kiko, have you ever considered going to school for drawing instead of painting?"

My throat catches. Maybe I'm not a good enough painter. Maybe Mom was right. Maybe—

Hiroshi interrupts my thoughts. "I'm only asking because you have an amazing style and a much stronger body of work with your sketches than with your canvases. You have a solid portfolio here already—have you ever thought about submitting it to Prism?"

I swallow what feels like a giant chunk of cardboard lodged in my throat. "Most of them are just doodles. They're unfinished."

"Artwork isn't finished just because you've colored up to every corner on the page. Artwork is finished when you get to the end of your sentence." He shakes the book in his grip. "You have a great many stories in here that are worth sharing."

I take the sketchbook back and I feel like I've been wounded even though he's trying to compliment me. Painting is my life— it's what I want to do. I draw in order to paint. It's the order of things.

Isn't it?

Hiroshi shrugs. "Perhaps it's something to think about." He moves back to his desk in the corner, and I step closer to my borrowed easel.

I think about it. I don't *stop* thinking about it, even after I finish painting the woman's dress with burnt orange and crimson and topaz yellow. I paint because it's the next step—what does it mean if there isn't another step? Drawing feels so open and skeletal. My sketchbook is a collection of imprints from my soul. They aren't finished—they need to be colored in, and decorated, and turned into something much prettier than what they are.

If I don't have emerald greens and magentas and lilacs, I just have Kiko. Black-and-white. Bare and smudged.

I'm not confident enough to let my drawings speak for me. I need my paintings to say something else entirely.

Maybe this is my problem. Maybe this is what Hiroshi has been trying to tell me.

My paintings aren't honest enough.

Cringing, I close my eyes and picture what the starfish woman will look like when she is finished. She's vibrant and beautiful and commands the attention of the painting. But this isn't her story.

And then my mind pictures the girl standing behind her, hidden behind the luminous splendor. She's gray and plain, but she's beautiful, too, in her own way. But the woman will never see it because she's too busy being beautiful herself.

This painting isn't about the starfish. It's about the girl who wants to venture out into the ocean, away from the starfish, so she can feel like she matters.

Because the girl will never matter to the starfish.

In the finished painting in my head, the girl will finally know this.

It's the honest story I want to tell.

I will make this painting the truest painting I've ever done. And after that . . .

I will swim into the ocean.

I paint a crown of starfish and golden hair, all jumbled together because the body and the mind are all part of the same being.

CHAPTER FORTY-SIX

In the middle of the night, my phone rings. It takes me a while to wake up, and by the time my fingers fumble against the plastic, I'm hurrying to press the answer button without bothering to look at the caller ID.

"Hello?" My voice is raspy and quiet because I don't want to wake up Jamie's parents.

"Hi," says a timid voice.

"Shoji?" I sit up, letting the quilt fall to my waist.

"Yeah," he says. "Umm, I just wanted to know when you were coming home."

I pause. Did Mom put him up to this? Does she think she can get to me through my brother? I wipe the sleep out of my eye with my finger. "Well, I'm not sure, to be honest. I'm sort of here on a trial basis."

There's a long pause. "But are you coming back?"

"Probably. Maybe. I mean, I don't *want* to."

Another long pause. "Okay."

I frown, my eyes adjusting slowly to the shadows around the room. "Are you okay? Is everything . . . okay? At home?" My mind goes straight to Uncle Max.

He clears his throat into the phone. "Yeah. Mom's kind of being worse than usual." He forces a laugh. "It's easier when you're home. She notices me too much when you're not around."

It's my turn to pause. I didn't think about how Mom would be when I left. Maybe she can't help herself. Maybe she has to be herself at all costs, no matter who is standing in her line of sight.

Did I leave Shoji to take my place on her target board? Because Taro's too strong for Mom to break, and with me gone and Uncle Max gone and Dad gone, Shoji's all that's left?

"Okay, well, I'm going to go. Bye." He hangs up the phone before I get a chance to say anything else.

I sit in the darkness for a long time, watching the shadows shift when the moon does, and I wonder if maybe Mom doesn't really hate me—maybe she doesn't hate any of us. Maybe she doesn't know how to be any other way.

I decide to call home after I'm finished painting at the studio. Not because I'm planning on telling anyone Shoji called, but because I want to know if everything is okay. My brothers don't normally call me—I'm still trying to figure out why Shoji made an exception last night.

I call Taro first. He sounds surprised to hear from me, which I guess is a good sign. If there's a problem with Shoji, he must not know about it.

"Why are you calling?" He laughs into the phone awkwardly.

"I wanted to see how everything is back home," I say carefully.

He grunts. "So are you and Jamie dating now? Mom says you guys are living together."

"Mom exaggerates everything," I say. "I'm just staying at his parents' house while I look at schools." I pause. "Have you hung out with Shoji lately? How is he?"

"Trying to pretend he's a foreign exchange student living in our house, like he always is." Taro laughs louder, sighing at the end like he finds himself incredibly amusing. "Did you know he speaks Japanese now?"

"I mean, I guess I assumed. I know he reads all those comics," I say.

"Yeah, but he can actually speak it. Even Dad doesn't know Japanese. It's kind of weird."

I raise my eyebrows even though we're not in the same room. "I think it's kind of cool. I wish I could speak Japanese."

"Maybe." Taro snorts. "I'm pretty sure he only learned it so he could cuss at Mom without her knowing."

I stiffen. "What makes you say that?"

"Because every time she talks to him he starts muttering in a different language under his breath. What else would he be saying?"

"I bet she hates that."

"Of course she hates it," he agrees. "Can you imagine anything she hates more than not knowing what people are saying about her?" After a pause, he asks, "When are you coming back? *Are* you coming back?"

"I don't know yet," I say. "I'm still figuring it out."

There's a long, awkward silence. "Well, uh, I hope you're having fun or whatever. I remember when I first moved out. It was great."

"Yeah. It is," I say. "What about you? Are you okay?"

"I'm always okay. You're the one who lets her get to you too easily. You're just wasting energy if you try to get her to understand anything. It's easier to not care." He takes a deep breath and lets it out like he's bored. "Plus, I get to leave whenever I want, remember?"

And when there's another long silence, I add, "Well, I'll let you go."

"Okay. I'll talk to you"—Taro laughs into the phone—"sometime?"

"Yeah, okay," I say, even though both of us know "sometime" will be a long time from now. Because this is how we are with each other—we don't linger.

After he hangs up, I call Mom because I'm still not positive everything is okay with Shoji. I don't know what I'm expecting to hear. I guess I'm just trying to find out if something happened—if there was some kind of a massive fight or Shoji's done anything out of the ordinary beyond muttering possible Japanese curse words under his breath.

Mom talks about her blog, and work, and a new show she's watching.

"How are Taro and Shoji?" I ask, as delicately as I can.

She grunts noncommittally. "Still unable to cook a meal or

clean a toilet. You know, sometimes I just want to sell the house, get a one-bedroom apartment, and tell them they can go live with their dad for a change. Let him see how hard it is."

My chest tightens. I don't want to argue with her—I want to ask about my brother. Because he opened a door last night—a door he might want me to look inside. But I don't know how else to follow up on it without going through Taro or Mom. Even if my brother made a phone call, he's still wearing his armor.

I think of something simple to ask, something that won't set off any alarm bells. "Is Shoji still doing tae kwon do?"

Mom ignores my question. "Your dad had it so easy. I wish you guys could see that."

I feel my head start to throb. "I don't want to talk about Dad with you." I want to talk about *Shoji*.

"Yeah, because you always side with him."

All my organs start to feel tight and cramped, as if there's not enough room for them. They're being pushed out of the way to make room for all the frustration boiling inside of me. Maybe that's why Shoji called—maybe his frustration is boiling over too. "Well, go get an apartment, then," I snap.

"What's that supposed to mean?"

"Nothing," I say quickly. "It was your suggestion. It's not like Dad didn't want to see us more."

"What's *that* supposed to mean?"

Oh my God, why am I falling into this sand trap? *Just stop talking, Kiko.*

She sighs heavily into the phone. "I didn't force your dad to stay away. He could've seen you guys as much as he wanted to."

"I think maybe he thought it was easier for us to go to him. So you two didn't have to fight," I offer.

"Is that my fault? That he couldn't have a mature conversation with his wife?" she growls.

"Ex-wife," I mutter.

She keeps talking, the volume in her voice growing with every word. "He always blamed me for making it hard to see you guys, but he could have made more of an effort."

My agitation builds. Sometimes I have an uncontrollable urge to defend Dad because he's always defended me. I know he left, and maybe that wasn't right, but he's always felt more present in my life than Mom, and she was living in the same *house* as me. "You had full custody, Mom. You argued for that. He was trying to give you what you wanted."

"Well, I wouldn't have asked for it if I'd known I was going to be punished for it!"

"Mom, calm down. Nobody is punishing you." I squeeze the bridge of my nose and close my eyes. I think I made a mistake calling her today.

"If I could go back in time, I would never have married him. I was too young. I could've done so much better," she says.

My eyes flash open. Okay, what's *that* supposed to mean?

"People look at me different, you know. Having his last name. They treat me differently. It's not easy when people look at you differently just because of a name."

WHAT I WANT TO SAY:

"*Of course* you were never going to love my face—you can't even love a *name*!"

WHAT I ACTUALLY SAY:

"You have a maiden name. Change it back."

She tuts into the phone. "I'm not paying to have that changed. What, so Serena can say she's the 'real' Mrs. Himura? No thanks."

I roll my eyes. I want to tell her Serena isn't as petty as she is, and that maybe Serena would be better off as the only Mrs. Himura because she probably thinks it's beautiful and special and not in any way inferior.

But I don't.

"I have to go, Mom."

"Okay. Oh, by the way, have you read my last blog post?"

I clench my teeth. "I don't read your blog."

"It's really good, you know. Everyone at works thinks so. I kind of feel like a celebrity." She laughs.

I want to tell her I'll read her blog when she looks at my sketchbooks, but I bite my tongue. I don't want to engage anymore—I want the phone call to be over. "I'll talk to you later."

"I love you. Bye."

I stare at the mirror, running my fingers around my round face and my wide nose and wondering if Mom really does think she could have done better than Dad—better than *Asian*—and if she does, does she think she could have done better than me?

It hurts. It hurts hearing her vocalize my fear—that people might not look at me the way they look at her. And it hurts to think she looks down on Dad, and maybe down on me, and Taro, and Shoji.

Closing my eyes, I think of all the faces in my sketchbook. The ones I've drawn since Hiroshi told me beauty isn't just one thing. They're all different and special and unique. I don't look at them the way Mom looks at the faces in a yearbook. Because it wouldn't be fair. It feels cruel, like I'm saying one type of face is better than another. Like I'm saying one kind of heritage is better than another.

It's an ugly thing to do. I'd rather have an ugly face than an ugly heart.

I let my hands drop to my sides and shake my head at the mirror.

And I decide, right there and then, that I don't care if I'm not someone's idea of pretty. I don't care if my name might disappoint someone, or if my face might disappoint someone's *parents*. Because that says so much more about them than it does about me.

Who cares what anyone else thinks? Who cares what Mom thinks, when she's immature enough to keep a last name she hates just to maintain an imaginary war with Serena?

I love my last name. And maybe I'm even learning to love my face.

That can be enough. It has to be. It will be.

I draw a girl pulling her reflection out of the mirror and holding it close to her heart.

CHAPTER FORTY-SEVEN

Jamie takes me to Chinatown because he can't believe I've never been to one before. I don't understand why he's surprised—I've never felt the need to go to Chinatown, which probably stems from the fact that Mom never told me I should feel otherwise.

She once told me she wished she had given me and my brothers more "traditional" names because she was "kind of over the Japanese thing." You know, because being Asian is a trend or something.

I guess it explains why she doesn't think I'm pretty, or why she always hated when Dad watched his old samurai shows. To her, we're an interest she's outgrown.

Why would she ever point out the benefit of going to Chinatown?

But she should have. *Somebody* should have. *Because Chinatown is amazing.*

There's so much red and green and gold everywhere, it feels like we're in a different country. Every shop is full of things I've never seen before, and every restaurant is filled with foods

I've never heard of. There's a grocery store that only sells imported foods with labels I can't read. And it's not just stuff from China—there's stuff from South Korea and Thailand and Japan too.

It's a pocket of culture—some of it *my* culture—surrounded by the world I grew up in. The world I've never felt a true part of.

And I can't help but notice something that stands out even more than the bronze lion sculptures and the overpowering aroma of noodles and soy sauce.

Almost everyone in Chinatown looks more like me than any of the kids at my high school ever did.

It feels like a dream. I've never been around so many Asian people before. I've always felt out of place, but I've never realized quite how much until this exact moment, when I feel completely *in* place. They have eyes like mine and hair like mine and legs like mine. When they smile their skin creases the way mine does, and their hair mostly falls flat and straight the way mine does.

They're like me. It feels so comfortable and good I could almost cry.

And they're so beautiful. Like, Rei beautiful. They know how to do their hair and makeup and dress themselves because they've probably been taught by parents who understand they shouldn't just copy whatever the white celebrities and models are doing. Because they have different faces and body types and colors. It's like painting—you don't just use any color you feel like; you pick the color that fits the subject the best.

I can't believe it's taken me so long to learn the lesson I've needed since childhood.

I don't have to be white to be beautiful, just like I don't have to be Asian to be beautiful. Because beauty doesn't come in one mold.

It doesn't make it okay that people are jerks about race. But it does make me feel like I'm not alone. It makes me feel like less of a weirdo.

It makes me feel like Mom was wrong.

When I look around at the people in Chinatown, I don't feel like I'm desperate for their acceptance. I feel at ease.

I think I know why Shoji accepted our Japanese side a long time ago. I think he realized there was another world out there—a world Mom wasn't a part of. I think he knew that, somehow, finding our heritage was like finding a safe place from *her*.

There are so many things to do and see. We pass by a store where a man is selling bonsai trees. I try boba tea for the first time—Jamie's is mango flavored, and mine is coconut. We look around the grocery store, spending a lot of time in the candy aisle observing how different the flavors are—green tea Kit Kat bars, wasabi drops, squid-flavored gummies, and melon soda.

And then we see an artist outside a bookstore doing a live drawing. Her black hair is separated in two buns, and she's wearing a long skirt and a Sailor Moon T-shirt. She draws the way Hiroshi paints, like she has all the confidence in the world.

There's a stack of books on a table nearby, all titled *Manga Pop Art* by Tanya Fujisaki. Positioned above them is a sign that reads: MEET THE ARTIST AND GET YOUR COPY SIGNED TODAY.

Jamie hovers over the table and picks up one of the books, flipping through the pages casually. "Hey, these are pretty cool." He holds up the open book so I can see inside. It's a collection of the artist's drawings, paintings, and tips on how to draw manga. They remind me of Emery's tattoos, but so much more detailed and colorful.

I look back at Tanya Fujisaki. She's speaking in Japanese to a nearby teenager, who's watching her like he's starstruck. I'm pretty sure he's a fan.

I pick up a book of my own, turning the pages and falling in love with the drawings the way I did the first time I watched one of the anime shows Dad brought home. I don't know if it's normal to look at cartoons and feel so happy, but I can't help it. Some people look at pictures of animals and scenery and feel an overwhelming sense of joy. I feel that way when I look at art.

Jamie holds the book up to me again, tapping his finger against one of the pictures. It's a girl with black hair flying up to the stars, her hands trailing at her sides and the rest of the world far below her. "It's you," he says, like it's the most obvious thing in the world.

I flip through the book and find a picture of a girl stuffing her face with food. "No, this is me," I say.

He frowns. "Nobody should look that mad while they're eating doughnuts."

"She's hangry," I say. "It's when you get so hungry, you feel angry."

"That's not a thing."

"It absolutely is."

Jamie laughs and sets the book back down. I decide I don't want to be finished with my copy, so I pay for it at the counter.

"The signing starts in an hour," the man at the register says.

Jamie and I wander around the rest of Chinatown to waste time, except it doesn't feel like it's being wasted. I'm having the most fun I've had in years.

When we find a store called Paper Tokyo, we walk down separate aisles that stop right below our chins. Every time we see something cool, we hold it up for the other person to see.

I lift a box of highlighters, all shaped like boiled eggs. "How cute are these?"

Jamie holds up a giant eraser that's shaped like a piece of toast with a face on it.

I hold up a notebook with the word "Wishes" written on the front. Just below it is a giant walrus holding a magic wand.

Jamie finds a pair of fake eyes that you put on your eyelids. The box says they're supposed to trick people into thinking you're awake, but really they just look scary.

I find a set of drawing pencils with erasers shaped like pieces of sushi at the ends.

Jamie finds a back scratcher that looks like a bear paw.

I laugh. "What does that have to do with stationery?"

He shrugs, grinning. "Even people who sit at desks get itchy."

I buy the notebook with the walrus because I don't want to leave such an amazing store empty-handed.

"You should've gotten the fake eyes," Jamie says as we're walking out the door.

When we're standing in line for the book signing, I tell Jamie I have no idea what I'm supposed to say.

"You say 'hi' and tell her you like her work." He points to my bag. "You could tell her you like the picture of the hangry girl."

I feel my heart start to race. My eyes count the people in front of me, assessing how much time is left before I have to speak to a complete stranger. "Is this going to be awkward? It feels like it's going to be awkward."

"Breathe. She does this for a living. She'll probably do all the talking. All you have to do is say 'hi.'"

When I get to the front of the line, I don't say 'hi.' I freeze, drop the book on the table like it just came out of the oven, and look at all the space around Tanya Fujisaki's head without ever looking directly at her.

I think she asks me a question—something about if I'm from California—but I'm having trouble concentrating on anything besides passing out, so I keep nodding my head at everything she says until she smiles, hands me the signed copy back, and thanks me for coming by.

I clutch the book against my chest and tear away from the desk like I'm trying to find somewhere to breathe.

When I find a place away from the crowd, I look up at Jamie with large eyes. "Was that as bad as I think it was?"

For a second he just stares at me, and then he's laughing so hard he shuts his eyes and tilts his head away from me.

And even though I'm embarrassed, I'm not angry at Jamie for laughing. It takes only a few seconds before I'm laughing too.

"I did try," I say, my eyes pooling with happy tears.

"It's my fault," Jamie says. "I was trying to help you figure out what to say when I should've been reminding you not to assault the artist with her own book."

The skin between my eyes pinches together. "I did kind of throw it at her, didn't I?"

He nods. "You really did."

I sigh, and a smirk spreads across half of my face. "Today was going so well."

"Come on," he says, rolling his eyes. "Let's get something to eat."

We find a Japanese bakery and buy a selection of *anpan*—red-bean buns. Some have sesame seeds on them and some are coconut flavored, but they're all so delicious. In fact, they're kind of all I want to eat for the rest of my life.

Jamie pushes the last anpan toward me. "I'm stuffed," he says, picking his camera back up from the table. He's been taking photographs all morning, and I'm pretty sure half of them are of me.

I eat the last anpan like it's still the first one—it tastes like happiness.

"Do you come to Chinatown a lot?" I wipe my empty fingers on my crumpled napkin. "Because I would come to this bakery every day and become the fattest person alive. I never knew how delicious this kind of food was."

Jamie snaps another picture of me, and I don't even flinch. "Not a lot, but I've been a few times. I like the architecture here. And there's all this graffiti in one of the back alleys—it's great for photos." He pauses, letting the camera sink toward his chest.

"Didn't your dad ever make you guys Japanese food when you were little? Or take you to a Japanese restaurant?"

I shake my head. "Mom hates Asian food. She says it's too greasy." She also makes a lot of comments about the hygiene at Asian restaurants, but I leave that part out.

"It's weird. You're the only Asian person I know who doesn't know anything about her own culture." He makes a face. "Sorry. That sounded rude. I didn't mean it in a bad way; it was a stupid observation."

"Well, it's true. And I think it *is* a bad thing." I would have loved to have known about anpan and mochi and boba tea when I was a kid. I would have loved to have known about any part of my heritage that didn't make me feel so alone in the world.

And I would have loved it if I knew something about being Japanese that didn't make my mother turn her nose up.

A group of teenage girls walks past our table. They're staring at Jamie and giggling in the most obvious way possible. *Of course* they are—Jamie is perfect. But they're kind of perfect too, with their smooth skin and cute sandals and layers of shirts and vests that I'm guessing is what Asian hipsters wear.

I bite the inside of my cheek and pretend I don't notice.

"I'm not looking at them," Jamie says softly. "I'm looking at you."

When I bring my eyes up, I'm looking at him, too.

Like, *really* looking at him. It's hard to breathe when all the colors of his face are so rich and intoxicating—pale blue eyes, a honey tan, and dark chocolate hair. How could someone so beautiful be looking at me the way he is, with half of a smile and affection in his gaze? What does he see?

And then I realize. He sees the same thing I see when I look at him.

He sees something beautiful.

I know if I look at him for another millisecond I'll vaporize into mist all over the bakery, so I shift my eyes to my bag and rummage for my phone for no reason other than to keep my mind busy.

He drops his gaze to his camera and makes himself busy too. The next time our eyes meet, we realize we're still smiling at each other.

I tell Jamie I want to go back to the grocery store before we leave. I buy enough Hi-Chews, Pocky Sticks, and cans of Royal Milk Tea to fill up my bag, because even though it seems silly, buying Asian food makes me feel connected to a part of my heritage I never knew what to do with before.

I draw five Japanese women with very different faces, but all of them are equally beautiful because beauty is not just one thing.

CHAPTER FORTY-EIGHT

Dad calls to ask how I'm doing in California. Mom's been telling people I came out here to celebrate graduating. As annoying as it is that my mother is a liar, I don't have the heart to tell Dad about Uncle Max. Upsetting him wouldn't help anything. Giving him something extra to worry about when he has two little babies isn't an option. I won't make him unhappy just for the sake of needing someone on my side. I won't be like Mom.

So we talk about beaches and the weather instead. I tell him about Hiroshi, how I ate ramen and mochi with his family and how I went to Chinatown for the first time.

He tells me he's happy I'm getting to have these experiences. He says he wishes I could've had them when I was younger. He starts to tell me a story about Mom telling him to stop making Japanese food because it "made the house smell awful," but he seems to change his mind before he says too much. He says it's not good to complain about the things we can't change. And after we hang up, he sends me pictures of the twins. It feels nice, like I'm included in his life. It makes me feel like I have a family.

Mom calls an hour after him. I swear it's like she can sense when I'm moving further away from her, like an ex-boyfriend who never shows any interest when you're dating, but calls the moment you feel like you're in a good place without him.

I don't tell her I talked to Dad, but I'm not sure I could fit it in anyway. All she wants to talk about is herself.

She tells me about the fight she had with a woman at work over wrapping paper. According to Mom, the office had an unofficial agreement to never bring their kids' school fund-raising catalogs to work. The woman did it anyway, and Mom decided it was her job to chastise the woman in front of everyone. Obviously the woman didn't appreciate it.

I don't bother telling Mom she should have said something in private instead of in front of the whole office. Who wants to be publicly scolded by their coworker over wrapping paper? But there's no point in saying this to Mom—she's in a good mood, at least by her standards. I'm too relaxed to get into an argument.

She tells me about her website, too. Apparently it doesn't look professional enough, so she wants to pay a web designer to make it better. I don't comment on any of this either—I don't want to get into an argument. I'm trying to relax.

Then Mom tells me Taro went to stay with one of his college friends for the rest of the summer. And that Shoji doesn't do anything to help clean. And that she wants us to get our hair done together when I get "home."

I'm not relaxed anymore. I'm having a brain aneurysm. When

did I become one of Mom's friends? Are we friends? Is that why we're having a conversation where she's managed to avoid saying a single negative thing about me?

Mom asks me to call her tomorrow, and we hang up. There isn't room to think about the twins anymore. All I can think about is what this is supposed to mean.

Jamie holds the camera up to his face. A second later I hear the click of the shutter.

His hands drop to reveal a smile. "So when do I get to see your painting?"

"When it's finished." I scoop up another bite of white chocolate and raspberry ice cream.

He leans back in his chair and sets his camera on the table. We're surrounded by pink and blue, like we're in a pool of cotton candy. There's a neon sign on the wall shaped like an ice-cream cone, black-and-white tiled floors, and a jukebox in the corner. It feels like we've stepped into a time warp.

But I guess being with Jamie feels like a time warp all the time. We're kids again, finishing what we started all those years ago.

He slices his metal spoon into a glass bowl filled with two perfect scoops of mint chocolate chip. "Are you going to miss it? When you finish the painting and you don't get to see Hiroshi anymore?"

I press my thumb against the spoon tightly. "I hadn't actually thought about that." I've been spending so much time with Hiroshi that he's starting to feel like a friend. I guess a part of me forgot this was a temporary arrangement.

"Sorry. I didn't mean to ruin the mood." Jamie blinks at the table, thinking.

My trial period is almost up. We both know it. We just don't talk about it.

Hiroshi isn't the only one I might have to say good-bye to—it's Jamie, too. Because I can't live in his parents' home forever, just like I can't paint in Hiroshi's studio forever. I've invaded their lives, and eventually, if I can't figure out how to survive here by myself, I'll need to return to the life I left behind.

I feel sick. I've gotten used to Jamie and Hiroshi and California. I don't want to go back to living with Mom, existing alongside my brothers without ever really speaking, never going anywhere because Emery isn't there to go with me, and occasionally seeing my dad. This—right now—feels more like a family than I've ever had.

I kind of need them. I need Jamie.

The world seems too scary without him.

Click. Jamie's face is once again obscured by the camera lens. I cross my eyes and make my nostrils flare. *Click.* He laughs, and I do too.

"I'm going to keep that one forever," he says.

"Forever is a long time to keep a silly picture of me," I say.

"It's not the picture." His voice is gentle. "It's the memory. I want to remember you forever, Kiko Himura."

I don't say a word. I'm too busy glowing.

I draw a thousand fairies circling around a girl so that she can finally fly away.

CHAPTER FORTY-NINE

When my car gets a flat tire, I'm overwhelmed by the realization that my bank account is rapidly depleting. It scares me, worrying about money and things going wrong and not having a source of income. It makes me wonder if I'm being an idiot for hiding out in California when I have a job waiting for me back home.

Since Jamie and his parents all know my time in California may be limited and my time with Hiroshi *definitely* is, Elouise offers to drive me to the studio while Jamie picks up a new tire for me.

I'm grateful to both of them. To their whole family.

I need every spare minute I can get. I want this painting to be perfect. It *has* to be perfect.

Every time I've been close to Elouise I can smell the sour bite of wine. But today she smells fresh, like honeysuckles and soap. Her dark hair is parted neatly in the center and tucked behind both ears. She's beautiful the way a vampire would be, with red lips, a cold stare, and dark circles under her eyes. But unlike a vampire, Elouise isn't pale. She's so bronze her skin is practically metallic.

She seems like she's been tired for a very long time.

"Have you heard anything back from any schools?" she asks, her eyes focused on the road.

"Not yet." I pause. Maybe she's trying to get a better idea of when I'm planning to leave. Or *if* I'm planning to leave. "I put down my mom's address in the application, so that's where they'll mail the letter." My chest tightens thinking about how fast the time seems to be going.

Her brown eyes look like they're coated in shiny polish. "I know we all haven't seen each other in years, but it's been nice getting to know you again, Kiko. I mean that."

"Thanks for letting me stay in your home. It's been the best vacation I've ever had."

Her tongue slips over her bottom lip. "You probably don't have many to compare it to. I remember how much your mom hated to take vacations."

"That's true," I say quietly. "We tried to go camping once, but we were only at the camping site for an hour before Dad had to get everything back in the car and drive us all home. She said it was because she didn't want to share a bathroom with strangers. We didn't even finish putting up the tent."

Elouise shakes her head so slowly I would have missed it if I wasn't staring right at her. "That sounds about right. Angelina hated public bathrooms. She only lets people see what she wants them to see." Wincing, she tilts her face toward me. "I'm sorry. I shouldn't have said that."

I don't say anything because I wasn't expecting her words. I didn't know Elouise even knew Mom besides the occasional run-ins at birthday parties and school events. But the way she speaks about her . . . I don't know. I get the feeling she *really* knew her.

I want to ask her if she was friends with my mom. I want to ask why she said what she did. But it's uncomfortable now, because I've waited too long and because Elouise is turning up the music on the radio and tuning me out.

She stops at the side of the road opposite Hiroshi's café and studio. Her foot pressed against the brake, she wipes a finger beneath her eye. Was she crying? It's too hard to tell.

"I think you're terrific, Kiko. I hope you know that. We were always very fond of you, even when you were little. There's something magical and irreplaceable about a childhood friendship. I'm glad Jamie gets to share that with you. I'm sorry if we ever got in the way of that, with the move and everything." She doesn't look at me when she speaks—she just says everything she is prepared to and blends into the background noise of the radio.

I step out onto the street awkwardly, thank her for the ride, and she drives away in a hurry to erase what was just said between us.

My hands are anxious for brushes and paint tubes, mostly to give them something to do besides tremble against my legs. When I find Hiroshi, I'm hoping for the calming inspiration I've grown accustomed to.

Instead, I find a tearful, middle-aged man with his hair draped against his back and his wife sitting beside him with a hand on his knee.

What is going on with people and their emotions today? I'm usually the emotional one—not the rest of the world.

"Sorry." I catch my breath, feeling the rush of the door as it closes behind me. "I can leave."

"No." Mayumi holds up her hand. "I go." She plants a gentle kiss on Hiroshi's cheek and slips past me like a deer.

Pressing his hands to his small eyes, Hiroshi shakes his head like he's shaking away his tears. "I've always believed emotion is good for painting, but I'm afraid I'm not in the best mood to create anything today."

"Is everything okay?" I ask quietly, the worry thick in my voice.

"Oh yes. Everything is fine." He forces a smile. "I'll leave the keys with you. Can you bring them downstairs when you're finished today? I think I need to rest my head at home. A little bit of recharging will do me good."

"I don't want to chase you out of your own studio."

"No," he insists, pressing his hands over my shoulders and leading me to my almost-finished painting. "This is where you belong." He drops the studio keys on the nearest table.

The studio feels eerily still without him in it. It's like all the color has been drained from the room.

I paint anyway, because I'm running out of time, and because I'm painting the girl today, lingering in the shadows. Today, gray is good.

Mayumi knocks on the door before she enters. She's carrying

a cup of tea and a slice of cake. "Energy," she says simply, placing it near me.

"Thank you."

I watch her eyes trail over to my painting. She nods a few times, taking it all in. "Why she so happy when little girl not?"

"I guess she's happy *because* the little girl isn't." I shrug. "I haven't decided for sure."

Mayumi sighs. "That's very sad. Everyone sad today, I think." She doesn't take her eyes away from the canvas. "My daughter leave for college soon. Both our children will be far away. Hiroshi is hurting inside"—she presses her hand to her chest—"because I think he will be too lonely without anyone around."

"He has you," I point out.

Her laugh is pretty. "Yes, but it's not the same. We have our work to keep busy. Hiroshi likes being a father. He likes to teach. Some people need to be heard. To be appreciated."

"People appreciate him all over the country. He literally has fans all over the place."

"I tell him that too, sometimes." Mayumi hums. "But it's not the same. I think it's because he did not have good relationship with his father. He makes up for it with his own children."

I never thought of Hiroshi as someone still seeking approval or acceptance. He's so comfortable in his own skin and confident in his art—he's the opposite of me. Is it possible we have such a big part of us in common?

I hope when I'm Hiroshi's age I'm not still suffering from my mother's disinterest in me. I'm deeply afraid I'll never be free of the hurt, or the rejection, or the indifference.

"You know . . ." Mayumi's hazel eyes close in on mine. "We need someone to replace Akane in café." She looks around. "Hiroshi hoped she go to college nearby and stay in studio. We were going to make bedroom." She points to the back of the room.

We stare at each other for a while. I can't explain how, but I know what she's thinking. I know what she wants to suggest.

Oh my God, please ask.

"Would you consider working in café full-time? You could stay in studio as part of arrangement. We work your schedule around classes too, if you like."

Oh my God, *she asked!*

My eyes are wide. I can feel them expanding out of my face. "Are you serious?" *Yes. Say yes, Kiko.* "Would Hiroshi mind?" *Why am I giving her the opportunity to change her mind? What is wrong with me?*

"I discuss with him later, but I do not see any problem with it. He sees something in you. Maybe something he wished he had seen in our daughters too, but they are not artists. Think about it, yes?"

I don't have to. The answer is yes.

I nod like my head is about to fall off. "I will."

She touches my shoulder and scrunches her eyes like we're sharing good news together.

I forget to drink my tea until the room turns it cold.

I can't concentrate on painting. I'm too busy dancing.

CHAPTER FIFTY

hat's ridiculous." Jamie can't believe my news. He looks almost as stunned as I feel.

"But not in a bad way, right? In a good way?" I press. I feel like I'm going to explode all over the room into a trillion tiny pieces of pure joy.

"In an *amazing* way," he clarifies. "Wait. Does this mean you're staying in California?"

The laughter erupting from my throat sounds so euphoric I don't recognize it as mine. "I think so. I mean, I haven't gotten accepted into Brightwood yet, but I'd have a job. And a place to sleep." Delirium envelops my mind. I'd be independent. I'd have my own life.

In California.

With Jamie.

He can't stop shaking his head and smiling.

"I mean, Hiroshi still might say no, so I probably shouldn't get too excited."

"He's not going to say no," Jamie interjects. "Are you kidding? I think that guy wants to adopt you."

I roll my eyes. "*That's* ridiculous." Not that I would have any objections to Hiroshi and Mayumi adopting me, if it weren't such a completely ridiculous thought.

Still, working at their café and remaining a part of their lives is more than good enough. It's a dream.

Suddenly Jamie's arms are wrapped around me. His mouth is pressed into my hair, and I can feel the warmth of his breath. It makes my skin tingle and my stomach flutter.

"God, I've honestly been so bummed out thinking about you leaving." More breathing. More tingling.

I press my hands just below his shoulder blades and squeeze him close. It feels incredible, like us hugging is the last piece of the puzzle before the picture is complete.

When he pulls his face in front of mine, his eyes dart back and forth. "Look, I know I should have told you this a while ago, but I honestly haven't been able to find the right—"

My phone rings.

Worst. Timing. Ever.

I want to ignore it—I try to, staring back into the two luminescent blue eyes in front of me. But Jamie clamps his mouth shut and glances at my bag.

I pull away, but not because I want to. I find the brightly lit screen—it's Hiroshi.

Sorry, I mouth to Jamie. It might be about the job. Maybe he's calling to say his wife was wrong to offer such an over-the-top opportunity. Maybe he wants to tell me I can't come back to finish my painting.

"Hello?" My voice trembles into the phone.

He doesn't take it back. He tells me he thinks it's a phenomenal idea and that he only wishes he had thought of it himself. He even suggests we could keep painting together.

I feel like I've somehow stepped into another dimension where only good things happen to me. How is this even possible?

All the while Jamie watches me from the edge of his bed, grinning with excitement and giddiness that I'm sure nobody else in the world could ever understand.

Only Jamie knows how much this means to me.

After the phone call, I ask Jamie what he was going to say.

He waves his hand at me like it's not a big deal. "Don't worry about it. I'll tell you some other time."

"Are you sure?" My heart thumps. I wonder if he was going to tell me how he feels about me. Maybe he was going to say he doesn't want to "just be friends" anymore. It would be a good idea, because I'm pretty sure I've changed my mind.

Who cares if Jamie could destroy me with just his fingertip? I love him. I've always loved him. And this is literally the best day of my life. I might as well top it off by admitting what I'm certain Jamie already knows.

I've had feelings for him for most of my life. I want to stay in California so I can be close to him. And I really, really want him to kiss me.

It's hard to hide my disappointment when Jamie nods. "Yeah,

I'm sure. It can wait. Right now we need to be celebrating."

"Okay," I say in a breathy sigh. "But first I need to call Emery."

Brandon and Elouise make homemade macaroni and cheese for dinner. Afterward Jamie and I go to the movies. And after that we go to a party on the beach.

What is my life right now? I feel like I'm experiencing what it's like to be someone else. It's intoxicating.

The sand is still warm even though the sun has completely disappeared. It's lit up by a small bonfire and the headlights of a few trucks. I don't know anyone here, but Jamie knows plenty of them. I still feel like I'm having a panic attack every time someone new comes to talk to me, but it feels better with Jamie's hand locked onto mine. He's like my IV, but instead of blood he's giving me strength.

Someone starts up a small grill with hot dogs and burgers. The smell makes my mouth water, even though I haven't eaten meat in years.

Jamie thinks it's hilarious. "See, you're going against natural instinct. We were meant to eat meat."

I scrunch my nose. "There is nothing natural about that hot dog."

"If you were starving and somebody gave you the choice of one kind of meat to save yourself, what would you pick?" The fire flickers in his eyes like he's magic.

"Bacon. Super crispy bacon. Like, almost burnt."

He tilts his head back like he's laughing at the stars.

"If someone told you every type of meat was going to be taken away from your diet except one, what would you keep?"

"Chicken, definitely. You can make so many different kinds of chicken. It would never be boring." He shrugs. "Coconut chicken, fried chicken, chicken katsu . . ."

"God, you're making my choice look so bad. I'm starving and I go with the meat that will probably give me a heart attack and kill me anyway."

He points to his head. "Practicality is one of my things."

"Mm-hmm. Of course it is."

He taps his shoe against mine. I nudge him back with my hand on his knee.

Next to my leg, my phone rings from inside my bag.

"Aren't you popular today," Jamie says.

"I know. Nobody ever calls me this much. Sometimes I put fake reminders on my phone just so it will ring."

I look at the screen—it's Mom.

Leaving Jamie and the bonfire behind me, I venture quickly toward the darkened sand.

"Hello?"

"Why didn't you call me back? I said to call." Mom sounds irritated.

"Sorry, I was busy today."

"Oh. Well, I was waiting for you to call."

WHAT I WANT TO SAY:

"You have never waited for me to call in the history of my

life. You're only saying that because you can somehow tell I'm happy without you."

WHAT I ACTUALLY SAY:
"Well, I'm sorry. I didn't know you were waiting."

She sighs. "I don't know if you heard, but I got in a huge fight with Shoji today."

I frown. "Where would I have heard that from?"

"I don't know. I thought maybe somebody would have told you."

"Mom, people don't spend their time talking about what's going on in your life. Not everything is about you." Oh my God, did I just say that out loud? I think I did. I'm sure I did.

She laughs. "Somebody is in a bad mood today."

"No, actually I'm in a really good mood." Or was. It's rapidly changing.

"Why? What happened?" She pauses. "Did you get into art school or something?" She sounds more wary than excited.

"No. It's not that. I'm still waiting for a reply." I suck my breath in. Gut instinct tells me I should keep my pending job opportunity to myself. If Mom gets ahold of it, she will destroy it with her negative Mom-hammer and spray me with venom in the process.

"Well?" I can hear her waiting. Thinking. Plotting.

I know I'm an idiot before I even open my mouth. "I got a job, and a place to stay. That artist I was telling you about is going to let me stay in his studio as long as I work at their café. It means I can stay in California and work while I go to school."

It's remarkable how little time passes before she starts speaking again. It almost feels like she's had a response prepared for this very scenario.

"That sounds suspicious to me. I hope you're using your brain and not living in the clouds. This sounds like something out of your fantasy world." She doesn't mean it as a compliment.

I swallow. My chest tightens. "They're really nice people. I think they care about me."

"I don't buy that. I think I'm going to need to talk to these people and find out what they're after."

My face gets hot. "You're not talking to them. This is *my* life."

"You're still seventeen."

"For, like, two more weeks!"

"You think you're so grown-up now that you're going to turn eighteen? Because you've been in California for a couple of weeks? Or because some guy takes photos of you? Does that make you feel important?"

The spinning in my brain is making me feel faint. "What are you even talking about?"

"I saw that picture in your room. Does Jamie take photos of you?"

"What does that have to do with anything?"

"I know what it feels like to have someone take nice photos of you. It feels nice for someone to think you're pretty. But I don't want you to feed off the attention—it could turn you into someone very self-absorbed."

My mouth is open and my eyes are shut tight. I'm trying to

concentrate on my breathing over the crashing waves near my feet, but it's too hard. Mom didn't use a hammer—she threw a grenade.

"How do you do this?" I ask quietly, tearfully. "How do you make everything ugly?"

"I'm just trying to get you to see things for the way they are."

"Which is what, exactly? That Jamie is only nice to me because he's using me? Or that people in general are only nice to me because they're using me?"

"I don't want you to be naive. What kind of a mother would I be if I didn't try to teach my daughter about the world?"

I don't respond because I'm too busy crying into the darkness, away from the fire and laughter.

She sighs into the phone. "Look, I have to go to bed. I've got work in the morning. I love you, okay? Let me know when you're coming home."

The phone clicks.

I don't have time to wipe my tears, or control my breathing, or pull my phone away from my ear.

Jamie's hand presses against my lower back, and he steps in front of me so I don't have to face the crowd in the background.

"What happened?"

Shaking my head back and forth, I sputter, "It's just my mom. It's nothing new."

His brow narrows with anger. "I hate that woman."

My inhales are uneven. "What? Why?"

"Because—" He stops himself. "She doesn't get to do this to you."

I'm frowning. I never realized Jamie was so aware of the issues I have with my mother. Maybe he's just paying attention, or maybe he remembers she was this way even when I was younger.

"No." He takes my face in his hands. "I won't let her ruin today for you. I won't."

Jamie presses his lips against mine so desperately that I don't have time to take a breath, and I end up exhaling into his mouth. He pulls away just an inch—just enough for the air to move between us. Our breathing is so fast it sounds like we've been running for miles. I close my hands over his wrists, his palms still cupped under my jaw.

He swallows. I can hear it. And he kisses me again, this time softer, but with the same hunger as before.

With our faces pressed closely together, I can smell his skin. It's so much like the ocean, but warmer, like it's mixed with toasted sugar. I feel his hands drift away from my face—one finds my hand, and the other closes against my lower back. He pulls our connected fists between our hearts, and it feels like we're dancing, even though I'm melting too fast to move.

I don't feel human. I feel like a red firework on the Fourth of July, shrieking into the air and flinging itself in every direction possible.

I close my eyes and let his lips take away my thoughts.

CHAPTER FIFTY-ONE

We stay on our own side of the beach, like we've drawn a line in the sand between the party and us. Nobody bothers us—we're not the only couple kissing beneath the stars, but I'm sure we are the only ones who've wanted this for almost a decade.

Jamie pulls my head against his shoulder and kisses my forehead. We're sitting in front of the water, too far away to feel the waves but close enough that it feels like we're all that's left in the world.

"I'm so happy I could cry," he announces proudly.

I giggle next to him, my hand attached to his leg like I'm afraid to let go. Part of me still worries this is all too good to be true.

"You have no idea how long I've wanted to do that for." He rests his chin on my head.

"Actually, I think I do," I admit. "I didn't keep your Batman key chain because I thought you'd make a good pen pal."

"Just think of all the time we wasted while you were deciding if you wanted to be just friends or not." I can feel him shaking his head above mine. "We could have been doing this weeks ago."

I close my eyes. "It wouldn't have been right weeks ago." I wasn't ready then.

He breaks away from our hug so he has room to kiss me again. He doesn't stop for a long time.

When we pull our faces apart, the beach is empty and it's just the two of us.

Jamie runs his finger around the sand, making figure eights and messy zigzags. He's gone serious.

"What is it?" I'm afraid of what he's going to say.

When he looks at me, his eyes are so pure and brilliant I think they're made of glass. "What happened with your uncle?"

I swallow. It isn't his eyes that are made of glass. It's my soul, and it feels like it's been shattered to pieces so many times I don't know how to fix it anymore.

"I'm sorry. I know you don't want to talk about it, but I'm thinking the worst. God, if it's the worst, please tell me, because I will literally kill him."

I catch my breath and laugh a little. "I would never let you go to jail for me."

"I wouldn't get caught. I've been binge watching cop shows with my dad—there are ways."

I shake my head. "It's not the worst." I think about what Mom said. "It's probably not even that big of a deal. Maybe I just wanted my mom to care more than she did."

He's quiet, waiting for me to continue.

The sand is so warm beneath me, and the ocean and salt spray and plum-colored breeze is so calming, that I tell him the story about my uncle. I tell him everything.

"When I was seven, I woke up to my uncle sitting at the bottom of my bed in the middle of the night. He had his hand around my ankle and—I don't know—I guess he was massaging my leg and foot or something, I don't really know. But the whole bed was shaking. I remember opening my eyes and seeing my stuffed rabbit next to me, and her ears were flopping up and down like someone was bouncing on the mattress. He was making these noises." My face turns red, but I keep going. "They sounded like he was groaning. I was so embarrassed and confused; I closed my eyes and pretended I was still asleep so he wouldn't know that I had heard him. After a while—I don't know how long because at the time it felt like hours—he stood up, watched me for a while—I could still hear him breathing next to me—and left."

If a meteor crashed into the ocean and caused a tsunami, I don't think either of us would even notice. We're too still, too silent.

"It happened a few times. I can't remember how many. I always pretended to be asleep." I meet Jamie's eyes. "That's all. That's the whole story."

He stares back at me. I can't tell if it's confusion plastered all over his face or something else. He's so quiet. And still.

"It's not that big of a deal, I guess," I say automatically. I don't know why it comes out of my mouth. I just feel an overpowering need to ease Jamie's discomfort, whatever it is.

"Not that big of a deal?" he repeats in alarm. "Your uncle groped your leg while you were asleep. While he . . . jerked himself off. That's fucking terrible."

The word startles me. I've never heard Jamie swear before. I've never seen him look so angry either.

I've also never heard what happened to me come out of someone else's mouth. It sounds so blunt. So black-and-white.

"And you told your mom? And she didn't call the cops or anything?"

I shake my head. "It took me a while to tell her. A few months, maybe. I can't remember for sure. She didn't really say anything at first. She kind of thought about it by herself, I guess. But afterward she told me that she thinks all boys are perverts. And after that she never talked about it again."

"Oh my God," Jamie says stiffly. His jaw is clenched.

I shrug. "I don't know if she could have called the cops anyway. I mean, I don't know if what he did even means anything. If it even has a name."

"Are you kidding? That's sexual abuse." He pauses. "Or something. I don't know what you'd call it either, I guess. But it's wrong. And you shouldn't sugarcoat it just because your mom thinks you should."

I flinch. "I'm not sugarcoating it," I say quietly. "I don't like talking about it."

His face softens. "I'm sorry. I didn't mean to say it like that. It's messed up that it happened to you, and that your mom—" He pauses, shaking his head again. "I'm just sorry."

He reaches his hand out to touch my wrist, and my skin comes alive.

I place my hand over his. "You don't owe me an apology. But thanks for listening. It's kind of weird saying that story out loud."

"You can tell me anything, you know."

"Yes. I know."

I draw an infinity symbol in the sand. Jamie says that's how long he wants to kiss me for.

CHAPTER FIFTY-TWO

Jamie and I kiss a lot. Like, *a lot* a lot. His parents catch us a few times on the balcony, but they never say anything. They pretend it's completely normal.

It *feels* completely normal.

I was wrong before about the hugging and the puzzle pieces. *This* is the last puzzle piece—kissing Jamie makes my life feel whole.

Hiroshi invites us both to dinner. He and Mayumi are throwing a going-away party for Akane before she heads off to university.

We show up to a restaurant that is so close to the ocean that when I look out the window it feels like I'm going to fall onto the sand.

The whole restaurant is rented out for the party, and almost every person in the room is a relative of the Matsumoto family. When Akane sees us, she gives us both a quick hug. She's wearing a yellow sleeveless pantsuit with flowers winding up one of the legs. Around her neck is a white choker with a silver charm hanging from the middle.

"Thanks so much for coming," she says. "Dad's back in the kitchen, hovering."

Rei falls into the empty space next to her, raising her perfect eyebrows in two arches. "Well, it's about time." She tilts her nose toward our hands, comfortably clasped together and not wanting to let go.

I bite my lip to keep from smiling too wide.

Jamie beams. "You're telling me."

We laugh, and it feels so easy and euphoric and pure that I want to bounce off the walls like my entire body is made of springs.

Mayumi is perched next to one of the windows. When she sees us, she waves her hands frantically, motioning for us to come closer.

At the center of a small table is a wooden post at least two feet high with strings dangling from the top like a tree. Most of the strings are threaded through long rows of paper cranes, all different colors and hiding their own secret messages.

Mayumi pulls me toward her, handing me a black pen. "You have to make wish. Origami Wishing Tree is Matsumoto tradition."

"What do I do?" I ask, mesmerized by the dangling birds.

She hands Jamie a pen too, and points to the table. A mess of colorful bits of paper sits directly below the tree. "You write wish and hang from tree." She smiles. "You hear of Japanese legend, 'Thousand Origami Cranes'?" When we shake our heads, she continues. "It's good luck. Fold one thousand origami cranes and wish come true. But"—she chuckles—"we never reach one thousand. Our tradition is different. Everyone gets to make wish."

I look at Jamie, but he's already busy writing his wish down, covering his paper with a cupped hand and making a goofy face at me when he catches me looking.

It doesn't take me long to think of something to write. *I wish I can be this happy for the rest of my life.* When I'm finished, I press the paper to my chest, just to make sure Jamie doesn't peek.

Mayumi shows us how to fold them. I make a mistake and mine ends up with a slight bend in the wing. Jamie notices and bends his wing on purpose. He says it's so ours can match.

We string them onto the tree, our blue and orange birds, and Jamie kisses me on the side of the head.

I feel like I'm the one made out of paper.

We sit at the longest table in the world. There seems to be a hundred bowls of things I've never heard of before—katsudon and oyakodon and tempura and yaki soba—with plates of sushi and grilled fish and *so much rice.* Everyone seems to help themselves, piling food in their individual bowls and going back for seconds as often as they want.

Akane sits on my left, pointing out which dishes are vegetarian friendly and which aren't, and Jamie sits on my right, literally trying everything. Their family and friends treat us like we belong just as much as they do. They smile and tell stories and pay attention to everyone in the room. It's welcoming, and kind, and I don't want it to end.

I think this is what acceptance feels like.

At the end of the meal there's mochi and taiyaki and kakigōri, and after that Hiroshi announces they're going to play a game called Tora Tora Tora. Everyone finds a seat at the other side of the restaurant. A paper screen is set up, splitting the front of the room right down the middle, surrounded by a collection of round tables and chairs.

Everyone begins taking turns going up, two at a time, each behind alternate sides of the screen, singing a song in Japanese and clapping while everyone in the audience sings along with them. At the end of the song they step forward, revealing themselves to their opponent while acting out a pose. Whoever loses takes a drink, laughing along with the rest of the people in the room.

Rei leans in to us, raising her voice over the growing noise. "It's like charades meets rock, paper, scissors," she says. "It's basically Uncle Kenji's way of getting everyone drunk."

Jamie laughs. "What are they singing about?"

"Honestly? I have no idea." She points to the two people playing—Mayumi and one of Rei's cousins—and nods. "All you have to know is that old lady beats samurai, samurai beats tiger, and tiger beats old lady."

I look up. Mayumi is crawling on the floor and scratching her fingers at the air. Rei's cousin is pretending to hobble with a cane. When they spot each other, Mayumi raises her hands in the air and squeals in triumph.

And then she catches my gaze.

"Come, Kiko! You try." She flicks her hands toward her chest, like she's trying to coax me to safety.

But a stage is not safety. A stage is terrifying.

I stiffen, shaking my head quickly.

Jamie's breath tickles my ear. "I'll go up with you. It could be fun."

Everyone is staring, still laughing from Mayumi's win, waiting for me to make my way to the stage.

But I don't move. It's too many people. Too many eyes.

Before I have time to think, Akane grabs my hands and yanks me up, dragging me through the space between the tables and placing me at one side of the paper screen before ducking behind the other.

Everyone starts clapping and singing before I have time to breathe.

I feel like someone's just set my body on fire, but I start clapping because Mayumi is urging me along in front of her, and at this point I'll do anything just to blend in.

I hear the song coming to an end. I hold my hands in front of me like I'm carrying the samurai spear some of the others held. And I take a step forward.

Akane is crawling like a tiger, laughing hysterically.

Everyone claps, and somehow I can hear them over the beating in my chest.

Akane stands up, pointing to the alcohol. "Loser gets a drink, right?"

Mayumi swats her hand away. "No chance." With a wink, she adds, "I drink for you."

Everyone laughs even harder. They're not paying attention to my fidgeting or my awkwardness. They're not analyzing me the way Mom would.

I breathe.

When I find my seat again, Jamie is smiling. "I had a feeling you'd pick the samurai."

"Why is that?" I ask.

"Because"—he shrugs—"you're the strongest person I know."

I rest my head on his shoulder.

When Hiroshi and one of his cousins take their turn, Hiroshi pretends to have a cane and his cousin holds an imaginary spear. Hiroshi acts like he's whacking his cousin on the head, and everyone laughs.

When Jamie goes up with Mayumi's mother, Jamie pretends to be a tiger and she pretends to be an old lady. When she sees Jamie, she starts to pet his head and then gives him a kiss on the cheek. Everyone laughs even harder.

Two more family members go up. One pretends to be a tiger and jumps straight through the paper screen, tackling his opponent without bothering to see what he was posing as.

I'm laughing so hard there are tears in my eyes.

Later in the evening, Hiroshi asks for the room's attention. He wants to give a speech. His eyes pool with water before he even says a word, and when Mayumi takes hold of his hand, he doesn't let go.

"To my daughter, Akane: You are kind, generous, and so determined. You have the strength of the ocean and the transparency of glass. You are honest. You love without stipulation. You chase your dreams, and you don't apologize for living your life the way you want to. You are an inspiration. You aren't afraid to stare life in the eyes and demand a break sometimes. You deserve everything good in this world. You are a third of my heart. And like Amaterasu, you shine as bright as the sun." He clears his throat, wiping his cheeks with his fingertips. "Thank you for giving us the honor of being your parents. We love you so very much."

Everyone claps. Everyone except me.

Because I'm not paying attention to the clapping, or Akane hugging her parents, or the fact that Jamie is squeezing my hand so hard I think it might crumble to ash.

I'm too busy crying myself, thinking of how it must feel to be loved so wholly, so unconditionally.

The tears burn my eyes and blur my vision, and by the time I manage to wipe them all away with the backs of my hands, one of Akane's uncles is making jokes to Hiroshi across the table and everyone but me seems to have moved on from the speech altogether.

"I'll be right back," I whisper to Jamie, slipping out of my seat and finding one of the doors to the balcony.

I take in the fresh air, hoping the breeze will help dry my tears. I don't know why I'm so emotional. I mean, it's a speech for Akane, not me. And I'm not family, or even a *close* friend, really.

But his words—and the place they come from—speak to everything deep inside me.

I know not every family is the same. We all have different

personalities and names. Different colors in a box of crayons.
Different shades in a box of graphites. And maybe love looks
different to different people, the same way beauty looks different.

But the kind of love I need isn't the kind I have. I guess I'm still
trying to find a way to be okay with that.

"I wonder if this is going to be a habit," Hiroshi says from
behind me. "Having serious conversations on balconies while
looking out at the ocean." He holds up his hands like he's framing
a portrait around me.

I laugh and wipe my face one more time to make sure the tears
are all gone. "Sorry. I'm just being weird."

"No. You're being human," he says.

"That was a really nice speech," I say.

Hiroshi looks out at the water, his hands folded behind him.
He's wearing another one of his loose-fitting tunics, this one navy
blue, with black bottoms. His hair is pulled back in a tight bun,
and his cheeks seem to have caught a little more sun than usual.

"I see you, you know. The way you paint with such love. And
you always stare back at the painting as if you aren't sure you're
truly worthy"—he hesitates—"of being loved back."

I push my tongue against my cheek, fighting the tears that are
trying so hard to give me away.

Hiroshi places his hand on my shoulder. "You *are*, Kiko. And
the sooner you accept it, the easier it will be to accept what you
cannot change."

I nod too many times, because I'm too shaky to do anything
else.

He nods back, just once, and disappears back into the restaurant.

It takes me a while to leave the ocean. It's dark outside, and if I curl my hands around my eyes like binoculars, all I'd be able to see is stars and sky and sea. And it feels like a safe place to be, where nobody else can see or hear me.

Akane has a sun goddess to remind her to be strong. Maybe my inspiration comes from a hundred stars—a hundred suns—all reminding me that I'm not alone.

I turn around and look through the window. Jamie is standing with Rei and her friends, blending in like he always does. He doesn't see I'm watching him, and I'm glad.

I think it's better if he doesn't know he's one of the stars. I think it's better if I don't admit it out loud.

Jamie loving me would make my mother not loving me hurt so much less.

I don't want to scare him away. I don't want to risk losing him. *I don't want to lose him.*

And maybe I should be worried about how much that would destroy me, but right now all I want to do is kiss him.

When I find him inside, that's exactly what I do.

I draw fire and water forgetting all the rules and morphing into something new.

CHAPTER FIFTY-THREE

I finish my painting. Hiroshi calls it "exquisite." Jamie takes a photograph of it because he says he can't stop looking at it.

I'm in such a good mood after dinner that when Mom calls I forget all about our conversation from last night.

By the sound of her voice, she's forgotten it too.

She's happy on the phone. It's like she's treating me the way she treats people who don't really know her—like she's a nice person.

I fall for it because my guard is down and because—let's face it—I *always* fall for it. I tell her about the party—but not the kissing—and about finishing my painting and how great it turned out.

"It sounds like you're having such a good time over there." She pauses. I can practically hear the *ticktock* of her brain. "Has Elouise asked about our family at all?"

I make a face even though my mother can't see it. "No. Why would she?"

She answers too quickly. "Oh, no reason. We used to be friends, that's all. I thought she might be interested in our lives."

"Well, she didn't ask anything." I want to talk about something else. I don't like where this is going. "Did Shoji get his new belt yet?"

Mom's silent.

"Umm, hello? Mom? Are you still there?"

"Yeah, I'm here." I know I can't see her, but I swear to God she's grinding her teeth right now. I can feel it—she's about to explode and I have no idea why.

I need to hang up. It's the only way to avoid whatever is coming. "It's getting pretty late actually. I'm going to go to bed."

"What's she been saying about me? I know she said something." Her words are sharp and quick.

A heavy, disheartened sigh escapes from me. Of course the niceness wouldn't last. "Nothing, Mom. Why do you always think people are talking about you?"

"Because people *always* talk about me. I have amazing intuition, and right now my ears are ringing." She sounds so proud of her imaginary superpower.

"Well, she wasn't." I really, really want to get off the phone. I was in such a good mood before when—

"I don't believe you. This is why I don't trust you." Her words rip through the phone like paper cranes attacking my face until I'm covered in stinging cuts.

"What do you mean you don't trust me?" I say from a thousand miles away.

"You're always trying to make people think bad of me."

"Seriously, what are you talking about right now?"

"I don't know; I just have a feeling."

I wish I could crush the phone in my hand until it becomes dust. "A feeling based off what, Mom? You can't just tell someone you don't trust them and not give them a reason."

"I don't need a reason. I already told you, I have a feeling."

WHAT I WANT TO SAY:
"WHY ARE YOU LIKE THIS?"

WHAT I ACTUALLY SAY:
"Well, you're wrong. I don't try to make anyone think bad of you. I don't even talk about you."

She scoffs into the phone. "You mean to tell me you don't talk about me to Jamie?"

"I talk about *me* to Jamie, and maybe how I feel about the way you treat me, but not about *you*."

"That is talking about me. I don't want Jamie knowing my personal business."

"It's *my* personal business!"

"Family issues should stay private," she snaps.

"They aren't family issues! And sometimes I just need someone to talk to. It's not like you ever listen to anything I say."

"Oh, here we go again. You always act like you have all these emotional problems. It's pathetic. Do you think it's cool? Is that why you act this way?"

I'm crying again. God, I wish I could seal up my tear ducts just so I could stop letting my mother hear me crying.

At some point we both hang up the phone.

The next day she calls again. Jamie suggests I change my phone number.

Mom doesn't apologize about yesterday, but she does ask a lot of questions about Jamie. In the middle of the conversation I leave his room because I'm embarrassed he's going to find out what my mom is talking about.

"Do you think you're in love?"

"Well. Yeah." My heart reacts quicker than my brain—because if my brain were faster, I would know better than to tell Mom anything this personal. It's like giving her the exact recipe to poison me in the most painful way possible.

"How do you know? I mean, what does being 'in love' even mean?"

"I can just tell, I guess. I'm happy around him. And I feel like myself. And I feel like I love him unconditionally, and he feels the same way back." *Yup. This is a terrible idea*, Brain says. *Retreat. Retreat.*

"What is unconditional love?"

"Loving someone for no reason other than that you just love them, I guess. Like you'd love them even if they got gray hair and wrinkles or didn't like the same movies as you or thought *Star Wars* was stupid."

She's quiet for a minute. "Yeah, I'm not sure I believe in that.

I mean, I love you guys because you're my kids, but unconditionally? No, I don't know what that even means."

Sometimes Mom can be insightful without even realizing it.

My mother is incapable of real love. It explains so much.

The next time Mom calls, she's shouting into the phone and I can't understand what she's saying. It's only after I tell her to calm down that I realize she's crying hysterically.

I mouth to Jamie that she's crying, and he rolls his eyes and shakes his head. I start to make a joke about changing my number, when Mom's voice cuts so roughly into the phone that I feel like I've been stabbed with a rusty, jagged blade.

"Shoji is in the hospital. He tried to kill himself."

I don't draw. I spend all night trying to get ahold of Shoji, but nobody will let me talk to him.

CHAPTER FIFTY-FOUR

Jamie brings pancakes to the guest room. It's almost nine in the morning, but I've been up crying since five. Jamie knows this because he spent the whole night lying next to me, telling me everything was going to be okay.

I push myself up. I feel groggy. "Thanks."

He puts the tray in my lap and sits next to me. "I can drive back with you, if you want."

It takes a lot of effort to cut off a bite of pancake—there's no strength left in my arm. "You don't have to do that. I think I just need to be with my brother."

I'm struggling to comprehend it. Shoji didn't seem particularly happy, but none of us did. It never occurred to me that Shoji was dealing with everything worse than me—I was always the problem. I was always the one in trouble for stirring the pot of our screwed-up family.

Shoji was the quiet one. The one who seemed to be able to ignore everything the best.

I had no idea how much he was hurting.

I'm the worst sister in the world.

Mom insists she doesn't know why he did it, even though Shoji begged the doctors and Dad not to let her see him.

In the afternoon, Mom calls to say she needs me to come home tomorrow. Even though I was already planning to go home, and even though I feel like this should be my choice and not hers, I'm too tired to fight with her.

She's not crying anymore, but she's somehow found more energy through the night. "Your dad is trying to tell me Shoji is going to live with him. Can you believe how ridiculous this is getting?"

I flinch at her choice of words. "I think everyone needs to do what's best for Shoji right now."

"The best thing for him is to be with his mother. Not around two newborns and a father he barely sees," she says testily.

"Maybe he asked to stay with Dad."

"Just because you hate me doesn't mean everyone else does," she snaps.

"I can't do this today," I growl into the phone. I've barely slept. My little brother is hurting. My dad is just trying to do what's best. Why does my mom have to overcomplicate everything?

"I'm in pain too, you know," she argues. "You don't have kids. You don't know how it feels to have one of your children hurt themselves. Nobody ever cares how I feel. This is hard on me, too."

"I have to go. I'll see you in a couple of days." I hang up before she can infect my mind with anything else.

The air on the balcony is heavy, making it harder to breathe than usual.

Or maybe it's just me. I'm having a hard time keeping my eyes open. I want to get to Shoji, to ask him if he's okay.

Oh my God, he's not okay, is he? He tried to kill himself.

Elouise taps on the glass door. "Jamie and Brandon went to get the groceries. They didn't want to interrupt your phone call." She's holding a wineglass in one hand and a book in the other. "Any news?"

I tuck my hair behind my ear. "I think he's okay. He's been asking to live with my dad, I think, so he's well enough to talk to people."

Frustration flickers in her eyes. "I'm sure your father will make sure he's fine. Do you know when you're going back?"

"Tomorrow." I expect to see relief in her eyes, but I don't. She looks a little sad.

"I can imagine this isn't the way you wanted to say good-bye, but at least you'll be back soon." She takes a sip of her wine and sits down in one of the chairs.

Sickness fills my stomach. "I can't leave Shoji all by himself."

She blinks in surprise. "You're not coming back?"

"I don't know. How can I? He's only staying with Dad because he hates Mom, but what happens when he realizes Dad abandoned us a long time ago too?" I don't mean to say it, but the words are pouring out of me like they're foaming right from the edge of my mouth. "Dad was never around. Not after his affair. Maybe if he was, Shoji could have had someone else to talk to. Maybe all of us wouldn't have been left to deal with Mom on our own. He replaced us with a new family. How's Shoji going to feel when he realizes he doesn't belong there? He needs a real family. He needs a better sister." I can't stop crying. I feel like I've failed him.

Elouise looks like she's being suffocated by something too heavy for her to push away. It draws me in—a secret that she wants ripped off for good.

"What is it?" I wipe my eyes with my sleeve.

"Your dad didn't have the affair, honey. It was Brandon with—" She doesn't want to say it. Not out loud, and not to me. But maybe the truth was too heavy for too long.

Everything goes still. The air presses down on me and I can't move.

"It was Mom." My voice is hollow. *I'm* hollow. Mom had the affair. With Jamie's *dad*.

The wineglass trembles in Elouise's grip. "I shouldn't have told you that. I'm sorry. You were upset. I thought it would make you feel better about your dad, but . . ." She shakes her head and gulps down the rest of her wine.

Something inside me dies. I think it might have been the dream. "Did Jamie know?"

She doesn't have to say a word—her eyes already give away the answer.

He knew. He knew the whole time.

I rip out every sketch I ever drew that reminds me of Jamie. Hiroshi thought they were honest, but they're not. They can't be. Because Jamie lied to me.

CHAPTER FIFTY-FIVE

Jamie reaches for me, but I push his hands away. If he touches me, if I feel his skin and remember how gentle and soft his lips are on mine, I'll crash into his arms and never reemerge.

It takes everything inside me to be strong.

"I'm sorry, Kiko. I didn't know how to tell you. I tried, but—"

"—but you didn't." The skin under my eyes boils with tears. "You knew my mom cheated. You knew she broke up my family, and you never told me."

His hands extend toward me, but I step backward in to his desk.

"You don't get it." Tears burst from my eyes. "All this time, I thought it was *my* fault. I thought my parents split up because of"—I try to push Uncle Max from my memories—"because of me. I thought I was the reason they were fighting. Because of what I told my mom."

Jamie's hands are open. "I'm so sorry." His face is lost in the blur.

"But now I know they split up because my mom cheated. And you knew, because your parents moved to get away from her and try to mend their family. *Your* family." I'm choking on my tears. "I needed you, Jamie. You were my friend, and you were the person who knew the truth. You didn't write back. You didn't come to see me when you visited. And why? Because you didn't want to tell me the truth?"

"I didn't know what was happening with your uncle," he says. Clear pools fill his eyes. "I didn't know how much it was going to affect you." He takes a breath. "God, Kiko, I was a kid! I'm not perfect."

"You're not a kid anymore." I bite my lip to stop it from trembling. "You had weeks to tell me the truth."

"You think it was easy for me not to? I desperately wanted to tell you. My family didn't even want me to hang out with you anymore. That's why I couldn't write or visit you. They didn't want to open up old wounds with my mom." He looks away and blinks. "Your mom and my dad almost destroyed two families. Mine is still broken."

"Your parents are still together. You had both of them, regardless of whether they hate each other. And you don't have a brother who tried to commit suicide because his toxic, self-absorbed, emotionally abusive mom pushed him toward it."

Jamie steps closer to me, his face falling back into kindness. "That's good, Kiko. Say what you want to say. Say everything. I'll listen to it, and I won't fight with you. Because I love you, and because I know this is what you need. So tell me you're angry.

Tell me how terrible I've been. Tell me I made the wrong choice. And then, Kiko, forgive me. Because I'm sorry. I'm sorry, and I love you."

He kisses me even though I try to raise my hand to stop him. And then I don't stop him. His lips mold against mine like they're perfectly shaped for each other. He tastes like mint and smells like himself. I want him to hold me forever. I want him to make everything better.

And then I realize this is all wrong.

Because the truth is, I'm not really mad at Jamie. I mean, I'm mad that he lied, but I'm not really mad at *him*.

I'm mad because I need him. I need him to be perfect and strong and to protect me from everything in the world that's terrifying. I need him to hold my hand as I walk through life because it's so much easier than doing it alone.

And needing him is a mistake.

I don't want to need anyone. I want to stand on my own two feet. I want control of my own life and my own emotions. I don't want to be a branch in someone else's life anymore—I want to be the tree on my own.

I want all the strength to come from me. I don't want to depend on anyone for anything ever again.

I pull my face away from Jamie and it literally hurts so much I have to grip the desk to keep from falling over.

I can't hide from the truth anymore. I let Jamie become my crutch. I let him fill all the voids in my life—family, friendship, love—and it hurts so much to know what I need to do now.

Panic is in his eyes. He senses what I'm going to say next.

Because even when we're hurt, we still know each other. We know each other without words.

I say them anyway. "I've spent years trying to forgive myself for ruining my family. I blamed myself for everything—my uncle, my parents, my mom not loving me, and now I even blame myself for Shoji. I don't want to be angry with you, Jamie, but I don't want to be angry at myself anymore either. I need to get rid of the guilt. I need to figure out how to forgive myself. I need to apologize to my brother."

"What are you saying?"

We're both so hollow and cold. What happened to us? How did a single hour change us so much?

WHAT I WANT TO SAY:

"I love you, Jamie, but I don't want to love you this way. I'm broken in too many places and I can't let you be the one to put me back together. If I'm going to survive in this world, I need to learn how to take care of myself first. I need to heal, so that my heart can be whole again. I need time. A lot of time."

WHAT I ACTUALLY SAY:

"I need to go home."

I draw a girl on a plane, leaving her heart on the runway.

CHAPTER FIFTY-SIX

I drive straight to the hospital because I'm not ready to see Mom yet. Not until I talk to Shoji.

The doctors are keeping him under observation, but Dad says he's going to be released soon. He says he already has a lawyer trying to work out the next step in getting custody of Shoji.

The lawyer says the easiest way is for Mom and Dad to work it out between them, amicably.

Dad doesn't think amicably is an option.

Shoji is covered up to his waist in a blue blanket. He doesn't have any tubes or anything sticking out of his arms—not like I thought he would. He's just sitting still, like he's waiting for what to do next. There's not even a book in his hands.

"Did you like California?" he asks sheepishly.

I sit next to him—Dad motions that he's going to wait out in the hall so we can talk.

"You could've called me, Shoji. Before you . . . you know." I try to sound strong, but it comes across as awkward.

"I didn't plan it. It just kind of happened." He rests his head against the pillow, the blacks of his eyes peeking out of his puffy eyelids. "Who called you?"

"Mom." I roll my eyes, and Shoji laughs because he knows what I know.

"Does she know I want to live with Dad?"

"She knows." I drop my hands between my knees. "I'm sorry. I feel like I should have noticed sooner. I'm sorry I wasn't paying attention." Maybe I was too wrapped up in myself. Maybe I'm a starfish too.

It's a thought that makes me want to rip out my insides and replace them with anything else. I don't ever want to be a starfish.

"It's okay. We kind of all ignore each other." He shrugs. "Taro called and said the same thing as you. Maybe we're all the same person, split into three pieces."

I nod quickly to hide the tremble in my jaw. If we are all three broken pieces of the same being, we should have tried to put ourselves back together a long time ago. Maybe we needed each other because being a third of something was never enough.

Maybe we had what the other person needed all along.

Taro doesn't take Mom personally. Shoji knows where he fits into the world. I dream about a new life.

Maybe by splitting into three pieces, we robbed each other of what it felt like to be a full person. If I had Taro's thick skin or Shoji's confidence, I might've fought back a long time ago. I might've realized sooner that it's okay to be different.

And if Shoji had my ability to dream, he might've cared more about his future than ending his pain.

We're no good as broken pieces. We failed as siblings.

I press my arms against my stomach and dig my fingers into my sides. Shoji looks back at me with his dark, familiar eyes. Even when they're filled with pain they're beautiful—why has it taken me so long to notice?

My little brother knew long before I did that our half-Japanese heritage was worth loving. I only wish I could have told him our future was worth loving too.

He asks me to tell him a story that's not about Mom or suicide. I tell him about California, and Hiroshi, and Jamie, and Brightwood. I don't tell him about my painting, because that's too close to Mom, but I do tell him about the job at the café.

"When are you moving?" he asks.

I flatten my lips. "I'm not. I don't want to leave you here with Mom."

"I'm staying with Dad," he says seriously, leaning forward.

I'm not sure I should tell him about the custody and the lawyers and the fight Mom is making about it. I don't think this is the appropriate time for bad news. "Okay. Well, I still don't want to leave you."

Shoji settles. "I don't want you to stay here. It sucks here. I'd much rather you went to California." He thinks. "Besides, if you lived in California, maybe I could come visit you one day."

It's a nice thought, even though it's unlikely to ever become a reality. My brothers and I just don't keep in touch, no matter how good our intentions are.

I nod anyway. "Okay, well, the nurse said I was only supposed to have a few minutes. I guess you need to rest still."

"Okay. Thanks for coming."

I stand up, but he lifts his fingers to stop me.

"Hey, Kiko?"

"Yeah?"

"Do you remember when some of your money went missing?" His face goes white. "It was me. I took it."

It wasn't Uncle Max. It was my brother. My face crumples in surprise, but I try to smooth out the creases before Shoji starts to feel bad. "Why would you do that?"

He shrugs. "I was going to run away." A weak laugh follows. "This was plan B."

I don't join in on his humor. "Well, thanks for telling me."

"I told Dad, too. I thought if he found out later he might not let me live with him." He stares at his hands. "If Mom tries to make me stay with her, will you stick up for me? Even if Dad has to get a lawyer?"

I push a smile onto my face to reassure him. "Of course," I say. I hope it won't come to lawyers. I'm afraid of what I'll have to say out loud if it does.

I draw a skeleton putting itself back together again.

CHAPTER FIFTY-SEVEN

Jamie leaves four voice mails on my phone. He texts sixteen times. Most of them say **Please call me back**. The very last one says **How do I fix this?**

I'm not ready to talk to him. I want to—I want to go back to where we were on the beach, two people finally telling each other how they really feel. But I can't find the beach anymore—there's too much road between us. A road I need to travel on my own.

I don't tell Emery about any of what's happened. She's so busy that it's easy not to. More important, I'm worried I'll go back to using her as a crutch now that I'm not talking to Jamie, and I don't want our friendship to be about her holding me up.

Mom doesn't act like it's been weeks since she's seen me. She just asks questions about Shoji and whether anyone—the doctors, Dad, Serena—has been bad-mouthing her.

I spend a lot of time in my room drawing. It's the easiest way to avoid Mom, since she's now the only other person in the house. I think it's making her weirdly clingy. She even comes up to my room to give me a stack of pages torn out of a fashion magazine.

"I know you always wanted to use makeup," she says enthusiastically. "And you're almost an adult, and I'm sure you're going to do what you want to do. So I thought you could at least look at these to get an idea of what looks good. There's nothing worse than someone putting on makeup the wrong way."

All the pictures are of a certain type of model. Blond, blue-eyed, narrow-chinned, with thin brows.

In other words, they look nothing like me. They look like Mom.

I don't point out to her that she's giving me makeup tips for the completely wrong face shape—I just thank her and push the pages under my bed.

Because blond and blue-eyed and narrow-chinned is what Mom thinks is beautiful, but it's not what everyone thinks is beautiful.

And more important, it's not what I think is beautiful. Not anymore. Not when I've seen all the colors and lines that exist beyond this small town.

Beauty is unique and special and it looks different for every person in the world.

I don't need Mom or her magazines to try to convince me otherwise.

Mom spends a lot of time arguing on the phone with Dad. They haven't talked this much in years. Mom's threatening to fight Dad for custody. She thinks she'll get it.

* * *

I call the bookstore to see if they have any hours for me. I need to start saving for college, and I'm so anxious these days that it's probably better if I stay busy with work. The manager tells me I can start again next week, two days after my birthday. It's something, but, to be honest, I feel like my mind is broken into a hundred tiny pieces, and most of them are still back in California.

Because all I ever think about is Jamie, and I'm supposed to be working on rehabilitating my mental health. I know I want to be stronger. I know I don't want to feel as if I need people to meet my expectations as a mother, friend, boyfriend, or even brother. I want to find self-worth without needing it to come from someone's approval.

I want my first steps into my new life to be ones I take on my own.

But still. It's hard to forget his blue eyes, and the way he's so tall that when he hugs me I fit against his chest, and how he smells like the ocean, and how when we kissed for the first time all I could hear was the water kissing the sand.

I want to call him. I don't.

When Shoji goes home from the hospital with Dad, Mom spends the morning googling lawyers. She doesn't call any of them—she just reads a lot.

Even though she will never admit it out loud, I think she knows Shoji should be with Dad and Serena and the twins. He'll be healthier there. He'll probably be more loved, too.

If she wanted to, she could've stopped Dad from taking him home, but she didn't.

We're all thinking it—we just know better than to say it. Mom is irrational when she thinks you're in any way criticizing her. Admitting Shoji is better off without her is admitting she's not the best mom.

"Do you want coffee?" Mom asks from behind her laptop. She's holding a mug in her hand. She laughs. "Isn't that what everyone in California drinks?"

"You don't need to keep making fun of California. I'm probably not going back anyway." My voice is dry. I haven't slept very well since I've been home. Being here makes me feel constantly on edge.

"Did you and Jamie have a fight?" She blinks at me with intensity.

I shake my head. The last thing I want to do is talk to her about Jamie.

"Until we get Shoji back, it's just us girls. We can talk, you know. About anything."

"Shoji isn't coming back, Mom."

"We'll let a judge decide that."

I'm scowling. "If you take Dad to court, I'll tell the judge everything. I'll tell them about Uncle Max. You'll never get custody."

She sets her mug down. Her eyes twitch. "Where is this coming from? Are you angry with me about something?"

Saliva fills my mouth. It must be my nerves. They make my chest itch too. "Why did you tell me you and Dad split up because he cheated?"

324 AKEMI DAWN BOWMAN

She pulls her hands away from the keyboard and shifts. "I told you he had an affair because that's the truth."

"Before or after you cheated with Jamie's dad?"

Her nostrils flare. "We all make mistakes in our lives. That happened when I was very young. I've already made my peace with it."

"I don't care what your reasons were or whether you regret it or not. I'm asking if you and Dad split up because of him or because of you." *Thump. Thump. Thump.*

"Does it matter?"

"Yes." My hands shake. "Because I thought he had the affair because you were fighting about me, not because you were fighting about you."

"Well, I never told you that."

"But you did." I blink. "Or you implied it anyway. You told me I was always causing problems. You said I was making it hard for you and Dad to get along."

"Because you and Jamie were constantly hanging around each other. It was hurtful."

"How was I supposed to understand that?" I growl. "You never explained it. I thought you had told Dad about Uncle Max. I thought he was angry that he was still living in our house."

Mom shrugs. "I don't know why you thought that. I never even told your dad."

My stomach disintegrates. My blood drains. All that's left is my painful heartbeat. "You didn't tell him?"

"I wasn't going to make an issue out of nothing when my brother needed a place to stay. I've already told you—you were little, it was late, you might have dreamed it." She crosses her arms. "Besides, I asked Max about it at the time, and he swore he had no idea what you were talking about. And it's not like accusing him of things he hasn't done isn't a pattern with you." Her blue eyes go cold. "I know Shoji took the money. Your dad told me."

Something horrible swarms my chest and throat. "I'm not lying about what happened to me."

Mom clicks her tongue against the roof of her mouth. "I'm not saying you're lying. I just think you might be remembering things that didn't happen. And since we're on the subject, I think you owe Max an apology."

"For what?" The veins in my neck feel like they're going to explode.

"I kicked him out of this house because you told me he was stealing," she says.

WHAT I WANT TO SAY:

"You kicked him out of the house because *you* thought he was stealing—you didn't even believe me when I told you!"

WHAT I ACTUALLY SAY:

"I will never apologize to Uncle Max. Never."

"Well." She sighs. "I think that's very immature, Kiko. I've already called him and made things better."

The sides of my head throb. My knees feel weak. "You need therapy."

Mom laughs the most over-the-top, hysterical laugh I've ever heard.

"It's not funny. There is something wrong with you. Who treats their kids this way? There's a reason none of us want to be around you. There's a reason Shoji wants to live with Dad, and why Taro spent the rest of the summer with his friend, and why I want to go to art school thousands of miles away from you." My face burns with frustration. "You are so obsessed with yourself that there isn't any room for anyone else's feelings. You don't care about anything unless it somehow relates back to you."

I start to walk away, intent on leaving her alone in her chair. But something stops me.

Spinning back to face her, my breathing erratic and my voice hoarse, I growl, "And I'm not imagining what happened to me. Your sick brother sexually abused me. I don't care what you think it's called, because that's what it is. Sexual abuse. *I was sexually abused*. Do you get that? And if you were any kind of mother, that would have mattered to you. You wouldn't have tried to justify it or rationalize it away by saying it wasn't rape and therefore isn't as bad—it *was* bad. That's it."

I leave because I don't want to give her the chance to respond.

I draw a dragon breaking free from its grave and finally seeing what its wings and fire are for.

CHAPTER FIFTY-EIGHT

Jamie sends another text: I know you don't want to talk to me, but I just want to know if your brother is okay. I love you and I'm sorry.

I text back: He's fine, thanks. He moved in with my dad.

He doesn't send another reply. Part of me knew not to expect one—I'm the one ignoring him, after all, and he did just want to know about Shoji.

But part of me feels devastated. As if I've taken the silence too far. As if I'm ruining us forever.

I give myself a pep talk in the mirror to remind myself I need to be strong. It won't do any good to cry about Jamie when I'm trying to make it so that the only person who can make me cry is *me*.

And besides, I still need to work on curing myself of Mom.

I find her downstairs in the living room while I'm on my way to get a glass of water. My eyes focus on all the space around her but never directly on her.

To my surprise, she doesn't ignore me.

"Can I talk to you?" Mom looks at me nervously. Her hair is spun in a golden knot on her head, and she's still wearing pajamas. I feel like she might have been waiting for me, which is ridiculous, because when we fight she always pretends I don't exist at least until the afternoon.

"Sure," I reply. Now *I'm* nervous.

I sit down next to her on the couch. She's still holding the remote in her hand, even though she's muted whatever reality TV show she was watching.

"I've been thinking a lot since yesterday," she starts. The smirk starts to form on her face—the one she usually blames on awkwardness—but she tries not to let it take over. "And I think I'm going to talk to someone."

I wait, but she doesn't say anything else. "You mean like a therapist?" My heart is pounding. She's actually going to talk to someone. She actually wants to get better. I can't believe it.

She *listened* to me.

Mom nods. "Yeah, I think I need to."

Something in my stomach spins and spins and I feel light-headed. She took me seriously. She's admitting she needs help. "Mom, that's great. Good for you." My face feels heavy, but I try to hide it because I'm afraid if I show any happiness she'll change her mind.

She nods again, and the smirk starts to grow. I'm too happy to let it bother me.

"I've been reading all this stuff on hypnotherapy and repressed memories, and I really want to find out if something happened to me when I was younger."

The spinning stops. My ears ring. "Wait. What are you talking about?" I thought this was about her narcissism. It's not.

"I mean, how can I know for sure if someone didn't do something to me when I was younger? Like when I was sleeping. *So* many people block those memories out—something horrible could have happened to me when I was a kid and I don't even remember it." Her eyes are wide now and full of something that isn't sadness or humor—it's craziness.

I try to take a breath, but I feel like throwing up. "Are you trying to say you think you were sexually abused when you were a kid?" My voice is so dry I'm sure my words are going to crumble into thousands of tiny, brittle pieces. I try to think logically. I try to be calm.

She shrugs and twists her face like this is a genuine possibility. "I mean, who knows? Maybe a hypnotherapist could find out."

"Do you have any memories at all that are making you think this? Did anything weird happen to you?" I ask through stiff breaths. *Like, I don't know, an uncle sneaking into your room?*

"No," she says pointedly. "But that's what I mean—just because I can't remember anything doesn't mean nothing ever happened. When I was younger, I was very attractive and very naive. I didn't even know there were mean people in the world. Someone could have taken advantage of that."

WHAT I WANT TO SAY:
"Nobody took advantage of you, nobody molested you, and you don't have any repressed memories of your childhood. I'm the child who was hurt, not you. You didn't believe me, but now

I'm supposed to believe that you're worried something 'might' have happened to you, even though you don't have any reason to think that whatsoever? Why are you trying to diminish the horrible thing that happened to me and make it about you?"

WHAT I ACTUALLY SAY:
Exactly that.

I leave her and her reality TV show and her stupid, stupid made-up problems on the couch, and when I'm miles away from her, blasting Wilco in the car, I shout as loud as I possibly can, "I HATE YOU."

I drive to Dad's. It was never my plan to bring up Uncle Max ever again, but something has changed. There's a desperation inside me that I want to rip out. I want this horrible thing out of my body and my mind, and I don't want to touch it anymore.

I tell Dad everything.

I tell him about Uncle Max. I tell him about Mom. I tell him I know the truth about their divorce. I tell him I thought it was my fault.

He's quiet at first, but when he starts to cry he has to bury his face in his hands to hide from me. I think he feels ashamed, even though I tell him I don't blame him. When he calms down, he hugs me and says he thinks I'm the strongest person in the world, as strong as a polar bear.

Dad says he didn't tell me about Mom and Brandon because he didn't want me and my brothers to take his side. He says he's not perfect either, and that no one is, really, but that he is trying to do right by the people he cares about.

He tells me he wants me to live with him and Serena and the twins and Shoji. He says we can all be a family.

I don't want to tell him it's too late for that, even though that's how I feel. I don't want the life I wanted as a child—I want the life in my future. I want art school. I want bills. I want friends. I want to meet people who inspire me. I want to inspire people I meet. I want to live.

Dad goes in the other room to call Mom. I stay downstairs with Serena, Shoji, and my two sisters, who seem to be growing at an impossibly fast rate. Leah is still bald. Emily is still chubby.

I move in with Dad. He goes with me to help pack up my room when Mom is at work. She left a letter for me on my bed. It's from Brightwood. I've been accepted into their art program.

I know I should be more excited, but it's hard to be happy when I still don't know what I'm going to do. California feels like it's slipping farther and farther away from me. I'm not sure I'm brave enough to go back and do it all over again but this time without Jamie.

I want to be brave. I just don't know where to start.

Jamie calls me on my birthday. I don't answer. He doesn't leave a voice mail.

I think we might be over.

I draw a ghost wandering through an airport because she doesn't know where to go.

CHAPTER FIFTY-NINE

I don't recognize the number when my phone rings. For a moment I wonder if it's Jamie. Maybe he's trying to trick me into talking to him. And for that same moment, I really want it to be him.

I answer, my voice hurried and cracked. "Hello?"

"Hi. Is this Kiko Himura?" A man's voice, but not Jamie's.

"Yes, that's me."

"This is Dexter Graham from the admissions office at Prism Art School. How are you doing today?"

Oh my God. "I'm God. I mean, good. I'm good. How are you?"

His chuckle is light and disarming. "Great, thanks. I'm calling because we've just looked over your application for the fall. Unfortunately, that program is already at max capacity for this semester. However, we were very impressed with your work. Your portfolio is quite stunning. So although we won't be able to offer you a place this year, I was getting in touch to see if you'd like us to hold your application until next year. We could interview you sometime in the spring, although—and I'm not supposed to say this—the interview is much more of a formality than anything. You'd basically have a place here if you'd like it." He pauses. "Is that something that would interest you?"

Oh my God. "Yes. Yes, absolutely. Umm. I don't understand though. I got a rejection from you guys already."

"Yes, for our painting program." He pauses. "But you applied again, for drawing? About a month ago? I've even got your recommendation letter here from Hiroshi Matsumoto, which was quite impressive."

"And you've seen my portfolio?"

"Yes," he repeats. "Well, the photographs anyway. We'd expect you to bring your actual portfolio with you to the interview, but the photographs were very well done. We got a good idea of your level of talent."

My stomach knots. It was Jamie. It must have been. Or maybe Hiroshi *and* Jamie, but either way, I didn't take those photographs, and I certainly didn't apply to Prism for drawing.

"So are you interested in us holding your application?" he asks again.

My heart races. "Yes. Thank you so much. This is amazing."

He laughs a little louder this time. He must be used to the dizzying excitement on the other end of the phone. "That's great. Well, I've got all your details here in the computer. We'll be in touch to set up an interview sometime in the spring, but if you have any questions at all, please do give us a call."

"Okay. Thank you."

"No problem, Kiko. It was nice to speak with you, and we really look forward to meeting you in person."

The phone clicks.

I collapse onto my bed in a fit of pixie-infused giggles.

I paint the world in completely different colors because nothing is the same as it was before.

call Hiroshi to ask him about Prism. He says it was all Jamie's idea, and he just made sure to provide him with a copy of his recommendation letter. He also mentions there might have been a phone call as well, again at the request of Jamie.

I don't deserve how much Jamie loves me. But I want to be in a position where I feel like I finally do.

I ask Hiroshi if the job at the café is still available, and he tells me I can start as soon as I'm back in California.

It doesn't take me long at all to make up my mind. I'm going to spend a year in California, working in the café, working on my art, and saving up for school. And next year, I'll move to New York and go to Prism.

It's not hard to say my good-byes, because I don't have that many people to say good-bye to. I tell Emery my new plans over the phone, and she tells me she wants to spend spring break on the beach with me. The manager at the bookstore wishes me luck. Dad and Serena get a little tearful and tell me I've been the perfect houseguest. Shoji even gives me a hug, which feels weird for both of us. Leah manages to smile at me when I kiss her good-bye, and Emily squeezes my finger and coos.

On my way out of town, I stop at Mom's. I don't want to leave without saying good-bye, even if she isn't the mother I need. I'm not sure when I'll see her again. Saying good-bye feels like the right thing to do—it's the last page before a new chapter.

She buys sub sandwiches for lunch and makes an oversized pitcher of sweet tea. She asks about Shoji and the twins like nothing is weird about our arrangement or relationship at all.

Mom has always been good at pretending things are fine when she doesn't want to apologize.

But I don't need an apology. Not anymore. I have my whole life ahead of me—there isn't room in it for anger about things I don't have the power to change. I've mourned the loss of the mother I imagined could exist. I accept the one I have will never be the one I need.

And that's okay—because I will be the person I need. I will be the one I can depend on, the one who has the power to make my life better or worse.

I'll still panic when I'm in a crowd. I'll still question whether people mean something different from what they say. And I'll probably always feel my heart thump when I think someone is criticizing me.

But I can live with that.

I accept myself.

Mom tells me to call her when I get to California. She doesn't hug me good-bye, but she stands in the doorway waving until her house disappears from my rearview mirror.

I don't drive north or south or east or west. I drive forward.

When I hear the bell ring, my heart catches. I set the mug behind the counter, take a deep breath, and turn my face toward the café doors.

Jamie is wearing a thin jacket to protect him from the January chill. His tan has faded, but otherwise he looks exactly the same as he did all those months ago.

Locking his blue eyes on me, he smiles like he has something stuffed in his mouth. Too many words, probably. Too many things that were left unsaid.

Still, it's a smile.

I pull my apron off and hang it on the wall peg. "Thanks for coming," I say. Jamie still towers over me, but somehow I feel taller.

He nods, his hands stuffed in his pockets like he doesn't know what to do with them. "I was wondering if you'd ever call."

"You knew I was in town?"

"I saw you through the window once." He shrugs. "Just passing by."

"I wasn't ready back then." My voice isn't timid—it's exactly the right amount of volume.

He doesn't say anything. He just keeps looking at me like he isn't sure I won't disappear.

"I want to show you something," I say.

We walk up the stairs at the side of the building, and I unlock the doors to the studio. When we step inside, I think I'll have to point out what I want him to see, but I don't. He sees it. He sees everything.

The right wall of the studio is covered in paintings I've done over the last six months. Some of them are hung up on the walls. Some of them are set along the floor because there's not enough space. Hiroshi says he wants to feature me in his next art show. He says I could sell some of them to help pay for Prism.

And I'd sell all of them. All of them except for one.

The biggest canvas is wider than my arm span. It's bursting with so much color it looks like a graffiti artist got too excited with a spray can.

But it's my story, told in brushstrokes and acrylic paint.

There's Jamie and me as children, hiding in trees and searching for ladybugs. There's me alone, searching for stars in the dark. There's my mom, the queen of the starfish, existing in a tornado of glitter that poisons anything else it touches. There are my brothers and me, living on opposite sides of a triangle, experiencing the same things but never together. There's my dad, never knowing or doing as much as he should but trying to fix the poison all the same. There's Hiroshi, painting my hands so I can paint my voice. There's me split in half—Japanese and white—stitching myself together again because I am whole only when I've embraced the true beauty of my heritage.

And there's Jamie and me in June, the sun on our faces and the sand at our feet, finding each other again after all those years. Our lives trail around us, sometimes broken and sometimes beautiful, but all puzzled and tangled up into the lump that is us.

We fit together not because we need each other, but because we choose each other.

Our friendship was always our choice. Love was a natural progression.

Jamie stares at the painting for so long that I think the room actually starts to get darker. When he turns to face me, he looks relieved. Calm.

Jamie turns back to the painting.

We don't need words. We just *know*.

Our fingers find each other's.

ACKNOWLEDGMENTS

S o here I am, writing the acknowledgments, and surreal is the only way to describe this. Seeing *Starfish* morph into a real book has truly been a dream come true, and it wouldn't have happened without the help of some truly fantastic people, many of whom I'm lucky enough to call friends.

I owe so much to my incredible agent, Penny Moore of Empire Literary. People use the term "dream agent," but you are an actual superhero. Thank you for believing in my words all those months ago, and for always fighting in my corner. Your guidance and support means everything to me. I honestly could not ask for a better agent, and I feel like the luckiest person in the world to call myself one of your clients.

To my editor, Jennifer Ung—thank you. A million times over, thank you. I couldn't imagine a greater champion for this story. You helped shape it into the book it is today, and being able to work with someone who loves this story as passionately as you do has truly been an honor. *Starfish* is so many pieces of my heart—

thank you for handling them with so much love and care.

Thank you to Mara Anastas, Mary Marotta, Liesa Abrams, Carolyn Swerdloff, Nicole Russo, Christina Pecorale, Chelsea Morgan, Sara Berko, and everyone else at Simon Pulse who played a role in making this story a real book. Your time, dedication, and love for Kiko's journey has made this entire process feel like a dream. And a very special thank you to Sarah Creech, who designed a cover so beautiful and perfect that I still have trouble believing it's real.

I also owe a big thank you to Christian Trimmer, whose feedback on an early draft of *Starfish* became the inspiration for Emery.

I am eternally grateful to all the people over the years who were kind enough to beta read for me. Thank you, Nikki and Dylan, for being there at the start; Jennifer G., for your generous enthusiasm; Jamie H., for editing a book of mine in eighth grade and teaching me that a first draft is just the beginning; Ian, for your never-ending support; and Anisaa and Taylor, for being the world's best critique partners.

To the writing friends I've made over the last couple of years, Nicki, Jessica, Michelle, Tabitha, and Lyla—thank you for being so kind and enthusiastic, and for being such an incredible source of comfort throughout this long and often nerve-racking process.

To the readers who followed Kiko's story to the last page (and then all the way to the acknowledgments—you're quite thorough!)—thank you for opening your minds and hearts to a book that means so much to me. It means more than you could ever know.

And finally, I want to say thank you to the three people I am lucky enough to call my family. Shaine and Oliver, thank you for being such a beautiful source of joy and love in my life. I hope you two will always know how much I love you, and how honored I am to be your mom. To my husband, Ross—you are the most supportive partner in the world. Thank you for reading terrible first, second, and third drafts, for being a soundboard for all of my story ideas (even the ones that seem to always happen in the middle of the night or during long car journeys), for the hundreds of cups of tea and bags of chocolate (my writing fuel), and for always believing so deeply in my stories. But most of all, thank you for being the family I always dreamed about. I love you times infinity.

ABOUT THE AUTHOR

Akemi Dawn Bowman is the author of *Starfish*. She's a proud Ravenclaw and *Star Wars* enthusiast, who served in the US Navy for five years and has a BA in social sciences from UNLV. Originally from Las Vegas, Nevada, she currently lives in England with her husband, two children, and their Pekingese mix.